SHADOW KISSED

SHADOW KISSED

The characters in this book are fictitious. Any similarity to real persons,
living or dead, is coincidental and not intended by the author.

Editing by Belle Manuel
Proofreading by Virginia Tesi Carey
Cover design and interior formatting by Dark Wish Designs
Map by Daniel Garcia
Character art of Olivia and Sebastian by Art by Steffani
Character art portraits of Olivia and Sebastian by Angelika Buergo

This book contains sensitive content:
This book contains adult language, suicidal thoughts, mentions of slavery,
blood, violence, and scenes of murder.

GLOSSARY

Places:

Sanmorte: The Vampire Kingdom ruled by Sargon

Baldoria: The Kingdom Olivia is from

Laveniuess's Lake: The birthplace of the God, Laveniuess

Ismore: City in Baldoria where Olivia lived

Black Mountain Retreat: Exclusive hotel for the elite

Orders:

Nightshade: Order that serves Kalon

Guild for the Protection of Mortal Beings: Protectors the mortal world

Midnight Lotus: Secret order to protect the king

Other:

Cane of Cineris: A cane gifted to the kings from the gods that will turn any vampire it touches into ash

PRONUNCIATION

GUIDE

Erianna–Air-ee-anna

Draven: Dray-ven

Ravena–Rav-ee-nah

Hamza–Ham-zah

Sargon–Sar-gone

Kalon–Kal-on

Sanmorte–San-moor-tey

Baldoria–Bal-door-ee-ah

Sangaree–Sang-ah-ree

Aniccipere–Ann-iss-sep-heir

Laveniuess–Lav-en-nwass

Jaiunere–Shaun-air

Salenia–Sal-ee-nah

Achais–Ark-ice

Seraphina–Sair-ah-feen-ah

Dedicated to Sarah Elyse Rodriguez

For loving this world as much as I do

And for all your empaths out there who

take on the energy of the world. This is for you.

PRAISE FOR SHADOW KISSED

"Shadow Kissed pulls you in from page one and holds you tight
with Garcia's fresh, sexy take on the chosen one trope.
Vampires, slow burn romance worth waiting for, and one bed?
Look no further! Five scintillating stars"
-*Sarah M. Cradit, USA Today Bestselling Author of Kingdom of the
White Sea*

"Rebecca L. Garcia has composed a dark, magical symphony of
vampire notes in Shadow Kissed."
-*Casey L. Bond, author of When Wishes Bleed*

"You've never read vampires like this before and Garcia shows
her fangs in this twisting tale full of tension. Five stars!"
- *Rebecca Grey, author of Ruined*

"A dangerous and enticing spin on vampires with action, twists,
and doses of spice that will keep you flipping pages."
~ *Cameo Renae, USA Today Bestselling author of Hidden Wings*

"Betrayal and sacrifice bite deep in this genuinely seductive
vampire tale!"
~ *Award-winning Author, Tish Thawer*

"Inventive, modern, and brimming with soul, Garcia's Shadow Kissed will bewitch lovers of vampiric dominion with the magic of a single, unforgettable touch."

- K.L. Kolarich, author of The Haidren Legacy

"Shadow Kissed is a surreal world of vampires. The story so well written by Rebecca Garcia and takes your imagination and emotions to whole new world of fantasy."

- Rebel Heart Book Blog

"Shadow Kissed is set in a gothic landscape with secrets, betrayal, a sexy vampire with all the sexual tension you (think) you can handle. I couldn't turn the pages fast enough!"

- A Midsummers Nights Read

SANMORTE

LAKE OF
LAVENIUESS

CIT
NIGH

ROYAL CASTLE

BLACK MOUNTAIN
RETREAT

OF
ARES

ONE

My nightmares slipped away as my eyes fluttered open, revealing the dim light of my bedroom. I turned on the lamp and checked the time: 11:00 p.m. I'd barely slept an hour and a half. Rubbing the sleep out of my eyes, I stood from my bed, stretching as I walked over to the small, square window.

A protector from the guild where my mom worked glided through the evening fog and stationed himself outside the front door. That meant my mom would be spending another night at headquarters, leaving me to the protection of the guild's security.

Everyone was on high alert, but whenever I asked her about it, I got the same answer: *"It's nothing for you to worry about."* It hadn't always been that way. She used to confide in me years ago when I was practicing magic and getting somewhere with it. I was expected to follow in her footsteps and protect mortals against vampires, but I had failed one too many times. It didn't help that I was also terrible at combat, and now with my powers weak and the grief of losing Astor, they looked at me as if I were broken. Maybe they were right.

It had been fourteen days since my boyfriend died. He was the only person who truly understood me, and he was gone, his soul now with the gods we worshiped. Whenever I tried to contest the way he died, I was shut down, and I was expected to believe the heightened security at our house had nothing to do with his death. Astor was one of them, after all, a guard at the Guild for the Protection of Mortal Beings—a secret society that safeguarded us mortals.

I pressed my forehead against the cool glass pane and squeezed my lips together. Sometimes it felt like someone had pushed pause on my life, like I was standing still while the rest of the world moved on. I was supposed to start college last year, but I put it on hold for Astor. He needed me here, only twenty minutes from the guild, and not in some dorm across the city. When he got sick, everything changed. He continued to work, but as his health deteriorated, he took more time off, eventually traveling north for a month to visit his dad and half-siblings.

My breath fogged up the window as I stared out at the full, pale moon. Nighttime was my favorite. There was something mystical about seeing the glittering stars against the black canvas. I thought about him, losing myself in view of the horizon. I stared hazily at the trees silhouetted against the hilly horizon, waving gently in the breeze. The streetlamps lining the sidewalk flickered beyond our gate, emitting a cool white hue. Moving my gaze to the protector stationed at our front door, and another by the gate, I opened my heart enough to reach out—to feel a taste of their emotions to ease the heaviness in my chest—but as always, their feelings were only a distraction from my own grief.

Everyone called me an empath, but I was more than that. Not only could I feel the way others did, but with my magic, I could manipulate their emotions. It had served me well when my mom had gotten angry or Astor had become panicked over his sickness. I'd taken it all away with just a touch. However, it wasn't always a gift. At Astor's funeral, I couldn't keep up the barrier I'd built over the years to protect myself from feeling what everyone did all the time. It opened like a floodgate when I felt overwhelmed, and all that grief almost killed me.

I stepped back, almost toppling into my desk in half-thought, and grabbed the edge to steady myself. I looked at an open notebook, one of many in which I'd scribbled some half-coherent ideas before tossing it into an ever-growing pile. I closed the cover on the last thing I'd written before Astor died. I couldn't find the motivation to pick up a pen since then.

I released a slow breath and moved my gaze to my unmade bed. I thought back to the last night I'd spent with Astor, how he'd ran his fingers through my hair and talked about his visit up north. He'd always wanted to travel more, but hadn't made it outside of our kingdom, Baldoria. If I'd known that would be the last time I would see him, I would have said so much more.

They hadn't found a body, but no one survived a fall off the white cliffs. Even if that didn't kill him, the rocks at the bottom would have. So all I knew was that he was gone, but I couldn't bring myself to believe he wasn't coming back. Every time the door to my bedroom opened, I half expected him to walk inside.

Tears crept into the corners of my eyes, threatening to break through again. I swallowed thickly, allowing them to pour over, trickling down my cheeks. I pushed my red curls out of my face, which caught against my nails. Then, pulling the pillow only he used against my nose, I breathed in the fading scent of his honey and shea butter shampoo. I'd used it on myself to recreate his scent last week, but it didn't smell the same on me.

My bedroom door creaked open, and my mom walked in, holding a steaming cup of cocoa in my favorite purple mug. A faint smell of cinnamon mixed with chocolate hit my nostrils, removing Astor's scent altogether. "Olivia, honey." Her brown gaze narrowed when she saw my tear-patterned cheeks. "If you won't eat anything, you should at least drink something, so here."

She placed the mug on my nightstand and sat on the edge of my

mattress. I noticed she was dressed head to toe in black spandex,

the typical uniform of protectors.

"You're leaving again," I stated.

"Yes."

"I assume you won't tell me why."

"It's nothing for you to worry about."

"I'm not a child, Mom," I said tentatively, "you can tell me

what's happening."

She tucked a lock of black hair behind her ear. "It's

complicated. You have enough going on. I don't want to worry

you." She reached over to touch my hand but thought better of it.

"Draven will be here soon to keep you company."

"I don't need a bodyguard," I said, although I did want to see

him. I just hated her looking at me like some fragile thing that

could break at any moment.

"He's your friend."

"I know." I rubbed the side of my neck. "But if he wasn't with

the guild, would you even allow us to be friends?"

"Of course," she said, but we both knew it was a lie. No one

had come in or out of this house who didn't belong to the guild.

On rare occasions, when I was allowed outside of the house, it was always with her.

After I turned eighteen, I'd expected her to loosen the reins a little, but it didn't happen. Now I was nineteen, and I was still stuck in this house all the time unless I was with her or a member of the guild. I supposed that was what happened when one is a sorceress. We were rare and desired by the vampires in the neighboring kingdom, Sanmorte.

I sat upright, pushing my back up against the wall. "I know something's going on." I chewed over my words. "If it has something to do with Astor, please tell me. I can take it. I just need to know the truth."

"It's not that." She hesitated, then sighed. "There have been a couple of vampire attacks."

My chest tightened. "In Ismore?" Ours was the biggest city in the south of Baldoria. I couldn't believe vampires would ever come inside the city. We were infamous for having a guild headquarters here.

"They've remained at the outskirts. It's unlikely they'll come into the city, but we must still be prepared."

My stomach dipped. "Do you think Astor was killed by one of them?"

"No. That was..." She trailed off, lowering her head.

"Suicide." I filled in the blank.

"He was dying, sweetheart," she told me as if we hadn't already had this conversation before. "These attacks started after then. You have to stop trying to find another reason when there isn't one."

I didn't want to believe it, but all the evidence was there— the handwritten note to Astor's mom, the voicemail he left telling me he loved me. Maybe I was a fool for thinking there was more to it, but when I'd listened to his message and heard the crack in his voice, it killed me that I couldn't help him. Part of me just hoped it wasn't real, that he wouldn't leave me behind without saying goodbye, and somehow, in an alternate world, I could still have the chance to take this pain away before it was too late.

She didn't say anything, only stared at the wisps of steam dancing up from my cocoa.

"He would have told me first... He wouldn't have just killed himself. I know Astor," I croaked, breaking the silence. "*Knew*."

She shot me a pained smile, and I sighed. There was little point in arguing with her. "I'm sorry, Olivia, but facts are facts. There were no signs of foul play, and the note he left—"

"I know." I looked at the ground, tight lipped.

Her lips parted. "I wish I could make it all go away."

"I know, Mom. Be careful out there tonight," I said to end that conversation.

"I will." She smiled, but there was no crease in the corners of her tired eyes. "Try to get some rest while I'm gone. I'm surprised you're still up."

I clicked my tongue. "It's the nightmares," I explained. "They keep me up."

She squeezed my knee. "Do you want melatonin?"

I laughed. "So I can have nightmares on steroids? No thanks." I'd taken one before and had the most vivid of dreams. "Maybe tomorrow we can go to see Astor's mom. I promised her I'd go soon."

Her shoulders slumped. "Not right now."

"You said the vampires won't come into the city."

"I can't take any chances with these attacks. I can ask if she can come by the house."

A change of scenery was what I wanted, but I relented. "Okay, that's fine."

Sometimes I wished I weren't a sorceress, so I could live normally. The vampires who want us—the sangaree, who drink blood, and the aniccipere, a far more terrifying creature known to suck the souls from their victims—craved our magic. They desired to use our ability to influence others' emotions and energies. Fortunately, we had remained hidden and the royals in Sanmorte didn't know about us.

She checked her watch. "I need to go. Try to eat something." She stood, glancing out the window. "Draven's here."

I climbed out of bed to find my hairbrush as the doorbell rang, then hurried downstairs.

Draven smiled when the door opened; his blue eyes softened when they landed on me from over my mom's shoulder. He was a good foot taller than her five-foot-four height, but somehow, she always appeared as the most authoritative person in the room. "Take care of her."

"With my life."

She moved to get her beeper from her pocket, and he winked at me. "Okay, I have everything. I'll be back at ten a.m."

He nodded and stepped inside the house. Before leaving, my mom turned back, her raven-black ponytail swishing behind her. "Don't stay up all night just because Draven has to."

"I'll make sure she gets some rest."

Her shoulders relaxed. "If you need anything—"

"We'll be fine." I arched an eyebrow at her. "Stay safe."

"Okay. Love you," she called and hurried out the door.

"You too," I shouted, but the door was already shut. I hurried over to Draven, and he wrapped his arms around me. My cheek rubbed against the tight elastic material of his black-and-gray top. I'd seldom seen him out of uniform. "You'll make sure I get some sleep, will you?" I snarked.

He grinned. "I just said that for your mom's benefit. I could never make you do a thing you didn't want to do."

"I've missed you." I matched his smile, then took a step back. "How's work been?"

"It's been hectic at the guild. Security's high." Under the yellow light in the hallway, I noticed his bronzed skin looked darker than the last time I'd seen him. He'd probably been training outside more.

"I know. Mom told me about the attacks."

His eyes widened, and he leaned against the hallway wall. "I'm surprised she said anything to you."

"I only found out tonight. I don't suppose you'll tell me anything more?" I arched an eyebrow, and he gave me a look.

"She asked me not to."

"Some friend you are," I teased and turned, heading toward the kitchen, our usual gathering spot. The bright lights flickered on, showing off the long marble island, black stools, and stainless-steel appliances. Sometimes it felt more like living in a showroom than a home, but this was all my mom's taste. I preferred cozy, with warmer colors and wood furniture.

Draven paused in the doorway as I drank a glass of water, looking down at his feet. "I'm sorry I didn't come sooner. I've missed you too."

"It's not your fault," I said, and his nostrils flared. He had to follow orders, and the guild probably didn't let him leave, especially with all the attacks. "I understand."

"I wanted to come. I should have."

My chest somehow felt heavier. "It's okay."

"It's not."

I licked my dry lips. "Draven—"

"I'm sorry." He paused. "Really, I am. It doesn't matter how I felt about Astor. He didn't deserve to die." He pulled out a stool and propped his elbows up against the island as he sat. "I should have come to the funeral, but I had to work."

I believed him. Even though their rivalry went back to when they both started the academy, there was an unspoken bond between protectors at the guild. A brotherhood of sorts, even amongst those who didn't like each other. "It was horrible, and in a way, I'm glad you didn't come." The memory of the funeral threaded through my mind, of watching Astor's mom falling to her knees in front of an empty casket. The same twinge of shock and desperation she'd emitted on that day pinched through me, and I placed my hand on my chest.

"How have you been doing?" He shoved his hands in his pockets, taking me away from the dark memory. "I mean, apart from the obvious. I'm sorry, I don't know what to say."

"It's okay. We don't have to talk about it."

I inhaled deeply. I needed a distraction from the constant pity coming from my mom. "Not right now. I'm just glad you're here."

He ran his hand through his honey-brown curls, which stopped at the tip of his ears. "Me too."

"So these vampire attacks are crazy, right?" I tilted my head at him.

"Come on, Olivia."

"Don't be like her. I'm tired of being treated like some naïve kid. We're both nineteen. Just tell me something."

He chewed on the inside of his cheek. "How about this? I'll tell you more, but only after we both eat. I'm starving."

I ran numb. Mom must have told him I wasn't eating.

"Grilled cheese?" he asked but didn't wait for an answer before moving toward the fridge.

I leaned over the counter, propping my chin against my fists. "Sounds great," I lied. "So don't keep me in anticipation. What's really happening with the attacks?"

"It's the sangaree." He caught my eye, his mouth tugging into a grimace. "They're getting braver, flying in from Sanmorte. I assume their food supply is low if they're coming so far inland."

My nose crinkled. The vampires usually snatched a few of us from the eastern towns, but we were in the southwest. It was unusual, but I supposed that's why the guild had a branch here, in case these things happened. "Is that what my mom's doing? Hunting them?"

"She's leading a team out to the last sighting of one."

Bile climbed my throat. I should have hugged her goodbye.

He spotted my worry, and his expressions softened. "She'll be fine. She's trained for this and is far better than any of us."

I couldn't help but agree. She'd beaten men twice her size in combat, had mastered spells I hadn't even heard of, and had a gravitas about her that demanded the attention of a room. She was going to be okay, I told myself.

The smell of toast filled the kitchen. Draven slid a plate holding a perfect grilled cheese sandwich across the kitchen island. "Here."

I stared at it, and my stomach churned. Carefully, I picked it up under his watchful gaze and took a small bite. Grief had dissolved my appetite, but I couldn't keep refusing to eat unless I wanted to end up in the hospital. "It's good."

"What can I say? I'm a great cook." He grinned.

I took another bite and set the plate back down. "So?" I arched my brow. "Have any of you killed one yet?"

"Yes. We killed a sangaree. Took off its head."

"Who? Not you?"

He swallowed a bite. "It's nice to know you have so much faith in me, but no. It was Aiden who swung the fatal blow."

I recalled the black-haired, muscular man who'd been my mom's friend for gods knew how long now. "It's not that I don't think you couldn't kill one," I defended. "I just don't want to think of you being in danger like that."

Something changed in his eyes. "You're too sweet."

I shot him a small smile and managed two more bites before pushing it away. "I'm getting tired. Let's hope I can sleep for more than two hours without waking up again." Exhaustion crept over me in waves before taking me completely. I glanced at the wall clock; it was almost one. Time had gone by fast.

"Don't miss me too much," he said teasingly.

"I was going to say the same to you." I half smiled, which turned into a yawn. The dreams began right after Astor died. It was the trauma, or so the therapist my mom paid to come by the house said. I only hoped they would go away soon. The thought of Astor brought all my dark feelings back to the surface. Not even Draven could distract me for long. "You should sleep, too. I won't say anything."

"I'm not tired," he said, but we both knew he was simply following orders. "I'll be here when you wake up."

Closing the distance between us, I kissed his cheek, breathing in the evocative scent of cedarwood from his cologne. "I'm glad you came this time. The other protectors are awesome and all, but they're not you."

His lips curved upward. "I'll always be here for you."

I headed upstairs, and vampires filled my thoughts. I'd never seen one; most people in our land hadn't. The people who were taken by them were never seen again.

My mom said most were kept as prisoners and were fed on or used for entertainment. Only a few mortals had been killed immediately, their bodies left for the guild to find. I shuddered when I thought about being trapped in their cold kingdom of monsters. I'd prefer a swift death by one of them rather than to be made prisoner.

I climbed into bed and closed my eyes, drifting off into a dream-filled sleep.

I felt hands shaking me as I was jarred awake to reveal a pale-faced Draven. "Get up, get dressed, and pack a bag of necessities. Now."

My heart raced as I sat upright, running cold. I opened my mouth to ask why, but he cut me off. "The vampires are in the city. Two of our own have been killed."

A lump formed in my throat. "Where's my mom?"

"She's leading the hunt. The sangaree ambushed a festival in the city. It's a bloodbath." I could hear his phone buzzing in his pocket, but he didn't answer. He must have been sent pictures. I shuddered, not wanting to see them. "I'm taking you to headquarters. It's safer there."

"Surely they wouldn't come here."

"Just pack your bag. Aiden is coming to get us."

A loud ringing sounded around the house, muting Draven's following words. Someone was in the house. "Draven." I hesitated. "The alarm." Aiden knew to turn it off before entering, so it had to mean someone had broken in.

"Stay behind me." He stood in front of my bedroom door and pulled out his sword. In his other hand was a gun. It wouldn't kill one, but the bullets would give him a few extra seconds to cut off its head.

The door creaked open. I willed my powers to thrum into my hands, but nothing happened. I'd always been terrible at magic, but now I realized how useless I really was. I took a step back as my bedroom door opened wide, and a man stepped inside.

TWO

Aiden stepped inside my room, a gun in one hand and a sword in the other. "They've gone. We scared them off. The others are outside," he told Draven, who lowered his weapons. My heart pounded as he turned to look at me and clicked a button from the remote in his pocket, sending the wailing alarm into silence. "We need to leave before they come back."

"Wait." My brain faltered as I processed his words. "Were there vampires in my house?"

"Yes." Aiden grabbed an empty rucksack from my closet and shoved it at my chest. "Pack only what you need for two days."

"Why did they come here?" I asked, my eyes widening. "Do they know about my mom? About me?" I looked from Draven to Aiden; their expressions said it all. No one but the guild knew we were sorceresses. We had no extended family. My dad had been out of the picture since I was one, and I didn't even know his name. "How is that possible?"

"We don't know anything right now. This could be a random attack," Aiden said, but I knew he was lying.

Why would vampires pick my house out of all the others? Unless more were attacked.

"No more questions. Pack your bag, or I will pack it for you."

Draven shot me a pleading look. "Please, Olivia. We have to get you out of here."

"I'm going," I promised, and bundled handfuls of clothes, pajamas, and toiletries. "Were other houses attacked?"

"Not from what I saw," Aiden said, confirming my suspicions.

They had targeted my house, meaning they knew. Draven shook his head as I parted my lips to ask another question. I decided to wait until we were at the guild, feeling the rage coming from Aiden. He didn't say a word as we walked to the black car. Several protectors surrounded us, and I climbed inside.

Draven squeezed my shoulder. I blocked his emotions as his anger spiked my own. The barrier I'd created was like a switch, something I could turn on and off at will, mostly.

The car pulled out of the drive and through the open gate, sweeping us toward the rolling hills where headquarters was based. I looked back through the tinted windows, gripping the beige upholstery under the window, and gazed out into the endless night.

Draven dragged his thumb over the top of my hand. "You're shaking."

I laughed flatly. "I'm not even cold."

"It's the adrenaline. Focus on your breathing."

I nodded and glanced at Aiden. "Where's my mom?"

"Amara's leading the team in the south of the city." He turned his focus on Draven. "Once we reach headquarters, take Olivia to the bunkers. Use this." He handed him a keycard. "They shouldn't be able to get inside, but we must take precautions."

Draven nodded, and they both fell silent as Aiden typed into his phone. I twirled my promise ring around my finger, over and over, until it left a mark. I watched hedges blur past the car as we sped down the road between the rolling hills of the countryside.

We slowed as the guild came into view, and I studied the deceivingly quiet view. It seemed like any other night, though it was far from it. Panicked voices shot out of Aiden's radio, and Draven squeezed my hand. Finally, we pulled into headquarters, and the car door was opened by a man dressed head to toe in navy blue.

"Get her inside," Aiden ordered, without looking away from his radio.

Draven nodded and escorted me inside. Thick, metal walls curved around, joining up to a dome at the roof, forming a dark, impenetrable building. Half of it was hidden from view, running deep underground. It wasn't my first time inside, but each time I visited, the fortress stole my breath away.

Keycards got us through the first two thick metal doors. The next was opened using Draven's fingerprints. I watched as a scanner darted a beam of red into both his eyes, then turned green. The door swung open to the fourth and final door.

This one was protected with magic. I could feel it moving through the steel door like electricity. Draven pressed a stone against the door, which disarmed it the moment obsidian touched the surface. My mom had spelled the stones to disrupt the magic long enough to let guild members through. Once inside the windowless, gleaming white foyer, I marveled at how empty it was. "Wow."

"Yeah." Draven's grip tightened on his gun. "They're out chasing the vampires. Their numbers have doubled," he admitted as he walked us to the steep steps leading down to the tunnels. Aiden didn't even look at me as he followed, pausing at the stairs. "Take her to A14. Stay there until further notice. I have to take care of something."

"I have my radio and phone," he said, and Aiden gave him a signal for us to go.

Draven escorted me away. Once we were in the tunnels burrowed underground, alone, I spoke up. "Is this really necessary? I'm just as safe above ground."

He marched on ahead. "Your safety is paramount. We can't take any risks."

"You know I'm claustrophobic."

"Have you been down here before?"

"Not in the bunkers."

"The rooms aren't as small as you think."

"I don't like the thought of being underground." I didn't want to think about the soil packed around the tunnel we walked through. My skin was crawling by the time we reached the small room. There was just enough room for a bunk bed, sink, and table pushed against the wall with a hard, plastic chair.

"Great." I touched my throat, feeling as if my lungs were half the size.

"We won't be in here long."

"This is ridiculous." All I could think about was escaping.

He closed the door, turning the circular locks until they clicked, and the door settled. "You're right. It is doubtful a vampire can get in here. We have a ton of security measures up. But not impossible, so better be safe than sorry. You're one of a few thousand sorcerers left in the entire world. So we have to make sure you're safe."

"They let my mom go out and fight. She's a sorceress too."

"She's also highly trained. Her powers are an asset."

I sucked in a deep breath, but dizziness forced me into the chair. The walls were closing in, and I wanted to tear my skin off. "Please, Draven, can't we go back up?"

His face crumpled. "I don't have the authority."

"Gods, please." I curled my fingers into fists, digging my nails into my palms until they left half-crescent marks. My red curls poured around my face as I bent over. "I can't stay here."

"Here, drink this." He handed me a bottle of water, which would do nothing for my claustrophobia. I threw it on the bed. I didn't want to be ungrateful, but I couldn't think about anything apart from finding a way out of this room. "I think there might be some dry goods in a box under the bed."

"I don't need snacks."

"I don't know what else to do," he admitted.

I focused on my breathing and turned my ring around my finger until the skin underneath was red and raw. "Draven, tell me more about the vampires." The order fell sharply from my lips as my anxiety grew. I needed something to take my mind off being in here.

"You know the stories," he said simply and sat on the edge of the bottom bunk. "That the goddess Salenia cursed her lover with vampirism."

I pressed my back against the wall, feeling the slithers of cold press against my bare skin at the top of my back. "Everyone knows that, but I assume there's more to the story. People don't make crazy decisions like creating a race of bloodthirsty creatures for no reason. Not even goddesses."

"Haven't you asked your mom about this?"

I guffawed. "I did, and what do you think she said?"

He didn't respond.

I kicked back against the wall then walked to sit on the bed. "We're stuck in here for gods know how long, and I'm going crazy. At least try to have a conversation with me."

He pressed his fingers against his temples, then straightened upright. "I don't know everything. A lot of it is lore, and some of it is classified."

I twirled a lock of hair around my finger, a habit I'd picked up years ago. "Please. I won't say anything."

He shot me a look. "We both know I can't tell you any classified information."

"I know, but you can tell me anything else. You know all the books about their history are banned. Except in the guild and the royal family's personal library."

"For good reason."

I rolled my eyes. "I'm not a fanatic. I'm not going to go looking for them or want to become one of their blood donors."

My gaze fell into his, neither of us looking away until he shook his head. "A lot of it is just stories. Nothing is proven."

"I still want to know." I sat next to him.

"Fine." He let out a heavy sigh. "As you know, Salenia fell in love with a mortal man—Vener. What you probably don't know is that she gifted him immortality long before he became a vampire."

My eyebrows knitted together. "How? Like made him into a god?"

"Of sorts." He tilted his head to the side. "He had many of their powers. However, after decades at Salenia's side, he grew restless, or so the stories say."

"Where did this information come from?"

"Writings, journals, and documentation collected throughout history."

"Is that all here?"

"No, it's all kept up north, in archives underground."

I nodded slowly. "So, Vener grew restless." I urged him to continue. "Then what happened?"

"He fell in love with someone else."

I shook my head. "Typical."

"Her name was Anastasia, and she was mortal. Those who wrote about Vener say he loved Anastasia so deeply, most believed they were soulmates."

"Now *that* is a myth."

Something changed in his eyes. "Not everyone thinks so. It's said that there is the perfect person for everyone, and for Vener, that was Anastasia. They understood each other deeper than anyone else."

My stomach knotted. "So I assume that's why Salenia cursed Vener?"

"Yes."

My mouth fell open.

"Salenia was furious and cursed them both with an ancient spell. Their hearts darkened as the curse took hold, and they found themselves driven by their base instincts and hidden desires. They were driven by a hunger for mortal blood and realized normal food was unable to sustain them like before. Without blood, they would die. Anastasia loved her family more than anything, but when she refused to consume blood for a month, she went into a frenzy, losing all control, and killed her entire family, draining them all."

"After that, she attempted to take her own life, lost in grief, but no matter what she did, she couldn't die."

I imagined the bloodied scene and pain Anastasia must have felt. I'd always respected the gods, but Salenia had certainly earned her reputation as ruler of the underworld.

"Salenia used all the dark energy created from the bloodshed," he continued, "to create the underworld. She made a place where immortals could go, so they could die. Then she killed Anastasia, and her soul went into the underworld where Salenia reigned. It was a prison for Anastasia, Vener, and Salenia, so they wouldn't be at peace upon their deaths. She waited for Vener to die, expecting him to also take his own life out of grief for Anastasia, but he didn't."

I shifted against the bed, leaning back against the pillows. "Vener wanted revenge." I calculated.

Draven blew out a tense breath. "She underestimated the nature of mortals."

"That we're fucked up?"

He snorted. "Something like that."

I looked up at the ceiling and bright lights, creating spots in my vision. There were thousands of vampires now. "Vener must have given the elixir to entire villages, and Salenia cursed them all?"

"No." He swallowed thickly, bobbing the lump in his throat. "This is the part they keep out of history, and for a good reason." He paused, and if I hadn't known Draven better, I'd have said it was for anticipation. But I think he just didn't want to tell me.

"I promise I won't say anything."

"I know." He puffed out his cheeks. "Okay, so he found a way to make others like him."

I leaned forward. "How? Did he use the same curse?"

He shook his head. "There's a way for the sangaree Vampires to make other vampires. After years alone and refusing to die so as not to give Salenia what she wanted, he grew curious about his blood. He realized it healed mortals of most injuries, so he would almost drain his victims, then give them his blood so they wouldn't die."

My nose wrinkled. "Gross."

"Yep." His mouth twisted. "One of his victims was killed with Vener's blood and venom still in her veins. When she woke up, she was a vampire just like him."

The hairs on my arms stood erect. "Wait, people can become vampires just by drinking the blood of a vampire?"

"Yes. Well, they need to be bitten first, so the vampire's venom is in their veins too. Then, they must die."

My eyes bulged. "That's... I mean, there are rumors that vampires can be made, but I was always told that was just a myth."

"We want mortals to believe that vampires can't be made," he explained. "Can you imagine what would happen if people realized they could become immortal? Hordes of them would go to Sanmorte, hoping to be turned, and the vampires would take advantage. They wouldn't change everyone. It would be like animals willingly walking into a slaughterhouse."

My chest tightened. "Do you think that many people want to be vampires?"

"I think a lot of people are afraid of dying and will take a way out when there is one."

"I would rather die than become a monster."

"I'm glad you see it that way." He rubbed his forehead. "Unfortunately, most people don't think that. A couple of centuries ago, according to our books and journals, it was widely known that vampires could be made. All I'll say is the number of mortals dwindled fast, but the vampire population didn't grow that much."

"So they killed most of them?"

He nodded. "It's why we keep it a secret."

I swallowed hard, attempting to remove the lump that had formed in my throat. "So many people have faith that vampires can be vanquished one day. They're convinced there are only a few thousand of them left, and once they're killed, they're gone. If they can make more, then that will never happen."

He shook his leg, tapping his finger against his knee. "There aren't just three or four thousand vampires. There are hundreds of thousands of them in Sanmorte alone, and if the other kingdoms found out the truth, everyone would be living in fear all the time."

"The guild is lying to everyone."

"We get our instructions from the royal family."

"Then they're lying too."

"For the good of our kingdom and for the rest of the world."

"I get it," I said, feeling unnerved. "Why would you tell me that?" I was certain he would get into a lot of trouble if anyone found out.

He turned, his fingers brushing mine over the top of the blankets. "I trust you." Astor hadn't told me any of this, and he had to have known. He was in the same ranks as Draven. I thought we told each other everything. Draven nudged my hand. "Why are you so sad?"

"It's nothing," I lied, but my chest felt ten times heavier. "It's a lot to process."

"Well, now you know."

A knock resonated around the room, jolting me upward. Draven jumped in front of me, and his shoulder brushed against mine. He looked over his shoulder, and I shot him an uneasy look. He returned my gaze as fear threaded through his eyes. It was unlike him to be afraid. The doors opened, and his hand flexed to my side.

I realized his panic had little to do with the vampires stalking the city and everything to do with me. The walls to the guild were impenetrable, built to sustain apocalyptic events. I was safe here, but Draven didn't relent. He moved like a panther—smooth, graceful, deadly. His muscles rippled under the spandex material slicked against his back. He acted on impulse, as if every movement were a potential threat.

Two protectors marched inside with enough guns to steal my breath away. One I recognized as Thomas approached Draven first, barely shooting a glance my way. "We've lost Starlight and Eagle."

Code names, I concluded.

"Taken or dead?"

"Taken."

He closed his eyes for half a second. "Where are the others?"

"In the east. sangaree are attacking in numbers we've not seen before. We're being sent there. Aiden asked me to tell you to stay here and protect the sorceress."

She has a name, I thought sourly but didn't dare interrupt.

"Thanks, Thomas. Stay safe out there."

He nodded once, looked at me, then left the room. Once we were alone, I let out a long breath. "Who's been taken? Anyone we know?"

Draven paled, then pulled out a handgun. "Take this," he said, avoiding my question. The gun was small and could easily be concealed up my sleeve. Surely that tiny thing couldn't do much damage. I turned it over in my palm, one eyebrow raised. "It's small, but it'll take down a man," he assured me, his wary expression steeling.

"Like my mom." I joked to ease the tension, but I knew what the gun meant. He no longer felt safe here. "Will you be leaving the guild?" I tried to push the anxiety from my voice, but it cracked through at the end.

"I won't leave your side unless I have to."

I licked my dry lips, feeling the cracks below the tip of my tongue. The cold, dry air had stolen any moisture from them. "Then why give me this?"

"It's just a precaution."

I grabbed his arm, squeezing, begging him to look at me. "Who was taken?"

He looked as if he might faint, an expression I'd never seen on him.

"We're going to get them back." He tried to push a lock of my hair back, something he only did when comforting me, and I knocked his hand away.

"Draven?" I asked again as an aching grew in my stomach.

"Your mom. Her codeword is *'Eagle'*."

The world crumbled beneath my feet. "My mom is gone." I mulled over the words as they shakily left my lips, sending pricks of cold through my body. My mind blanked for a minute as the reality of what happened hit me.

I needed to find her and get her back. She couldn't be gone. Not my mom.

"Let me out," I ordered Draven.

"I can't do that."

My mouth dried as I tugged at the lock, swearing loudly. "I swear to the gods, Draven, let me out."

"You can't help her."

"She's my mom! She's all I have in this world."

He stood, arms crossed over his broad chest, and watched as I pummeled the steel with my fists.

"I'm not a fucking prisoner here. Let. Me. Go," I warned, my face heating as beads of sweat formed above my eyebrows.

"No."

Something snapped inside of me, releasing all the control I had. Without thinking, I pulled the gun on him, my finger trembling over the trigger.

His eyes widened, but he didn't show anything else in his expression.

"You going to shoot me, Livi?"

A shiver snaked down my back. He rarely ever called me by my nickname, not since we were little in school together. I tightened my grip, sweat slicking against the trigger. "Open the door."

He looked me up and down, his lips curling inward. "Put the gun down. Before you hurt us both."

"No. Now open the door or I will shoot you," I threatened, but he didn't budge.

"Don't make me restrain you." Something in those green eyes told me he would.

"I'm the one with powers here and a gun, so you can try."

"You're only putting yourself in danger by being out there. You don't know anything about fighting vampires. You'll only cost more of us our lives."

A pain ripped through my chest as the truth tore through me. I opened my mouth to argue, but shame swallowed my words.

"Give me the gun, Livi. We both know you're not going to shoot me."

Tears ran down my cheeks as I threw the gun at him, sniffing back a sob which bubbled in my throat.

"I'll be back soon." He tucked the gun into his waistband and shook his head as he passed me on the way to the door. "If you try to force your way out of this room, so help me, Olivia, I will have to stop you."

My fists balled at my sides. "If you leave me in here, Draven, you can kiss our friendship goodbye. I'll never forgive you for this." The words bit harshly from my tongue.

A muscle in his jaw feathered. "Now that? That hurt more than any gun," he said and left the room.

The door clicked shut, and I dropped to my knees, sobbing into my open palms.

THREE

I awoke from a sleep plagued with nightmares of monsters with soulless eyes and sharp fangs. My mom had been one of them. Sitting upright, I shuddered away from the thought, sweat soaking through my nightgown.

Fumbling in the dark, I found the smooth metal switch and flicked the fluorescent white lights on. I shielded my eyes as they adjusted to the brightness, and the truth blasted through my sleep-hazed mind: my mom was gone. But she wasn't dead, not yet anyway. I assumed they wouldn't turn her because then she'd be useless to them. It's impossible to be both sorceress and vampire. Once turned, she'd lose her magic, and that's what the vampires wanted from us.

Right now, she was probably waking up in Sanmorte, surrounded by monsters. The idea of her being alone in a place where no mortals ever returned from made my throat close. Panic coiled around my core, stealing my next breath. I grasped at my throat, feeling heat creeping up my chest, then checked my phone on the off chance she'd contacted me, but it was dead. My stomach rumbled, but nausea overpowered the growing hunger. I looked around, but there were no windows to tell me what time of the day it was.

I climbed out of bed, careful not to bump my head on the rail of the top bunk, and dropped onto the cold floor. Before I lost my mind, I uncurled my fingers and stared at my palms. I had to get out of here to at least attempt to save my mom. Being a sorceress was pointless if I couldn't use my powers to save her when she needed me most.

All our practice sessions flitted through my mind as I searched the fragments of important information for something that would help, but that information threaded into a dozen thoughts, mixing the information together. I closed my eyes, focusing on the energy around me, but everything felt scattered. Being able to feel everything had hindered me in the past and broke my concentration when using my powers. I'd spent years trying to block other people's emotions, which I'd achieved. It was probably the only thing I had been successful at.

It felt wrong being stuck down here while others died to protect me, when I was useless with my magic. I could help the guild like my mom, or assist the royal family like other sorcerers did, but my magic didn't work properly.

We were descended from gods and mortals and valued by society. My mom was a perfect example of everything a sorceress should be—powerful and wise.

Closing my eyes, I willed for my powers to surface, hoping for a flicker of some magic I could use to get out of this damn bunker. In here, I was no help to my mom, and I wasn't sure what I could do once I got out, but at least it wouldn't involve sitting around and doing nothing.

I stared at the lock until my eyes burned and my nails bit into my skin. My heart pounded as I let out the breath I'd been holding. Nothing happened. It was worse than a year ago when I could produce some glimmer of magic.

Staring at the marks on my palm, I slumped back on my bed. Then, pressing my forehead against my knuckles, I let out a scream behind closed lips, feeling it vibrate in my throat. Astor was dead, my mom was gone, and Draven probably hated me.

In two weeks, I had somehow lost everyone I cared about. My mom always told me not to feel sorry for myself, to keep getting back up when life throws punches, but I wasn't as strong as her. Grief and pain had chipped what little resilience I had left in me.

I wasn't sure how long I'd been lying there for, curled up under the thin white sheets, when the door finally opened.

Draven's bloodshot eyes met mine. My brows furrowed as a faint ringing fell through the open door. "Is that an alarm?"

"They've breached the guild."

I froze on the spot. "But that's impossible."

"It's not. Someone let them in." He grabbed my arm, dragging me from the bed. "Get behind me and do as I say, else neither of us are making it out alive."

Nodding, I pulled my slippers on and grabbed my black jacket from the back of the chair.

He motioned for me to follow as he carefully stepped outside the door, a rifle in his arms. I noticed he had no sword or ax on his belt to slow him down. He didn't plan on killing any vampires. Instead, he would shoot them, allowing us to escape, for me to get away.

I touched his bicep, hoping the gesture was enough to tell him I was sorry. He flinched but didn't look back at me. I followed him down the tunnels, peering around him in the low light.

Draven looked over his shoulder, pressing a finger against his lips. Swallowing thickly, I slowed my breathing as much as I could and crept behind him. Even with the alarm, we couldn't guarantee there wasn't a vampire in the tunnels who might hear us with their heightened senses.

Draven reminded me of a cat in how he moved; each step was calculated with such grace and poise. We stopped at the joining of two tunnels. I shuddered back against the black metal wall as he looked both ways and behind me. He pointed left, and we rounded the corner. He halted before we could move farther down the tunnel. I caught my next step before I ran into him, pressing my hand against his back. He extended an arm out behind him and shuffled us backward.

The wailing from the alarm grew louder as we neared ground level. Suddenly, everything fell silent, pausing us. The stench of gunpowder and smoke drifted down to where we stood, lingering around us as a reminder that death was close. How many bullets would it take to stop a vampire? Even with their high-tech rifles, explicitly designed to be slow shot, I doubted anything less than three bullets would do much against such a powerful creature.

I swallowed, and sweat beaded on my forehead at the sound of my saliva being gulped down my throat. Draven touched my wrist, a silent signal not to move. Adrenaline coursed through my veins, accelerating my heart rate. I closed my eyes, focusing on staying as quiet as possible.

A dark realization entered my mind. What if the vampires had switched off the alarm so they could hear any remaining protectors? The guild wouldn't have switched it off mid-attack.

The thought made me nauseous.

Gunfire and screams had become a distant memory in the silence. Dripping from a pipe was all that could be heard as we lightly walked toward the ground floor. For the first time since running out into the tunnels with Draven, I realized we might not make it out alive.

Draven slowly took a step back, and I followed his movement, begging for once in my life to have some of the grace he did. With each slow, calculated step, we hurried down another tunnel. I pressed the sleeve of my jacket against my mouth to muffle my breaths. We stayed close to the wall until we reached more bunkers. B56, I read on one of them. There were only two blocks, A and B, for the bunkers, from what I recalled my mom saying once. They were to be used in case of an attack, so I supposed we were in the best place.

Upstairs, a lone gunshot sounded, followed by another. Someone was still fighting. I blew out a sigh of relief, and Draven moved us faster. We stopped by a bunker I'd seen on my way in. That meant we were right by the steps leading up to the main floor, but I didn't want to think about what was waiting for us up there.

Everything fell silent again, and Draven halted. I stepped back but lost my footing. I grabbed a rail sticking out by the bunker, catching myself before I fell and made a sound.

Thank the gods.

Until the rail squeaked, jolting me. I didn't catch myself this time. My slipper scraped against the ground, the sound of the fall exaggerated in the tunnel.

I didn't stand. Draven didn't move. Seconds fell into a minute, and nothing happened. Maybe they didn't hear us?

It started with a whistle, then gunshots erupted around us, ringing fireworks in my ears. I slumped to the ground as Draven fired in the direction of something I couldn't see.

"Run!" Draven shouted, but I couldn't leave him.

I reached for the gun in his waistband. Trembling, I fired in the direction Draven did when I saw it for the first time. I blinked twice as the creature from every horror story I had been told stepped into view, but the creature was nothing like I expected. The vampire appeared deceivingly mortal and even smiled when his shining blue eyes fixated on me. I blinked, and he was gone.

Hands gripped me from behind, fingernails digging into my upper arms. Before I could scream, the vampire's mouth was pressed against my neck, his tongue swirling on my skin.

I fumbled for the gun, but before I could fire it, his fangs sunk into my neck, piercing agony into my soul. It felt like flames licking through my veins, unrelenting and searing. My eyes pinched shut, and I was shoved backward, the vampire forced away from my neck. I barely opened my eyes when the door closed in front of me. Draven had locked me inside the bunker.

I couldn't recall his gunshot, but the pain was all-consuming. Slowly, I reached my hand to my neck. My hair slicked around the bite, wet hitting my fingers. Soon enough, the pain waved into ecstasy, and I felt lighter than ever. The creature's venom was attacking me from the inside, immobilizing me.

I pulled myself up as venom reached down my veins, slowing my movements. Draven was still shooting his rifle. I could hear the shots, like thunder in the distance. Splaying my fingers over the back of the door, I looked down at the heavy lock and stumbled. I caught myself as the bite pulsated with heat. "Gods, help us" was all I said as I clasped a hand around the bite.

Draven let out a war cry, giving me hope. He was still alive and fighting. But then everything went quiet—too quiet. Sweat dripped into my eyebrows as minutes ticked by with no sound. He would have opened the door by now if he was alive. I swallowed the cry bubbling inside. I couldn't lose someone else I loved. As the silence went on for too long, my heart shriveled to nothing. My forehead was cold, pressed against the door, my tears falling thick and fast, when the lock turned. My gun was gone, lost to the scramble outside that door. All I could do was push myself as far against the wall as possible. There was no way I could fight a vampire with no weapon.

Draven appeared, and I did a double take. His blood-smeared face and bulging green eyes were everything I wanted to see.

"You're alive," I spluttered, tears falling down my cheeks and lips. I opened myself unwillingly, feeling his emotions rolling away from him—relief, fear, anxiety, all mixed in a pulse that knotted inside of him. "I'm sorry." I wept and threw my arms around him.

As I did, he relaxed, and his breaths steadied. "I know," he whispered, resting his head against mine for a few seconds before pulling away. "We can't stop moving. I killed this one, but there will be more coming. We're close to getting out."

My eyes widened. "How did you kill it?" I moved my gaze down to his blood-soaked fingers, following him out into the low-lit tunnel.

He pointed at the shattered glass box on the wall reading *For use in an emergency*. The ax from inside lay on the ground, next to the lifeless vampire. His head was separated from his body, his eyes open in surprise.

If I didn't know any better, I would say he appeared normal, like any other man. "Your first kill," I said, sorrow lacing my tone.

"Yes."

I noticed blood seeping from his neck and arm. The vampire had bitten him too. "You cut its head off with the venom in your body," I stated, admiration rising in me. There was little point in being quiet, with all the ruckus that had happened. They'd already have heard us.

"This way" was all he said. He passed me the keycard from his pocket. We reached a heavy door, and I shimmied between it and him. He pressed the card against the pad, waiting for the beep. Instead, a little light turned orange. Draven pushed his hand over the sensor without looking at it, which now lit up green.

The door opened, and I was surprised to find crisp air filling my lungs. I gulped it in, closing my eyes when gunshots sent me diving onto the gravel.

"Stay down!" Draven shouted as he fired off a round of bullets, slamming them into the heart of a man I couldn't see.

When the creature emerged, a woman this time, I gasped. She lunged for Draven with a speed I'd never seen before.

He narrowly dodged her, rolling onto his side, and pointed the rifle at her head. "Run!" he ordered.

"Draven!" I screamed for him to move as another vampire ran at him from the side, but he didn't make it in time.

Instead, his wings spread out in a blackish gray, with bone lined underneath, reaching up into points. One of them blocked out the rising sun as the creature grabbed Draven, who hit him in the groin with the back end of the rifle. The vampire growled lowly, stumbling back as Draven's rifle tumbled from his grip. I reached for it but was kicked back by Draven.

"Leave me. Go. Now."

The creature sank its fangs into his neck then took off into the sky, Draven limp in its arms. "No," I spluttered as I watched them disappear into the horizon, helpless to do anything.

All the attacks were a distraction, so most of the protectors would be on the other side of the city when they attacked the guild. A female vampire drained a protector until all the life left his face. I stood, then ran until my legs burned. I reached a wall, moving out of view from the vampires in front of the guild, when a voice rooted me to the spot.

"Good morning." His tone was light, almost mocking.

I looked up at the sky, as if the gods might see me from down here. "Please, just kill me quickly," I begged, hoping the creature might have some mercy, however unlikely. The best I could wish for would be for it to kill me here and now, quickly, maybe with a snap of a neck.

He closed the distance between us. The smell of pine and a hint of citrus wafted from him. I would have mistaken him as any other handsome man around my age if I'd run into him in the city.

His night-blue eyes regarded me as he tilted his head, tousling his dark-brown strands. "I don't plan on it, love." He swept back my hair, revealing the puncture wounds from my bite. "I see someone has had their way with you already."

I slapped his hand away, and he grinned.

"Try not to scream." He peered around me. "You can thank me later."

"What—"

He swept me into his arms, pulling me close against him. I opened my mouth to scream, but his hand covered my mouth, stopping the sound before it could leave his fingers. I could hardly breathe when he whisked us both into the sky, expanding a frightening set of black wings.

I watched in disbelief as the guild turned into a dot in the distance. The wind tugged through my long hair, blowing behind me as we reached dizzying heights.

"You haven't fainted yet," he said against the wind, a smirk playing on his lips. "I'm impressed."

"Let me go," I ordered, although it was futile.

He laughed. "You don't want me to do that."

I peered down, then wished I hadn't. The city grew smaller, then everything faded to black.

FOUR

My eyes fluttered open to the place that has haunted my darkest dreams since I was a child, and it was far worse than I could have ever imagined.

The two times when I woke up, I had crossed my fingers before opening my eyes. I had prayed that I was home in Ismore, and at any moment my mom was going to come through my bedroom door with some hot cocoa and soup, but it all had been true. I was trapped here as a prisoner, held up in some bedroom in a four-story house in the City of Nightmares.

It had been roughly eighteen hours since I'd landed here in the arms of the vampire who called himself Sebastian. I checked the clock on the wall and realized I'd been asleep for thirteen of them. Slowly, I reached my fingers up to the bite mark on my neck, but it had already healed.

I jumped down from the four-post bed, hitting my feet onto the cold stone. Apparently, they didn't believe in heating here, but I didn't dare complain. In fact, I hoped if I stayed quiet, they wouldn't think too much of me. If it weren't for the need for food and water, I'd happily slink into the shadows of the large room and pray to be forgotten altogether.

I pushed back the white voile drapes, which floated outward from the breeze, and closed the window. My breath fogged the air, and I rubbed my arms, hoping to instill some warmth back into my skin. My gaze ran over the lamp-lit street below. I gripped the windowsill, digging my nails into the wood. The pressure did something to alleviate the fear pulsing through me. Aniccipere—or soul vampires, as many called them—walked in groups. Unlike my kidnapper, these creatures barely resembled their blood vampire heritage, inheriting many of their features from their demon parentage.

I'd heard the stories of the soul vampires, the offspring of demons, and the sangaree. They were ruthless, deceitful creatures of the night who feasted upon a different life source altogether. I could see from the defeated expression of the mortal man they pulled along behind them that he must have been fed on frequently. He walked with a slight limp, his shoulders slumped, and he was tugged by a leash around his neck, as if he were a dog lagging behind.

Back before the vampires had broken the treaty we had in place, agreements were made between the mortal kingdoms and the vampire king. In exchange for them not attacking us, criminals of the highest order, those who were convicted of rape and murder, were sent to Sanmorte to be kept as prisoners by the vampires. Now, innocent men like the mortal below were forced to remain here, imprisoned and used as if they were nothing.

The willowy creatures moved gracefully under the yellow lights of the streetlamps, smiling their lipless, toothy mouths at one another, their gray, beady round eyes the same color as their ash-tinted skin and long, thinned hair. Thick, yellow talons protruded from their bony fingers, sending goose bumps over my arms. I didn't want to think about the damage they could do with those things. One glanced up in my direction, and I dropped from view, pulling on one of the voiles as I dropped to my knees.

"They won't hurt you," a familiar voice said from the doorway. "Not while you're here, as my—"

"Prisoner?"

"Guest," he corrected, casually leaning against the doorframe.

My eyes narrowed. "If that's true, then I will be leaving."

He sidestepped, extending his arm. "Go. You won't make it far."

I hated that he was right. I wouldn't make it a minute down the road before being killed. "You need to fly me back to Baldoria."

"That I can't do," he said nonchalantly. "However, I'm sure you have a hundred questions for me. Now that you're awake and not crying, ask away."

Asshole, I thought but didn't say aloud. My eyes focused on the glint of his fangs when he smiled. He could kill and drain me of my blood in a second, and it would be no skin off his back.

"More like a thousand questions," I said, eyeing him carefully as I walked over to the gray, suede armchair in the corner of the room. "I'll start with the obvious. Why did you bring me here? Where is my mom? Am I to be a blood bag, or instead forced to fulfill your magical wishes? Because you're out of luck; I'm a terrible sorceress." As I said the words, I wished I hadn't, but it was best he found out now instead of trying to make me use them and seeing what a failure I was.

He leaned back, kicking one leg up against the wall. "You were in danger, so I decided to save your life. That's why I brought you here."

I arched an eyebrow. "You could have, I don't know, taken me somewhere else if that's true. Not here, into the heart of the most dangerous place in the world." I didn't believe a word he was saying, but if he wanted to lie to me for whatever reason, then he had to at least make it good.

"Where would you suggest I'd taken you?" He ran his fingers through his thick hair, losing them for a moment in the dark brown. "Back to your house, where the order was looking for you? Or return you to the guild with your fallen friends?"

The thought of everyone I'd come to know over the years roiled my stomach and sent an ache to the back of my throat. "How did they find out about me?"

"There's an order called Nightshade. They want to keep the vampire blood pure." He drew in a deep breath and slowly released it before leaning forward. "They believe all vampires should be made."

"So they don't like the soul vampires?" I deduced as I knew they had demon blood in their veins.

"No, but neither do I."

On that, we both agreed. Although, I felt that way about all of them. "What does that have to do with me?"

"That's not the only thing they care about," he said, his tone thick with a tension that felt as if it might snap at any moment.

A shiver danced down my spine as the cold air reached through my dressing gown, chilling my bones.

"You're cold," he said.

I repressed the urge to throw back a snarky remark. He was a vampire and not a normal guy, no matter how much he came across as one.

The muscles under his black shirt bulged when he moved toward the door. Before I could catch my breath, he was gone. Rubbing my forearm, I turned my attention to the ceiling, shivering against the cold air circling the room. I whipped my head around at a scuff against the floor, seeing Sebastian returned with a thick, red throw in his arms. "Take this." He walked toward me, and I couldn't help but flinch, so he threw it the rest of the way. I couldn't bring myself to say thanks, considering, but hugged the material around me nonetheless.

He continued, this time sitting on the side of the bed. "How much do you know about your father?"

I stiffened. "Nothing, really."

"Interesting."

"Why?" I played with my promise ring. "All I really care about is my mom," I admitted. "She's here, somewhere in Sanmorte, and I want to know where."

"I don't know, but as she's a sorceress, you can assume she's alive."

A lump formed in my throat. I had to find her, because even if they hadn't killed her, she would be a prisoner. I imagined her, scared, cold, with bite marks on her neck.

"About your father," he said, snapping me away from my awful daydream. "Your mother wouldn't want you getting curious if you knew the truth, which is why she probably didn't tell you. Although I am surprised you know nothing at all."

"What is it you know?"

He licked his lips. "He's a vampire."

My heart raced; cool sweat beaded at the back of my neck. "Vampire," I repeated, unsure if I heard him right. He'd said it so nonchalantly, as if this sort of thing happens all the time.

"Yes."

"How is that possible?"

"Your mother is a sorceress."

"Thanks for stating the obvious."

He tapped the side of his leg. "That means she is derived from a goddess. An immortal." He clarified as if I was stupid. "While we cannot have children with mortals, male sangaree can conceive with sorceresses. It's rare, mostly because your kind is rare."

An odd sensation flowed through me. "Where is my dad?"

"Here, in Sanmorte."

"Did he send you?"

He shook his head. "I decided to come on my own."

"Lucky me," I muttered under my breath before I could think better of it.

Fortunately, he smirked. "I've been tracking you for the past few days."

I buried my chin in the throw, snuggling against the pockets of warmth. "That doesn't make me feel any better."

"The leaders of Nightshade were tracing you, too, and your mom. They knew how to get into the guild."

My fists balled. "They attacked the city. Vampires had never come so far inland before."

"That you know of," he said darkly. "However, you are right. Normally they wouldn't bother. Sticking to the coastal towns is easier, but they came for you both."

All those people, who I'd known for my whole life, had died because of me and my mom. "My mom's not the only one who was taken. My friend, Draven, he's here, too," I explained, hoping it was true because the alternative was too hard a pill to swallow. "Where can I find him?"

"I'm not a map, you know. I don't know where they are. Your friend could be anywhere, in a blood den or sold in an auction. As for your mom, she's probably being held by some rich family, or Nightshade."

"I need to find them both."

"It's not safe for you to leave the house. I'll ask around to see if anyone knows anything."

"That's it? I'm supposed to wait on you asking around?"

"Yes."

I ground my teeth. I'd have to figure out a way to find them myself because he sure as hell wasn't going to help me. Instead, all I could do was squeeze out any more information which would be helpful, although the truth about my dad, if this vampire was being honest, did itch at me. "So the order—Nightshade—they want me dead because I'm part sorcerer, part...?" Every hair on my body stood on end as I realized what this meant. "Am I part vampire?"

"No. You can't be both magical and a vampire. You have to be one or the other."

"Then why are they after me?"

"They wanted a sorceress," he said, but I got the impression he was lying.

For every question answered, I had a hundred more, but my head ached. "I'm tired," I said, hoping he'd leave.

He shoved his hands in his pockets, standing. "Do you want some food?"

My stomach rumbled in response. "Don't you just have blood?"

His lips curled at the edges. "We had mortal food brought here for you."

"We?"

"You can meet my friends another day. As for your other questions, no. I don't plan on using you as a blood bag or for your magic."

"Hmm," I mumbled, unconvinced.

He clicked his tongue. "I'll have Anna bring you something to eat. She's mortal, like you."

"You have slaves?" I couldn't keep the disgust out of my expression.

He shook his head and turned. I glared at the back of his head as he closed the door. There was no way he was helping me out of the goodness of his heart, if he even had one. He was going to use me. I didn't know how yet, but I sure didn't want to stick around to find out.

Once his footsteps faded, I ran to the door. I wanted nothing more than to shove a chair up under the handle or push the marble dresser against it, but nothing would stop him from getting in if he wanted to. Vampires were strong, and heavy furniture would be nothing but a mere inconvenience to them. I slid down the back of the wood frame, burying my head in my arms. He was deceivingly mortal—he even looked it—but I knew what type of monster hid beneath, and I was trapped with him.

After twenty minutes, a mortal woman walked in, her smile meek as she dropped in a tray of sliced apples, crackers, cubed cheese, and butter. She didn't utter a word and left without so much as glancing at me. She appeared to be in her forties, and I wondered how long she'd been imprisoned here.

I didn't leave my bed for the rest of the night. Instead, I watched a spider crawl around its glittering silver web in the corner of the ceiling, weaving it bigger and bigger until an unsuspecting fly flew into one of its sticky traps.

Finally, I gave in and nibbled on a slice of cheese, but barely touched my crackers. When the sun came up, I thought of my mom, Draven, and the order of vampires who wanted me dead. When I tried to summon my powers to escape, only a flicker burned through my veins before sizzling out. Finding comfort in the soft covers on my bed, I closed my eyes, hoping this was some prolonged nightmare.

Inside my head was the only place where I could escape. I daydreamed about breaking out and finding my mom and

Draven, then finding us a way back home. I created scenarios in my head until sleep took me, and for a minute, I allowed myself to pretend I wasn't held captive by a vampire and my fate wasn't in his hands.

FIVE

My heart leaped as I turned in my bed and found myself face to face with a blond vampire. He tilted his head as I pulled the sheets over my chest. "Gods, what the—" I trod carefully as I took him in. I didn't want to piss one of them off right now. "You scared me." I moved back against the white-bricked wall that the bed was pushed up against.

White hair fell like silk around his shoulders, matching his star-silver eyes, which narrowed when I gulped. "You're the sorceress," he stated coolly. "Olivia."

"Yes." I cleared my throat.

When his lips parted, I spotted the tips of his fangs, and the hairs on the back of my neck stood erect. "I'm Zachariah. I am Sebastian's friend."

Whether or not he really was his friend, I didn't put it past him to sink those glinting fangs into my neck, even if Sebastian was under the illusion I was just his guest. "Where is Sebastian?"

His words didn't make me feel safe in the slightest, nor did I trust his intentions, especially when his gaze trickled down my neck every few seconds. I brought the covers up, hoping it would mask the scent. He ran a bony finger over the bare chest showing at the top of his unbuttoned shirt. "I will not drink your blood," he stated. "It would not be appropriate."

I inhaled sharply. "Good to know."

"You are a guest. We do not drink from guests, so you can lower those covers."

I didn't. "As long as I am a guest, I don't suppose that means I can request to be flown back home?" I asked, on the slim chance he'd be willing.

He paused, his arched eyebrows furrowing as he searched my expression. "We insist you don't leave."

"Would you stop me if I tried?"

"I am in charge of keeping you safe, and allowing you to leave this house would place your life at risk, so yes."

"So I am a prisoner."

"No."

I repressed the urge to roll my eyes. "If I must stay here, can you tell me why Sebastian is keeping me here? I don't assume it's out of the kindness of his heart?"

"Because we are vampires, you would presume we are not capable of such things?"

I hesitated. "I mean, well, yes."

He rose from the wooden chair by my bed. "You would need to ask Sebastian that."

"I get the feeling he's not going to tell me the truth."

His lips curled between his teeth. "I'll ask Anna to bring you some lunch," he said deadpan, changing the topic.

At least she was mortal, so being around her didn't make my skin crawl. I looked over at the window as light arrowed through the gap in the drapes. "I always thought your kind would burst into flames or something, but Sebastian flew me here when the sun was out."

"Us bursting into flames in the sun was a rumor started by us to make the mortals feel safe during the day." He glided over to the window, opening the drapes a slither more, peering out at a world I wanted no part of. "Your family is missing," he stated.

"Yes. My mom and friend are missing."

"I am sorry to hear it."

Was he trying to lull me into some false sense of security, and if yes, to what end? "I want to find them."

"Naturally." He turned his back on the window. "However, now is not the time to play the hero. The remaining members in the order have returned, and they are on the prowl. They know someone took you."

"Nightshade, right?" I recalled.

"Yes." The bridge of his thin nose wrinkled.

"Do you think they have my mom?"

"It's likely," he admitted, and the heaviness in my chest lifted a little. It was somewhere to start.

"Do they have a headquarters in the city?"

"I wouldn't tell you if they did."

"Why not?"

"Because if I were you, that would be the first place I'd try to escape to, especially if I thought they were holding my family. I will not allow you to leave under my watch. You will be killed instantly, and Sebastian's rescue would have been for nothing. He's already risked enough."

I bit my bottom lip. Why was any vampire risking anything for me unless they wanted to use me? There was no other reason for it. "He said he would ask around for them."

"If he said that, then he will."

"You're confident in him."

He moved his willowy form to the door at dizzying speed, ignoring my statement. He stopped before leaving. "If you need anything, just call my name."

With that, he left. Of course, they could hear every move I made. That's why Draven and I had been so quiet in those tunnels. The memory flooded back, along with many others with him and Astor. Suddenly, the room felt smaller. Panic slicked a cold sweat over my chest, back, and arms, and shaky breaths forced me into a ball as I attempted to shield myself from the memories. Whenever this happened, I was helpless to others' emotions. My barrier dropped, and I could feel the energy in the house.

It seemed everyone in this house was filled with a pain I recognized. It was unending and unrelenting, and they'd suppressed it so much that it felt numb. It was the type of suffering a person learned to live with, which I knew because the same belonged to me too. It was a grief anyone could grow comfortable with over time. Between the bursts of anger and sadness, I'd pushed the feeling deep down, enough to where I hardly noticed it, until I did, and then it became unbearable.

I closed myself off as best I could, not wanting to be around that energy for another moment, not when it amplified my suffering. When I thought about it, it made sense. Vampires had been alive long enough to go through all sorts of torment, things I probably couldn't even imagine.

Was I going to die here? Never see my mom or Draven again? I'd already lost Astor. The vampires attacking had distracted me from the grief, but like everything else, it was temporary. I lay back on the bed, creating a half-made fort with the pillows, and tears came thick and fast. I wiped my nose against the covers, howling deep into the threads until the emptiness came, and I stared at the wall and no longer cared what happened to me.

A light knock sounded some time later, but I ignored it. When I finally lowered the blankets, I noticed a tray of cold food on the chair. Someone must have brought it in while I was crying. A shade of embarrassment crept over me, but I shrugged it away.

"You've hardly eaten," Sebastian announced at the open door as he tugged at the sleeve of his tux.

"Going somewhere nice?" I snarked, unable to contain my hatred. I'd already had a shitty day. I didn't need him adding to it.

"No. I always look this good." He strode over to me, his smirk uncontainable as he sat on the chair, kicking his legs up on the bed. "How are you doing?"

"What sort of question is that? You don't care about me."

"I heard you were crying."

My fists clenched briefly. "How did you know?"

"Zach told me."

I drummed my fingers against my leg. "I'm sure the entire house was listening to me, except for all your mortal slaves."

"There's only Anna," he explained, "and she's not a slave."

No, I was sure she was just a "'guest" like me. Whatever made the asshole feel better about himself. "That doesn't make it any better."

He glanced at the plate. "Is the food not to your liking?"

I pulled my knees together then curled them against my chest. "I'm just not hungry."

"You need your strength."

He sounded like my mom. "Please, leave me alone. If I'm a *guest* here and you really have no intent on harming me, then prove it. Just leave me be."

"I only came up here to let you know I'm entertaining some out-of-town guests tonight. We will be in the dining room, so don't wander." He gripped his wrist with his other hand and leaned forward.

"Great," I said, my tone thick with sarcasm. "What's to stop them from coming in here?"

"Because I told them not to."

I scoffed. "It's not like I can do anything about it if they did."

He stood and turned to leave. "Wait," I called out. He turned back, fixing his collar. "Did you find out anything about my mom or Draven?"

"No." His stony expression told me he didn't care either.

"Are you going to tell me why I'm really here?" My voice quivered, and I sat on my hands to stop them from shaking. "Before you say it's to protect me, I want to know *why* you're protecting me. What is it you want from me? Because you monsters don't do anything unless it's for your own gain."

"Is it not enough that I saved you before they killed you?" His voice deepened. "What makes you think I want anything from you? Be grateful, unless you'd rather I hand you over to the people I'm protecting you from. Then you can see what real monsters look like."

My heart raced as I clambered back against my nest of pillows. "I just assumed—"

"You assumed wrong. Don't leave this room tonight if you value your life."

He was gone before I could say another word. There was no way I could get out of here by going against them, even if I hated them with every fiber of my being. So I stood, walked to the window, and looked down onto a bustling street. Mostly sangaree walked up and down the sunlit road, laughing and chatting.

My mom's voice sounded in my head. *"Sometimes, you need to join them to beat them."* That's what she used to say when I asked why agents from the guild would go undercover in this world, posing as mortals who wanted to become blood donors. Unfortunately, none returned from Sanmorte, but they knew what they were getting into.

This was like that. I had to play smarter because this wasn't just about me; this was about my mom and Draven, and until now, I'd been helpless in helping either of them.

Anger thrummed through me when I thought about the bloodsuckers and how they'd come into our home, taken people I'd cared about, and killed hundreds of good people who were only ever protecting us from them.

Sebastian, or whatever mortal name he used to pretend he was anything but a disgusting leech of a creature, claimed some crap about not wanting anything from me, but he was hiding me up here, from the order. There had to be a reason, one which suited him. They weren't ever going to be honest, and I'd turned into the prisoner they'd wanted by doing nothing.

Zachariah hadn't said there was a headquarters for Nightshade, but there had to be. If they had one nearby, then my mom was probably there.

I stepped away from the window and placed my hands on my stomach to center myself, drawing in deep breaths. I focused on the surrounding smells of polished wood, old spaghetti sauce, and lavender coming from the bag hanging on the closet door.

If only I could use my magic, I might have a chance of helping them. I willed my powers to come to me, keeping my mind as clear as I could while I searched for a spark of magic, anything to ignite what I knew was inside of me. I'd never concentrated on my lessons before, but now I had nothing else to do.

After half an hour of nothing, I took a break and ran a bath. Perhaps the water would energize me, and I'd have more success there. I plugged the tub and turned on the water. Heat steamed in swirls, and the tap leaked thick droplets when I turned it off. I added a jar of rose salts from the shelf over the white faucet and half a bottle of bubble bath.

After an hour of soaking, I'd only managed to make the water heat a degree. It was something, but not enough to get out of here. My head was pounding, and I called it a night, wrapping a towel around myself.

When I got back into bed, I found a note scrawled in elegant handwriting.

Sorry for losing my temper. Please join me for breakfast in the morning. My guests will have gone. Sebastian.

I crumpled the paper in my fist. Great, I was held captive by a temperamental vampire with anger issues. If I couldn't beat them, then I'd join them. I wasn't going to find anyone by being a bitch or sulking in this room. No, I would play whatever weird part I was expected to in this house.

If Sebastian wanted me to be grateful, I would fake it. If he wanted me to join him for breakfast, then I'd go. I would do what I believed my mom would do. I would earn their trust and use that to get out of here.

I went to bed, feeling a little comfort knowing that wherever she was, I'd underestimated her. She was probably working on a plan to escape too, and if anyone could do it, it was her.

SIX

A gown of shimmering blue had been laid out for me. I wanted nothing more than to throw it across the room, but it beat wearing a nightdress. Once on, I tied the ribbon at the back. Sebastian had guessed my size right. My cheeks reddened at the thought of him looking at me like that.

I made my way downstairs, tiptoeing down the spiral staircase linking two floors, which led out to a corridor of rooms. The second set of stairs opened out to a bright foyer. I'd only guessed the number of stories this house had based on the other buildings across the street from my window, but it was far bigger than I had imagined. I hadn't gotten a chance to see it before now because Sebastian had flown me onto the roof and taken me down through a hatch to the top floor and then to the room I'd now spent three days in.

The antique gold chandelier was far grander than anything I'd seen in Baldoria. Lights reflected from diamonds that trickled down from the arms like teardrops. My feet, squeezed into a pair of slip-on flats, made little sound as I walked across the marble floor. I rubbed my arms as goose bumps spread over my body and the cool air hit my lungs. I supposed they didn't need it.

Voices sounded from within a closed room. I spotted a makeshift sign from paper with *This way, mortal girl* scribbled on it and an arrow pointing to that room. I rolled my eyes and stepped forward, but panic suddenly shot through me, rendering me still.

My plan was to be nice to them, and I'd spent the night thinking about how I'd pretend to be their friend and give them what they wanted—or try, considering it was most likely my magic, and I was a terrible sorceress. I saw no other option if I were to escape, or better, get them to help me find my mom and Draven. It was better for them to think of me as an ally, a friend of sorts—if their cold hearts knew of that—or at the very least, a willing prisoner. But they were monsters, the things from bedtime stories and legends, evil, soulless creatures cursed by a goddess who hungered for blood or souls. I was nothing to them.

Inhaling deeply to calm my nerves, I pushed down the silver handles and opened the double doors to a long table covered with platters of food. The vampire who'd been in my room, Zachariah, sat stiffly in one chair with a goblet filled with wine—or worse.

Sebastian leaned back in a chair at the head of the table, draping one arm over the side. "I'm surprised you came down to dine with us *monsters*."

Zach didn't look at me when he spoke. "It seems she's *finally* showing some manners."

A woman stepped through doors behind me. Her dark eyes complemented her skin, and her thick lips pulled into a grimace in Zachariah's direction. "Don't act all virtuous. Most vampires *are* monsters. Besides, give the girl a break. If I'd been kidnapped and taken to another kingdom, I'd be pretty pissed too." A ghost of a smile crossed Sebastian's expression.

I almost smiled too—*almost*. I decided I hated her the least out of the three of them.

"You must be hungry." She pulled out a chair and gestured for me to join her. I stared at the platters of food, and my stomach rumbled.

"Don't you only drink blood?" I asked tentatively.

"Yes, we only drink blood. We weren't sure what you liked, so we got different options." She moved her braided, dark hair over one shoulder.

I couldn't help but steal a look at Sebastian. He leaned his elbows on the table as he circled his finger around the rim of his cup. At least he tried to seem of this age, with a standard, blue mug, whereas Zachariah drank from some silver thing I imagined a king sipping from a couple hundred years ago.

Sebastian's wings were tucked behind his back, his piercing eyes focused on the platter of food in front of me. I noticed tattoos peeking out from the rolled-up sleeves of his shirt, black markings which swirled in patterns, and a crescent moon that sat nestled between two curls of black reaching his wrist.

I averted my eyes when he caught me staring, feeling heat flood my face. Of course, I didn't want my observing them to be taken as my having any interest in who they are, and from the way his lips tugged into a lazy grin, I presumed he took it the wrong way.

"I'm Erianna," the woman next to me said, breaking the awkward silence. "I live here, with Seb and Zach."

I almost choked on the water I'd poured. *Seb.* It sounded almost amusing for such a frightening creature. "Sorry." I patted the sides of my mouth with a napkin. "It's nice to meet you, Erianna."

"I wish it were under better circumstances," she said, her brown eyes regarding me as I reached for the scrambled eggs and slices of toast. Being stuck in that room had returned my appetite, and when I woke this morning, I felt a need to fill the emptiness in my stomach—a feeling I hadn't had in weeks. "However, with Nightshade after you, you're safer here than in Baldoria."

"Wouldn't they be looking for me here?" I asked, remembering how Zach had told me they knew a vampire had taken me.

"Yes, but they'll be looking in all the wrong places."

"You mean in blood dens?" I made a face but remembered my goal here. I needed to show them I could be trusted. "I know you all need to feed," I added.

"Think of them as grocery stores for vampires." Sebastian leaned back in his chair. "It helps to not be so disgusted by them."

The muscle in my jaw ticked. "Except we don't keep live cattle in our stores," I pointed out, making the only comparison I could think of.

His voice charged with challenge. "Would you prefer if we bottled blood and kept the mortals in stables and fields?"

"Are you comparing us to animals?"

His cheeks dimpled when he smirked. "You're the one who said it. I would never regard mortals so lowly."

I couldn't help but scoff. I wanted to be pleasant and act like I could be a friend to these people, but something about him sparked a rage somewhere deep inside me. "Yet you keep one as a slave."

He arched a thick brow. "I told you before, Anna is not a slave. She's here of her own free will."

"No one would choose to be here of their own free will."

He took a sip of blood and licked away the crimson from his lips. "Well, you are the expert on vampires and the inner workings of our kingdom."

I touched my cheek, shuffling in my seat. "I never said that. All I'm pointing out is that we're just food to you. So why would any of us choose to be here?"

"Some of you are more than food."

My nose wrinkled. "Oh?"

"Yes," he purred. "You make great cooks and cleaners too."

"Okay." Erianna rose from her chair, glaring at Sebastian. "Stop antagonizing her." She turned to look at me, forcing a hard smile. "Ignore him. He's just playing. He doesn't mean it."

"He's an asshole," I said before I could stop myself, pushing my plate away from me.

"He doesn't know how to converse like a normal person," she explained, shooting him an incredulous look.

Zach glared at me, gripping the edge of the table. "He has every right to say something. We saved her life. She would be dead if it wasn't for Sebastian." His chair screeched when he pushed it backward. "I'll be back this evening. I have business to take care of. As for Anna—" He turned his attention to me. "She's no slave, so keep her name out of your mouth in the future, or I'll be the one who brings you food and clothing, and I'm nowhere near as nice."

"Zach..." Sebastian called, but Zach was already gone in a literal blink of an eye. He turned to face me, his expression falling flat. "He'll get over it. You should eat something. I didn't have this all brought here for you to stare at."

"I'm no longer hungry," I snapped. "All the talk of blood and cattle put me off."

He swirled his tongue around his fangs, then drank the rest of his blood. "Perhaps we should find more neutral topics of conversation for dinner."

I wanted to laugh at how he thought I'd be joining him for any more meals but stopped, mentally kicking myself for everything I'd said so far. If I couldn't keep my own emotions in check, I had no way of getting out of this alive. "I'm sorry," I said, hating myself with every word.

Sebastian stood, grinning. The bastard. "No, you're not, and you don't need to be."

Don't be snarky, I told myself over and over, rolling down my temper until it was a ball pushed deep inside me. "Your friend was right. I judged you."

"It's no big deal. I've heard worse from people I care about far more," he proclaimed with a shrug.

Erianna spoke, and I was glad for her. Even if she was a vampire, she at least pretended to be otherwise. "I asked around for the location of your mom and friend." She paused, plating some food, most likely to make me feel less lonely with my breakfast. "Unfortunately, your friend is not locatable. He's only a mortal, so he's nameless and wouldn't stand out."

My chest tightened. "What about my mom?" I asked, hoping for *some* good news.

"I've heard rumors of a sorceress being captured."

I almost leaped out of my chair. "Where is she?"

"She was captured by the leaders of Nightshade but was given as a gift."

My stomach churned, and nausea crept over me in waves. "Is she close?"

She looked at Sebastian, who nodded. "She was handed over to the vampire king, Sargon."

My heart palpitated. Even I knew that couldn't be good. "How do we get her back?"

Sebastian interrupted. "We're working on something. You sit tight. We'll get this sorted."

Erianna shot him a look, her eyebrows pinched down to her straight nose, but she didn't respond.

"What about Draven?" I persisted. "How do I find him? I can't leave him. He's my only friend." I felt pathetic admitting it, but it was the truth.

"There are hundreds of places he could have been taken to."

"Please," I begged, my dignity slipping. "Help me find him. I can't stay here for another night without knowing if he's alive or not."

A crack formed in the barrier of my power, allowing the energy of the room to slip in. I closed my eyes and felt a mix of sadness, pain, and curiosity in the air. I looked around and could feel it moving, like the emotion was a living thing.

Then I looked a Sebastian. The curiosity was radiating from him, and the suffering I'd felt in my room yesterday when I'd opened up was shared between Erianna, Sebastian and Zach. They all knew grief.

I tried to look away, but the feeling grew stronger until it merged with my own. I held my breath, unable to say another word. His gaze burned with uncertainty, a muscle feathering in his jaw as his relaxed expression slipped away.

"Are you okay?" Erianna asked, snapping me out of it.

I blinked twice, building my barrier back until I felt nothing but my own emotions. Their pain was tangible; there was so much aching, longing, and anguish pressed under the surface, and I wondered how they managed to walk around without crying.

"Yes." I straightened my torso and cleared my throat. I could see him in my peripheral vision. He was still staring at me, his brows furrowed, his index finger tapping lightly against the tabletop. "I just need to find my friend."

She sighed softly. "Maybe we could look around the city."

"Yes!"

"No," Sebastian barked. "Absolutely not."

"She'll be safe with us. You can pretend she's your plaything. No one would suspect otherwise. Not with your reputation."

I nodded along. "You did say I'm a guest, not a prisoner." If he wanted something from me and insisted on making me think I wasn't being held captive, it meant he wanted me to do whatever he was planning of his own free will. Suspicion swirled in my mind as to what his endgame was, but he gave nothing away. So neither did I.

"The order is searching for her."

"Most of them won't know what she looks like."

I decided I liked Erianna. "I won't cause a scene," I pressed.

"I didn't save you so you could get yourself killed," he said darkly, glancing from me to her.

Erianna placed a hand on her hip. "The only ones that might know what she looks like are Velda and possibly Eldor. Both of which are visiting the royal court. She needs this."

He swallowed thickly. "They'll know to look out for a sorceress. I can feel her magic from here."

Erianna licked her lips. "Not if we use the bracelet you got her."

"Bracelet, as in jewelry?" I asked, thinking I must have heard wrong.

"It's enchanted jewelry. It blocks the magic of sorcerers. They were created by Azia, the king's sorcerer," he clarified. "They use them to keep sorcerers taken from other kingdoms captive. However, I've had it tampered with, so anyone can remove it, including you."

They'd already prepared one for me. Was this planned? I didn't put much energy into the thought. Right now, Draven had to be my focus. He was the one who would be in immediate danger. "I'll wear it. I don't care."

Sebastian shook his head. "It's okay, Olivia. We can search for him alone."

Hearing him say my name sent an odd sensation through me. He spoke of me as if we were old friends and not natural enemies. "Neither of you know what Draven looks like," I blurted. "If you don't let me go, I will find a way to escape and look myself." Challenge burned in my eyes as I stared at him.

Erianna placed her icy fingers on my shoulder. "I won't let anything happen to her." When she rose, I noticed a dagger strapped to her side and a bottle of poison on the other. Her corset was armored, and her black pants were made from spandex, like the protector's uniform from the guild. This woman wasn't just another vampire; she was a warrior.

"Seeing as you have a death wish," he said bitterly, "it's better if you go with us than alone. But we look for one night only, and if we don't find him, then we come back and that's it. I don't want to hear any more talk of going out in the city again."

I breathed relief. It was something more than I could have asked for. Perhaps I should have pressed why any of them were extending any kindness or courtesy to me, but I didn't care. "Okay, I agree. When can we go?"

"This afternoon, before the sun sets," he said, staring over at the arched window. "You need to look the part. I'll have Anna bring you some clothes."

"What's wrong with what I'm wearing?"

"Nothing, but if you want it to come across as if we're on a date, you'll need to dress like it."

"Okay."

"You will also need to act submissive. So keep from using that sharp tongue of yours. At least until we're back at the house."

I nodded. "I'll do anything."

"Good to know." He smirked with a glint in his eyes.

My voice charged with hope. "Thank you."

I left before he could change his mind, running upstairs to take a bath before morning ticked into the afternoon. The thought of leaving the safety of this house to walk the streets with thousands of bloodthirsty vampires should have had me trembling at the knees, but, in contrast, I felt weirdly optimistic because, after everything, there was a chance that I might find and save my friend.

Once I'd finished my bath, I hurried to the window and stared as the crowd below swelled and the streets became more packed. People just like me walked alongside their masters, many not in chains—although where would they run to?

I was watching the sun lower in the sky when a knock sounded at my door. I turned, and Anna brought in a red corseted dress that stopped above the knees, puffing out like a tutu. A mix of dread and excitement trickled through me. I was about to step out from the trenches of the snake's pit and into the center. I pressed my fingers against the bone of the corset, refusing to think of where it had come from.

I sucked in a deep breath. *Here goes nothing.*

SEVEN

The city was vibrant with music and color. Store windows glittered with decorations for the upcoming holiday, Vitarem, a day when we honored our dead. I was surprised they celebrated it at all, but I supposed even vampires could die, and they all had to have had families at one point or another.

Some people believed in reincarnation, especially in the kingdoms of Asland and Kabet. In contrast, Baldoria and most of the lands surrounding us believed that once we die, our souls go to the other side, and we take our place amongst the gods. Either way, once a person was gone, who they were in their life here was over. So whether it was reincarnation, if my soul went to other side to be with the gods, or perhaps if there was just nothing at all, the Olivia I am in this world would be gone. I wondered how soon I would find out the mystery of the afterlife. Judging by the way the vampires looked at me, it could be sooner than I ever anticipated.

I looked at the decor in one window, noticing all their trinkets and banners were red and black, most with words describing the underworld. "Of course, you all go with Salenia when you die."

Sebastian pulled me closer to his side, winding his hand around my waist. Going against my instincts, I leaned into him, remembering I had a part to play if I wasn't going to be snatched from these streets. "Supposedly."

"You don't think so?"

"I know we're meant to because we're irredeemable, but I like to have hope."

I recalled my words to Astor once when he talked of evil in the world, and I said I thought most could be redeemed. He disagreed, but I stood by my beliefs. "Maybe even a vampire can have their soul saved."

He half smiled and gestured for us to continue walking. Erianna spoke up from her step ahead of us. "I'm glad you believe that."

The smell of rain-soaked garbage and urine wafted around us as we turned onto a narrow street lined either side with run-down buildings, a stark difference to the main strip we'd just come from.

"Don't look them in the eye," Sebastian warned as we approached a group of aniccipere.

Their thin, veiny nostrils flared when they sniffed the air. One of them focused on me, moving her beady, gray eyes to meet mine, and tilted her head. An unnerving smile curled her lipless mouth upward. Bile bit up my throat as her intrusive stare bore into my soul. She licked her lips as if she could taste my fear. Her ashy skin resembled the smoke dancing away from a sangaree puffing on a cigarette.

I tore myself away and instead looked at Erianna, whose grip tightened on her dagger. I wondered what damage it could do to an immortal.

"They can taste fear," he said as we walked.

Many storefronts were boarded off, some with signs reading *Mortal Peep Show* and *Mortal Auction Here*. My stomach knotted, and my mouth dried, making me huddle closer into Sebastian. The sun emitted an orange hue over the city streets, casting a glow onto a sangaree holding newspapers on the side of the road.

I pinched my nose as a pungent, rotting stench hit my nose, forcing a gag up my throat. "What is that?"

Erianna chewed the inside of her lip, pity lacing her brown eyes. Sebastian strode, nodding toward a man in a waistcoat who waved at him. "Don't look to your left," Sebastian warned, but curiosity tugged for me to peek.

A half-eaten corpse rotted out in the sun. Bone, slathered with blood, gaped through stretches of pink and blood-soaked skin. Ants crawled over the person's feet, and I noticed there wasn't much left of their face. Pieces of flesh and half-chewed body parts were putrefying around the mutilated corpse.

My hands flew to my chest, feeling the heat rising through my body against my open palms. Suddenly, I couldn't move from the spot, forcing people to move around us. Sebastian extended his wings outward, pushing a black wing out in front of me, blocking the horrifying scene from view.

The taste of vomit bit at my tongue, twisting my mouth and nose. I covered my mouth, my fingers muffling my voice. "I'm going to throw up."

"Come with me." I walked in the shadow of his wing, reaching a garbage-pickled alleyway. A rat scurried from under a trash bag, rustling as it sped away from us. I stopped in front of a urine-splashed concrete wall and projectile vomited. After gagging twice, I leaned over, pressing my hands against my knees, attempting to catch my breath.

Sebastian shoved his hands in his pockets, anger lacing his sharp features. "One of the aniccipere was careless."

"That was the work of a soul vampire?" I asked breathlessly. Strands of hair had fallen into the path of my vomit, so I wiped them with my sleeve.

"You seem surprised?"

"I mean, the body was eaten. Don't they only suck out your soul?"

His shoulders slumped slightly. "Their process takes a toll on the body. That's usually what a mortal looks like after being killed by one of them."

Dizziness forced me backward, and my heel caught against the bottom of a blue dumpster. I wiped the cold sweat from my forehead and face with the backs of my clammy hands. "Gods, this place is awful."

"We shouldn't see any more. Usually, they clean up after themselves."

"Let's just get to these blood dens before I have to see any more rotting bodies."

He closed the distance between us as he searched my expression. "You don't have to go. Now you've seen what this city is really like, I wouldn't blame you if you want to return to the house."

"No." I clambered for the words to persuade him I would be okay, despite standing next to a puddle of my puke. "It won't happen again. It was a moment of weakness."

"No one would think this was weakness. You shouldn't have had to see that."

Was that a sliver of pity I saw cross his expression? It was gone before I could decide if it was real or not. "Let's keep moving," I begged. "Draven needs me."

He let out an inaudible sigh, then placed his hand, escorting me out of the alley. Erianna stepped out of the way from keeping watch. "All good?"

He nodded. "Let's go."

My shoulders rolled back. As we walked, I tried to distract myself from our surroundings, thinking back to the soul vampires. "Why did you say not to look them in the eye?"

"They can taste your fear when you do."

"Right, you said." I shook my head, trying to gather my scattered thoughts.

"Eyes are windows to the soul," Erianna stated.

I made a mental note to never look at them again. "No staring at the creepy demon vamps. Got it."

Sebastian laughed, a sound I had heard little since meeting him. It was nice, almost, to see his expression lighten, if only for a moment.

We walked out into the heart of the city, a large square filled with old buildings stacked several stories high. It wasn't exactly clean, but then again, neither were the roads back home in Ismore. There were fewer aniccipere strolling the sidewalks, and musicians played various instruments on the corners. There was even a theater. I marveled at the ticket booths and inviting velvet curtains on either side of the entryways. "You have shows here?"

Erianna answered, "They're not shows."

I arched a brow.

"They're auctions," Sebastian answered. "More upscale ones."

"For?"

He gave me a look.

"Say no more." I grimaced, my lip curling as I gave the red-bricked building a last glare. The cool, early evening breeze caught the red curls of my hair, sweeping back any strays from my shoulder and chest to my back. Red streaks blotted the blue sky, and a thin layer of clouds hid the sun, arrowing light onto where we walked.

"We're here." Sebastian stopped in front of a black-painted door of a three-story building with rectangular windows and curlicue trims. He tapped the ancient metal locker three times and took a step back. Sangaree squeezed past us on the narrow sidewalk, and I moved closer to Erianna. "Remember"— Sebastian looked down at me—"don't talk unless it's to Erianna or me, don't cause a scene, and try to slink into the shadows as much as possible."

"Don't be noticeable. Got it."

"Essentially, yes."

Erianna squeezed my shoulder, reminding me I wasn't alone in here. An eye-level slot in the door opened, clacking metal against wood.

Sebastian whispered something to whomever was on the other side, and a few seconds later, the door swung open. "Come." I hesitated, as any sane person should before walking into a blood den with a vampire, but this was what I wanted. "I won't let anything happen to you," he assured, but it did little to make me feel better.

A short man dressed in blue stood aside in the narrow foyer, allowing us into the musky blood den. The smell of iron, sweat, and sex choked the air around us.

"They bring newcomers to the bottom level," Sebastian said, walking us out of the foyer and through a small, red-carpeted room with crimson wallpaper and gold finishes. Three vampires made out with each other on one of the plush, four-legged sofas. A woman moaned loudly, running her fingers between her legs as two men moved their mouths over her curves.

My eyes widened, and I walked out, ignoring Sebastian's amused expression. We emptied into a snug corridor. Sensual instrumental music played in the background, the sound carrying us down a set of steep stairs, masking the moans hidden behind doors to private rooms. I noticed scratch marks against the wallpaper, blood dotting the cream tears.

"How do you know he's not in one of those?" I inquired as we approached another cold, dark staircase.

"These rooms are for more practiced mortals."

My upper lip curled. Lowering my barrier enough, I blocked out Sebastian and Erianna's emotions as best I could and closed my eyes. Despair and emptiness radiated from the rooms, telling me the mortals inside had given up fighting. I shuddered as lust licked at my barrier from whatever vampire was inside the room, and I closed it off.

"There are two levels underground," Erianna disclosed when we reached the bottom of the steps. "This is where the newcomers are brought. This is the biggest den in the city, so if he's going to be anywhere, it's likely here."

The cold seeped through my skin, chilling my core. When Sebastian turned the switch to a low-lit lamp, walls emerged from the shadows. He walked us out into a long room filled with hundreds of curtained cubicles.

I arched an eyebrow. "Have you been down here?"

"I prefer the upper levels."

"Nice to know." My jaw tightened. "So these people are cheaper to feed on then?" Of course Sebastian frequented this place. I wasn't sure why I'd given him the benefit of the doubt.

His nature was just as devious as the other monsters in this room. Their mortal appearance only made them far more dangerous predators than I ever could have known. Mainly because they didn't appear like one, unlike the soul vampires who I would know to stay clear of.

Being around Sebastian was annoyingly alluring at times, and I couldn't help but be drawn to everything about him, his scent, body, and bedroom eyes, no matter how much I hated him.

Regaining my composure, I focused my attention on the cubicles. I desperately wanted to shout his name, but I assumed that wouldn't be the best idea. "Can I call for him?" I questioned, just in case.

He shook his head, warning threading through his stoic expression. He pointed at the first cubicle and moved back the curtains just an inch. I peeped inside, watching as a male vampire traced his tongue over a drugged-up woman's neck, licking up a trickle of blood that ran from fresh bite marks. A mortal man with bloodshot eyes, irises halfway back in his head, flopped against the wall in the second cubicle we looked at. Turning my back to them, I snarled. "They're barely conscious."

Erianna gave me an apologetic look, even though none of this was her doing.

"Remember what you said," Sebastian whispered in my ear, pulling the curtain from my grasp, giving the creature its privacy, "about not making a scene." His breath hit the top of my ear, wisping a shiver down my back. "He won't be in any of these."

"How do you know?"

"I think these are for women only."

My chest heaved as I begrudgingly followed him and Erianna to the very bottom level. He pulled back a curtain to the room mirroring the one we'd just left and nodded. "These are the men."

A scream ripped through the air, and I flinched back against Erianna. "No, stop," a man begged as sobs pierced from the back of the room. A minute later, two sangaree passed us, one nodding in Sebastian's direction, holding needles. They entered the area where the man screamed, and after a few seconds, the crying subsided.

My barrier itched to be lowered, my gift scratching at the edge, wanting to feel these strangers' pain, but I couldn't, not without it dropping me to my knees. I hated to think of the suffering in this room alone.

I trudged across the blood-spattered carpet, wrinkling my nose at the stench of sweat. A male vampire walked out of his cubicle, buttoning his blazer. I didn't make eye contact and waited for him to leave before sneaking a look behind the curtains of the first line of cubicles.

A sangaree woman didn't even bother to wipe her blood-smeared lips as she made her way from one to another, her eyes manic. She glanced at us, dragging her painted nails up to her lips before disappearing behind a curtain.

Sebastian raised a finger and pressed it against his lips as I gently pulled the material of one back and looked inside. I glanced over my shoulder at Erianna, who was standing watch. I shook my head. We moved on to the next, where a mortal man pressed a sangaree against the makeshift wall, one knee on a velvet footstool, thrusting deep inside of her. The sounds of their tangled moans had me closing the curtain fast. I didn't need to see his face to know it wasn't Draven. He wouldn't stoop that low as to fuck a vampire, not willingly, anyway.

Sebastian hid an amused smile when I turned, flushed red.

Thirty cubicles later, and Draven wasn't in any of them. I peered through the gap of the last cubicle, and one man struggled as the vampire's fangs reached his neck, but he was nothing against the sangaree's immortal strength. The creature allowed the man to hit him, laughing as his fist hit his impenetrable jawbone.

"They left this one conscious for any vampire who enjoys a challenge," Sebastian clarified, and I closed the curtain, wishing I could save them all, but I was as helpless as they were. I turned, rubbing my forehead as frustration threatened to pull me apart, and then I saw him.

Not Draven. Worse.

I had to be hallucinating. This was impossible. Sebastian tugged my arm, but I couldn't move. Everything moved in slow motion as I looked at him. I took in every crease of his face, watching as his honey-brown eyes widened and the lips I'd kissed a thousand times muttered something to another woman.

"Olivia." Sebastian's voice echoed in my mind as I slowly came back to reality, blinking several times. He looked between Astor and me. "What's up? Is that Draven?"

I shook my head, the hairs on the back of my neck standing erect. "It's Astor." My jaw slackened. "My dead ex-boyfriend."

Glancing from the woman who stood at Astor's side, to Erianna then Sebastian as if they might somehow provide an answer for the impossible, I rubbed my chin. Had he been taken here as a prisoner, and the vampires made his death look like an accident? But that didn't explain the note or voicemail he'd left saying he was done with life. Unless they made him do it to cover their tracks before the attacks began.

The pieces clicked together in my mind, and tears brimmed in my eyes. "Astor," I whispered as if he might disappear if I made a sudden movement. Every dream of him being back, every memory, suddenly materialized. He was alive, and my prayers had been answered.

"Olivia." His voice was music to my ears. I'd listened to his voicemail a hundred times, just to hear that deep but sweet tone, and I never thought I'd hear my name from his lips again. My knees buckled, shock forcing me to my knees. Astor watched, tilting his head, blinking several times.

A sob wretched me, and Sebastian tried to lift me to my feet, but I pushed him back before he could.

"How?" I spluttered. "Is she?" I observed the blonde woman next to Astor, and my tone filled with venom. She couldn't have been much older than us, but she was perfectly immortal, with not a blemish on her deceivingly youthful face. "Are you her prisoner?"

"Not exactly."

He looked as I remembered him before he got sick. In fact, he looked healthier than ever.

Sebastian spoke softly, standing at my side. "Olivia, he's not mortal."

I closed my eyes to the scene. "They forced you to become like them." My heart skipped a beat at the realization.

The woman next to Astor spoke, her voice sickly sweet. "Astor, who is that?" She turned to Sebastian. "And why are you here?"

I despised the way his name sounded on her lips. Erianna pulled me up. I opened my eyes, staring at them both through tear-hazed vision.

"Say something," I demanded. "Did she force you to become a vampire?"

Astor shook his head, unable to look me in the eye. "You were never meant to get tied up in any of this."

"What does that even mean?" I struggled to reach him as Sebastian placed his arm out in front of me. I glared at him and spoke through gritted teeth. "Astor won't hurt me."

"She will," he stated, staring down at the woman.

Vampires emerged from the cubicles. "What's all the noise?" one asked, and Sebastian shook his head in warning.

"Don't," he told a few other sangaree who were edging closer to our small group.

Astor puffed out his cheeks as he looked at Sebastian and back to me. "I didn't mean for them to take you too."

A fluttering erupted in my stomach. "I don't understand."

The woman tutted, her red-painted lips curving into a mocking smile. "You're not the brightest, are you? He's one of us because he wanted to be. He came to me. I didn't need to do anything to him against his will." She whispered a kiss against his cheek, and he flinched.

"No." I took a step back, almost tripping into a cubicle, but Erianna caught me. "He would never."

Astor stared at his feet.

"We should go," Sebastian announced. "Gwen, get your friend out of here. Now."

I splayed my fingers over my chest, feeling my racing heart beneath my palm. "Tell me it isn't true," I asked, ignoring Sebastian.

Gwen laughed. "Do you want me to write it down for you?"

"Enough," Sebastian warned.

"What, am I upsetting your latest mortal girl? Gods know you'll have another in a week, when you get bored. I don't know why you like them so much." She looked me up and down, venom in her eyes. "We sangaree have much more stamina."

"Leave, now, before I make you." He let out a low growl, and Gwen took Astor's arm. He mouthed "sorry" before following her, leaving me staring after them.

"That didn't happen."

Sebastian glanced at Erianna. "It makes sense now."

"What does?" My fingers trembled as I brought them to my forehead. "Astor, they must have." I stumbled for the right words. "They've brainwashed him."

"I'm getting you out of here." Sebastian took me in his arms before we could check any of the other cubicles.

"No, I can't go. I need to…" What? Speak to Astor? Pass out?

"It's not up for discussion." He lifted me, speeding us out of there.

Erianna followed us, one hand on her blade.

Shock frayed my thoughts as I struggled to make sense of everything. *I didn't mean for you to get tied up in any of this,* Astor had said.

"He's meant to be dead," I said, the words feeling wrong as they left my dry lips. "I guess in a way, he is."

Finally, we reached the black door and emerged into the crisp, cold night, and Sebastian's wings folded out. "We need to get you back to the house. I didn't think she'd be here."

Erianna nodded in agreement.

"What?"

Erianna spoke. "The woman he was with, Gwendolyn, she's Velda's daughter."

My mind whirled as I tried to remember where I'd heard her name.

"She's the head of Nightshade," Erianna clarified, filling in the blanks. "They're the ones trying to find and kill you, and your dead ex-boyfriend is tied up with them. He must have been the one who told them how to get into the guild."

Sebastian agreed. "That explains how they got inside and how they knew about Olivia and her mom."

His words burrowed deep, and the floor felt as if it crumbled out from under my feet. I loved Astor; he was meant to be my forever until he killed himself... supposedly. I touched the white-gold band of my promise ring, and my next breath hitched. We had talked about one day starting a family. He was my best friend, my lover, my first everything, and now he was my first, and only, heartbreak.

They continued to talk as if my world hadn't just imploded. I looked up at the night sky; stars winked at me, clouds wisped against the navy blue, and I screamed before I could stop myself.

EIGHT

Erianna woke me at noon. I had barely opened my eyes when she thrust a hot mug of coffee into my hands. "What the—"

"I've been told mortals require coffee."

Careful not to spill the contents, I sat upright slowly, pushing back against the bed's headboard. "You don't meet many mortals, do you?"

"You don't like coffee." She sighed. "I shouldn't have presumed."

"No, I do." I took a sip, finding relief as the hot liquid melted away the coarseness from all my screaming.

It had taken both Sebastian and Erianna to pull me away while I cry-screamed in front of the entire square of vampires. It wasn't my proudest moment, but discovering the depths of Astor's betrayal triggered something deep, surfacing all the pain I'd kept buried from the past few weeks.

Erianna tilted her head. "So you do like coffee?"

"It was the delivery of the coffee," I explained, and smiled. "I was still lying down."

"I'm only around Anna," she told me as she dragged the armchair next to my bed, tensing the muscle in her bicep. "Sometimes I forget your reflexes aren't like ours. I've done it to her too."

"How long has she been here?"

"Since she was seventeen, and she's adopted a lot of our habits, minus the blood," she said with a grin, showing off her elongated fangs.

"How was she captured?"

Her eyebrows knitted together. "Oh, sweetie, no. Anna was orphaned and abused in her kingdom. Zach found her and brought her here because she wanted to come. It's quite the love story."

My nose wrinkled. "Love story?" I thought about what Gwen had said to Sebastian regarding his mortal tastes. "Is she with Sebastian?"

Her laugh tinkled in the room. "Gods, no, but she'll get a laugh out of that. She's Zach's wife."

I almost choked on my coffee. "Wow. I didn't see him as the type who would take a wife, let alone someone so"—I mulled over the words—"sweet, while he's so...."

"Stoic?" she finished with a hint of a smile. "Surprisingly, they work well together. She brings out a softer side to him."

"I'd like to see that."

"He likes to pretend he doesn't have a soft side."

It was odd how mortal she seemed, more so with each interaction. I wished I could hate her like I did the others, but while she had the fangs of a monster, her soul didn't feel that way. Breathing in wisps of coffee, I opened myself up to touch her energy. There was little darkness there, mostly compassion, a healthy dose of pride, and now a lingering of confusion. When I opened my eyes, she was arching a thick, black brow at me. "What are you doing?"

"Oh, yeah, it's nothing." I paused. "I can feel people's emotions sometimes."

Her eyes widened. "That's interesting."

"I block it out mostly, but I can let it in when I feel like it. Sometimes I can't help it, like when I'm overwhelmed or in shock. When I found out Astor died, I couldn't switch it off for a few days." I looked into the deep brown cup. "Thank the gods I didn't have to leave my house and be around people. Being locked inside had never been such a blessing."

She blew out a tense breath, leaning back in the chair. "Why were you locked in your house in the first place?"

"My mom was protecting me against those who'd want to take me."

She stuck her tongue against the inside of her cheek, pushing out her dark skin. "Who did she say wanted to take you?"

"Vampires mostly. Only the guild knew about us."

"The Guild for the Protection of Mortal Beings, yes, they're infamous, even in Sanmorte."

"That's the one. My mom worked for them."

"I know."

I leaned forward. "You've heard of my mom?"

She nodded but didn't elaborate. I knew she was famous within the guild, but not enough that vampires would know who she was. "I never even told you her name. How do you know who she is?"

"Sebastian was tracking you before the attacks happened. He saw your mother and found out basic information about her."

"Right, that makes sense, I guess," I said, but I wasn't entirely convinced. Still, I wasn't about to call the only vampire I liked in this house a liar. "So," I said, thinking back to Anna. "Why is Anna serving me like a maid?"

"It was Seb's idea. He thought you'd prefer to be around another mortal, and he asked her if she wouldn't mind."

"That's considerate." *If not a little disconcerting*, I pondered. "Why is he being nice to me? I'm assuming, based on what you said yesterday of his reputation and the way the vampires in the den reacted to him, that he's not normally known for his kindness."

"He has his days."

A non-answer if I'd ever heard one. "Why am I here? Please don't tell me it's because you're protecting me, because I know there must be another reason. You're the only one who's been nice to me since I've arrived."

She shuffled uncomfortably. "Would it be enough for me to tell you he is trying to do the right thing?"

"Not really."

"There's a lot you don't know, and it's not my place to tell you. I'm sorry."

"Like how my dad's a vampire? Sebastian told me that much."

She tilted her head. "What else did he say?"

"That's it." My eyebrows furrowed. "Is there something else he should have said?"

She sighed. "No."

That felt like an outright lie. I lowered my barrier and could almost taste the anxiety waving from her.

She cleared her throat, forcing a small smile. "Are you ready to talk about what happened yesterday?"

"No." I swallowed the rest of my coffee.

"We need to know as much about your ex-boyfriend as possible. He's a risk to your life, and if he tells the leaders of Nightshade who you are, they'll come straight here."

"Is he one of them?"

She glanced down, pity creasing her forehead. That was all the answer I needed.

"What do you need to know?" I asked, placing the empty mug on the floor.

"You said he was supposed to be dead. When did that happen?"

I worked out the dates in my head. They were a little hazy. "Close to three weeks ago, I think."

"How did he die?" She added, "Supposedly."

"Suicide." The word stung, even now, when I knew that was a lie. "They told us he threw himself off a cliff and into the sea. That's why no body was recovered."

She tapped a long nail against her chin. "It's clever and sounds like the work of Nightshade."

My stomach churned. "Why would they change him?"

"It's rare, I'll admit. Normally, they'd have to get the king's permission to do it. So, I imagine they offered him something he wanted enough." Realization swam in her eyes, but she kept her calm.

"Astor knew about vampires being able to make other vampires. He was in the guild, and all members were told."

"I didn't know it was a secret."

"To the rest of us, it was. The royal family and guild keep that fact hidden, so people don't have a reason to come here."

She stuck her lips out, nodding. "They did the right thing. This is no city for mortals."

"No shit."

Her laugh was infectious, and before I could overthink it, I caught myself smiling.

"He's a coward," she said, and my eyebrows raised. "The woman he was with, Gwen…"

Ah, the blonde woman with the bitchy smile. "I recall."

"I've known her for a century. She's the daughter of the leader of Nightshade."

"I remember."

"We'll find out why they agreed to turn him," she assured, but from the look on her face, I wanted to bet she already had an idea, one she wasn't going to share with me.

"Do you promise?"

She chewed on the inside of her cheek. "Yes."

I wanted to trust her, but I'd been duped by people I trusted far more. "How long have you been a vampire for?" I asked, changing the subject.

"A hundred and fifty—" She looked up in thought. "Nine years."

"Are Zach and Sebastian that old too?"

She shook her head. "Seb's young. We found him a few years ago, newly turned. He learned fast and climbed the ranks in society. The boy knows how to survive."

A flicker of compassion swept through me, but I pushed it away, reminding myself of how horrible he'd acted at breakfast yesterday. "What about Zach?"

"Zach's older than me. He's been around for a few centuries."

"He hates me," I finally said aloud.

"It's nothing against you. He's old-fashioned, and you're different to how he expects women to act."

"It's a good thing I don't care what he likes."

She smirked. "He'll warm up to you. He did with me, eventually."

I shrugged. I really couldn't care less about a vampire's opinion of me. "Where is Sebastian anyway?"

"He's getting ready. We have guests coming tonight, which is another reason I'm here. We need you to stay out of the way for tonight."

I forced a heavy breath through my nose. "What about finding my mom and Draven?"

"That needs to wait."

I ground my teeth together but quickly reined in my temper. "Why does he have so many guests coming?"

"He's the master of travel. It's just some silly title made up by the vampire king, so Sebastian can remain in the city while carrying out his courtly duties."

"I had no clue he was a member of the court," I confessed, but then I had no knowledge about much in this kingdom.

"He's tasked with entertaining royals, nobles, and dignitaries from around the kingdom who wish to see the city."

"I can see why vampires would want to come here." I thought back to the cubicles in the blood den and swallowed my nausea. "I'll stay up here."

"You could come down." She shifted in the chair. "But you'd have to play prisoner or Sebastian's lover again, and I can't imagine you'd enjoy that."

"It might be worth it if I get to leave this room." It would be great, in fact. It would allow me to find out more about the people coming from the royal court, where I now knew my mom was being held. "Can I attend? If I play the part?"

"I suppose. It's not uncommon for Seb to have a mortal woman around."

I made a face. "Gwen said the same thing yesterday."

"Not all mortals in this city are treated poorly. Some women choose to be here, like Anna. They usually live with someone powerful or rich to keep safe, but they have free rein for the most part. Seb likes what he likes."

"Why?"

"They remind him of a time before all of this. I think being around your kind links him to who he used to be, but then, he never wanted any of this." She stood, knocking a chair cushion on the ground. "I'll tell Seb you want to come down. Anna will bring you some clothes."

"You know—" I stood too. "I wouldn't hate you coming to see me more too."

"I'm glad to know you trust me." She lightly touched the dagger at her side. "However, now I must go. Duty calls."

I was about to ask her what that meant, but she was already gone. I walked over to the dusty, white dresser and sat in front of a mirror. My green irises had dulled in my time here, and my bloodshot, puffy eyes were proof of how many tears I had shed.

My crimson curls laid limp around my shoulders, and when I pulled a comb through them, chunks fell out. It had to be the stress I'd been under. Fortunately, my hair was pretty thick, so it wasn't noticeable, but it made me realize I needed to take better care of myself. I just wished I cared enough to listen to that little voice in the back of my mind.

Thoughts of Astor crept in, and I kept pushing them back inside. I didn't want to think of him and welcomed any distraction to keep myself from feeling the heartache that came with his betrayal. He had been my one and only, my everything, for so long that I didn't know what to do, knowing it was all a lie.

Yet, despite it all, I still loved him, and I hated that most of all.

NINE

After I'd finished my bath and eaten half of the sandwich Anna had brought up, Sebastian knocked on the door. She still barely spoke to me when she did come, but he was right in sending her first. Being around someone who wasn't a vampire made being here slightly less weird.

"Good, you're ready," he said, throwing a red dress on my bed. "Erianna told me you loved playing my girl so much you want to do it again."

My lips curled behind my teeth. "I only want to get out of this room. If it means tolerating you for a few hours, then so be it."

"Oh, save some of your charms for our guests tonight."

I placed a hand on my robed hip. So much for playing nice, but he was so infuriating to be around. Whenever I felt like being sweet to earn his trust, he opened his mouth and thwarted my plans. "I'll behave." I gritted my teeth, swallowing my following remark. "Speaking of behaving, I wanted to apologize for my display last night."

"What display?"

I rolled my eyes, biting the inside of my cheek. "Don't play dumb."

His lips curved into a smirk, knowing dancing in his eyes. "I have no idea what you mean."

"The screaming," I stated, rubbing the side of my neck.

He leaned against the wall. "Ah, that. Well, you did just find out that boy had betrayed you."

I wasn't sure if he was being kind or mocking me, but I was trying to earn his trust, so I didn't react. "I'm sorry, nonetheless. I promised I wouldn't cause a scene."

"Olivia," he purred, "I never expected you to behave. It's not really in your nature." He grinned, amusement sweeping his sharp features. "Besides," he said, waving a hand dismissively, "lots of mortals lose it here at some point, some publicly. It didn't attract too much attention."

"Aren't you going to ask me about Astor?"

"Didn't plan on it, unless you wanted to have a heart-to-heart?"

My jaw clenched. "No."

"Then we can both save ourselves from that talk. I presume you have told Erianna everything she needs to know so she can research him for your safety."

"We talked."

"Good." He clasped his hands together, then rolled up his sleeves.

I eyed his tattoos. "Do they have any meaning?"

"Yes, but that's a story for another time." He glanced at the bed. "Put on the dress. You'll like our guests tonight. They're not the nicest, but they're a lot of fun."

It was doubtful, but I had to play nice. "I do have one question before you go."

He raised an arched, dark brow.

"You're a vampire."

A ghost of a smirk flashed across his face. "Am I?"

Tilting my head at him, I clicked my tongue. "Hilarious. Anyway, I've established you don't burst into flames in the sunlight," I stated bitterly. "Zach explained why that rumor was started, but I was wondering what else we have got wrong about your kind?"

His gaze climbed the length of my body, stopping on my eyes. "Well, it's not all rumors. Demons can't survive long in the sunlight, and the aniccipere are half-demon, so the sun irritates them. It won't kill them, but they prefer to be out at night."

"There were some out in the afternoon yesterday."

"Yes, some put up with what they describe as a mild burning sensation all over their body, so they can be outside any time of day. However, you'll find the majority of them after the sun sets. As for knowing what else you've got wrong about vampires, I have no idea. So why don't you ask me specific questions?"

I recalled what Draven had told me about them dying if they went without blood for too long. "Obviously, you drink blood, but do you need it to stay alive?"

"Yes. We will desiccate and slowly die without it. It'll take some time, maybe a couple of months, the same as you mortals will eventually starve to death without food. Fortunately, I've never had to go that long." He smiled, showing off his pearly-white fangs, anticipating glowing in his eyes. "What else?"

"Are you dead?"

He laughed, slapping his knee. "Do I look dead to you?"

"No."

"I'm immortal." The smirk hovering on his lips told me he was enjoying this far too much. "We do have to die for that to happen, but my heart is still beating, and blood is flowing." He paused, scratching the side of his temple with a grin. "In every part."

Clearing my throat, I pressed a finger against my clavicle. "Okay." I cut in quickly. "So you're dead, but not dead."

"It depends on your definition of dead. Did I die? Yes. Am I dead? No. I believe death means you're gone from this world, and I'm still very much in it, enjoying all it has to offer."

I chewed the inside of my cheek, avoiding the impenetrable hold of his stare. "Can you see your reflection in the mirror?"

He ran his hand through his tousled, dark strands. "Do you think I could look this good without one?"

"I don't know. You think so highly of yourself that it wouldn't surprise me if you thought so."

He drummed his fingers against his thigh, a low chuckle escaping his mouth. "When I met you, I thought you were sweet, you know, maybe even a little submissive. You act that way sometimes, but it looks like I was wrong."

"I'm sorry to disappoint."

"Oh, trust me, you haven't."

My lips parted, but I didn't respond to his comment. "Does blood cause you to go into a frenzy?"

"Yes," he admitted. "When I was first turned, it was all I could think about, but over time, that went away. Now I think about blood as much as you think about food." He played with the strap of his watch. "It means I can control myself, as can most of the people you'll meet here. Most choose not to."

"Can you eat our food?"

"It does nothing for us, so none of us choose to eat mortal food. It doesn't taste the same." His face crumpled. "But we can drink alcohol."

"Oh."

"You can have a glass of whiskey with me tonight if you'd like. I drink it to take the edge off."

"Yes, you must be so stressed, entertaining and drinking for a living," I said, my tone thick with sarcasm.

"It's a hard life," he replied playfully.

I tied my hair back and forced a smile. I didn't want to do a thing with him, especially drink, but if he was drunk, he might agree to take me to look for Draven again. That was an opportunity I didn't want to pass up. "We should have a couple of drinks tonight. I need a distraction from everything."

"Aren't you full of surprises?"

My gaze narrowed. "I'm going to get dressed. I'll meet you downstairs. Same room?"

"We're actually going to take a slight detour first. I'll wait for you outside."

He left quickly, closing the door behind him. I pulled on the red, glittery dress with a slit running from my thigh to my foot. It looked like it should feel scratchy, but the silk lining caressed my body like a glove. I twirled, noticing the fabric around my waist and hips was a little loose. I checked the size of the dress, and it was already one smaller than the clothes I wore before Astor died.

I had lost too much weight since he died. It had only been three weeks, but my skin was blanched, and I had little muscle. I sighed, averting my gaze away from my reflection.

I closed my eyes, and all I saw was Astor with his honey-brown eyes and freckled nose. We laughed at the same things and had these stupid, inside jokes that disappeared when he left me. I honestly thought we were going to grow old together and that he would be the father to my children one day, but when he became a vampire, he'd stolen my future with it. I knew he was afraid of dying, and I understood, but he had a chance. The doctors said he could survive, and even though the odds weren't in his favor, I had hope.

As much as I wanted to hate him for becoming a vampire, even if it was against everything we fought for, I didn't.

I hated him because hundreds of our people had died because of him. He'd betrayed those who fought alongside him for years. Nightshade got inside the guild because Astor told them how. They'd taken my mom as the price for his immortality, and hundreds died for it. I wondered if their souls weighed as heavily on him as they should.

My chest tightened, and my heart raced. I leaned over, pressing my hands against my knees, feeling the cold slip through my skin, spreading goose bumps over my limbs. My mind whirled as I tried to push him out. I couldn't cope with it yet, not with everything else. This was too much pain for one person.

I never understood how people survived the most terrible things, like losing someone they loved so much that it should have destroyed them. I often felt the shattering heartbreak that accompanied that kind of grief, and when I did, it felt like I was going to die. Now I understood the grief of losing Astor, my mom, and Draven would kill me if I let it in. So instead, I kept them separate in my mind, allowing depression to take me because that numbness was a temporary relief. It was better to feel nothing than everything.

Then there was Sebastian and the City of Nightmares, a distraction that I craved. Once I was dressed, I looked at my reflection in the frosted window. Sanmorte was a winter kingdom, and summer didn't last long here, which is why I presumed they took up residence on this large, chilly island to the north of our world. They didn't feel the cold as much as we did, so being here wouldn't bother them.

I pulled at the fabric around my cleavage, trying to hide it a little more, and flattened the area with my hands, as if that might somehow make it look better. I painted my lips with gloss only and picked at my fingers as I walked out the bedroom door and into the hallway.

"Olivia." He spoke my name as if it were a declaration. "You clean up nicely."

I rolled my eyes.

"I have a surprise for you," he said, walking me toward the roof.

"I thought we were going downstairs."

"We will be, but first, I want to show you something. I said we were going to take a slight detour."

Yes, but I thought he meant another part of the house. He pushed open the hatch and climbed out. The icy air hit my lungs as I followed him. His wings extended in midnight black, crumpling his buttoned-up black shirt. "We will fly there. Unless you'd rather walk." I nodded, and he closed the distance between us. The air whooshed from my lungs as he lifted me into the sky, twirling us into a swirl of stars and clouds.

TEN

I nestled into the pockets of warmth from his jacket as Sebastian landed us at the edge of a lake. The scent of him clung to the fibers, and I breathed in the evocative smell of spring, in an elegant mix of citrus and pine with hints of spice. I pulled on the drawstrings and looked up at the endless night sky. Sebastian tucked his wings behind his back, re-rolling one sleeve which had come undone.

The water rippled in the distance as the moon reached its apex, reflecting off the skyline-silver surface. I closed my eyes, breathing in a whirl of cold and listening to the familiar slap of fish hitting the water and the rustle of leaves in the trees surrounding the lake. Around us were smoky-gray mountains and a dark pine forest. "How far did you fly us?" I asked, registering that we couldn't be anywhere close to the city.

"Eighty miles, give or take."

"Why here?" I gazed around, noting the beauty of the pebbled beach under our feet, noticing how the stones somehow glowed against nothing but the light of the moon and stars.

Slowly, I made my way to the lake's edge, catching threads of blue and silver beneath the surface, illuminating the water.

"This is one of the few places in Sanmorte that remains mostly untouched by vampires. This lake was the birthplace of a god and was used by sorcerers to strengthen their magic. As the years have passed and the population of your people has decreased, the lake has been deserted. The king keeps it off-limits. He still believes in honoring the gods, a sentiment from being hundreds of years old and having probably met one before they ascended from this world." He took my wrist in his fingers and gently unclasped the bracelet. "You won't need this here."

The water's edge lured me as if it were singing its own ancient melody only I could hear, made from teardrops and enchantment. I kneeled at the edge, my fingers reaching out until I touched a wave. As soon as the icy water hit my fingers, I gasped. Power thrummed into my hand, running through my veins, linking with my own dormant magic.

Before I could think too hard, I was dancing my fingers in the air, elated in the feeling of being one with my powers. I'd always longed for it. My mother had spoken so fondly of her powers, it made me envious of the bond she had with her birthright. I'd felt detached from my own until now.

"What god was born here?"

"Laveniuess."

"God of Shadows," I said, closing my eyes to allow my other senses to attach to my power thoroughly. "I can feel his energy. It's beautiful."

"Most wouldn't call anything about him *beautiful*."

I opened my eyes. "No?"

"No."

"Why?"

"He represents our most hidden, darkest impulses. Before he ascended, he was known for bringing the worst out in people."

"My mom taught me differently. She said he pulled out the darkness in each person to help people embrace their hidden selves and guide the lost back into healing light." I glided my hand over the glass-like surface, smiling. "You can't fix something unless it's brought out into the open, and people often shy away from the ugly side of our nature."

His eyes changed shape under the moonlight, widening at the corners. "I've never thought of it that way."

"He was always the god that fascinated me the most," I admitted. "I even wrote stories about him. Made up ones, of course."

He paused. "You write?"

"You didn't know? I thought you were spying on me."

"Not that intimately, nor for that long."

"It doesn't matter anymore anyway." I looked out over the lake, knotting my fingers together. "That part of my life is gone."

"Aren't you going to ask why I brought you here?"

I figured he needed something from me, and being here just solidified the *what*. "I don't need to. You want to use me for my magic, and I can become more powerful here using a god's residual energy. It's so typical I'm almost disappointed."

A laugh tinkled out. "I don't want it for myself."

"Then what is it? Just tell me why you're protecting me."

He inhaled sharply, taking a step back from me. "I'm not trying to do anything to hurt you."

"That isn't an answer."

"I want to help you."

"What's that supposed to mean, Prince of Vague?"

His dark hair moved gently against the cool breeze sweeping over the lake. "That I'm not going to hurt you. Simple as that."

I didn't buy it, and his mysterious attitude drove me crazy. His eyes twinkled under the starlight, the pale light shining illuminating his immortal, blemish-free skin and chiseled jawline. I saw him for what he really was, a handsome monster with the beauty to lure anyone in. Of course, it was all a facade, a way to give people a false sense of security, and I would not fall for it. I was many things, but my mom didn't raise me to be an idiot. Everyone had hidden motives, whether it was love, power, greed, or a number of other things. Rarely ever was anything done out of kindness—not in this world, no matter how much I wished it was.

"Say I believe you—" Although I didn't. "Then you should know one thing. The only way you can help me is by getting my mom and Draven back. I've already lost too much."

"I know."

"So, you'll help me?"

"Erianna and I have already spoken about it."

"Can you clue me in?" I was starting to think I'd have better luck getting blood out of a stone.

He kicked a rock out onto the lake. It skidded over the water before disappearing into the darkness. "Erianna has been looking for your friend. She's diligent, so she will find him if he is still alive and in the city. It's a shame you don't have a picture of him."

That, I believed, and she didn't seem like the giving-up type. "My phone fell from my pocket when you grabbed me."

He turned on his heel, looking me dead in the eye. "I can get you a new one."

"I don't have much use for one," I admitted. My mom, Astor, and Draven were the only people I talked to. None of them would have a phone anymore, except maybe Astor, but I had no intentions of talking to him right now.

"Olivia," he said slowly, changing the subject, "I want you to help me bring down the people who did this to you and your mom and friend, and bring Nightshade to its knees."

There it was. The *why* of why I was saved. I'd gotten it wrong. He didn't want my magic for himself. He wanted me to enact some revenge fantasy. "You hate them."

"Yes." He didn't bother trying to hide it.

"Why?"

"I don't agree with the way they handle business." His forehead creased, and the corner of his lip twitched. It wasn't just about how they ran the order; this was personal.

"Did they hurt you?"

His jaw clenched. "They've hurt many people."

I looked over to the forest, ink blotted out into the distance. "I don't know what makes you think I can help."

"You're a sorceress," he said nonchalantly.

"I already told you, I'm useless with my powers. Even with the energy from a god in my veins, I still can't do much. Look." I closed my eyes to focus on my other senses and cleared my mind, willing the magic to do something. It did feel more potent than before, but no matter how hard I tried, I couldn't do anything with it.

"You lack confidence. That's all. It's why I've brought you here, so Laveniuess's energy can recharge your powers. This lake won't make you all-powerful, but it will strengthen what's already there. With practice, you can become powerful enough so we can destroy them. You can get your revenge on your ex too."

I thought about Astor and the girl he was with. "Gwen," I spat. "Did she change him?"

"I don't know, but one of them would have."

"Because he asked them to be changed."

He nodded again. I already knew the answers, but saying them aloud sparked the building rage. "They used him to get to my mom and me," I stated.

"They did."

He looked out at the scenery, and there was a peace in his expression I hadn't seen before now, one which the lake and trees gave him. We were the only people around for miles, trapped in this bowl of silver poured between mountains. I wasn't afraid anymore. If Sebastian wanted to, he would've hurt me by now. At least he kept his gaze away from my neck for the most part, and in this corner of hell was a paradise where I only had to contend being around one vampire.

I'd always enjoyed being around water and out in nature but didn't get much of it back home. When my mom had taken me hiking on a rare occasion, I wished I could bottle the feeling and keep it for when I was depressed. "I'll do anything to get them back."

He shoved his hands into his deep pockets. "Good, then take this time to revitalize. Until you're strong enough to fend for yourself, there's not much we can do. To get to your mom, we'll need to go to the royal castle, and you need to be ready."

"I thought we were bringing down the order first?" I asked, almost laughing at how ridiculous us bringing down an organization of ancient, evil vampires sounded.

"Long game," he said as if it were some explanation. "Your mom is safe for now. Trust me, they won't harm her. She's too useful, but the same can't be said for your friend. So Erianna will continue to search for him."

"Astor's responsible for this," I said with half a breath as I thought about Draven, lost, tortured, and potentially dead. "I want him to pay for this."

The corner of his lip tugged upward. "There I was thinking you didn't have a vengeful bone in your body."

My eyebrow arched. "You'd be surprised."

"Heartbreak does amazing things to our morals."

My chest tightened. Yes, it does.

ELEVEN

Sebastian flew us back to the house after I'd spent an hour at the lakeside, playing with the water and absorbing the energy that flowed through it. I felt stronger than ever, but I still had to practice harnessing it and making something happen, which was still difficult.

To see if my magic had come to life yet, I tried to send a shock wave through Sebastian's hand when I touched him before he flew us back. But, of course, he didn't know I did that, and fortunately for him, it didn't work anyway.

"It's a confidence thing." That's what he'd said, but a lack of confidence couldn't be enough to block something as natural as magic, surely?

Once we were back inside and I'd had a chance to warm up, we walked down to the banquet room. An archaic name for it, but just like everything else in this city, it had to be dramatic. "These guests of yours," I inquired, "from the royal court. Are they nice? I mean, for vampires."

"They're a lot of fun, but none of us are really nice," he half answered and dusted the remnants of dirt from our journey outside from his black shirt. "You can go back to your room if you prefer."

"No," I replied too quickly, then forced a small smile. "I want to meet them." His fingers flexed at his side, but he didn't stop walking. I needed to meet these people, hoping they'd have some intel on the royal castle and mainly, any information about my mom.

"One of them is from the city, though. He's the owner of an auction. I would recommend you don't wander off alone. You'll be safe with me. Just make sure you put that bracelet back on, and he shouldn't bother you."

I didn't even want to think about what happened at those auctions and instead reached for the bracelet.

A familiar voice set my heart ablaze. "Olivia."

I turned slowly, unsure whether I'd heard it correctly. Yes, I had, and he really had the nerve to come here.

"Get out!" Sebastian snapped, but I pushed my arm out between them before he could lunge at Astor.

"I want to talk to him," I declared, feeling the anger building inside of me. Before now, I hadn't wanted to, but seeing him changed that. "Please."

He stood between us, muscles tensed.

"I'm not going to hurt her," Astor said, his head dipping as he took a step inside.

"Get the fuck away from her," he growled, his eyes darkening, giving away the terrifying power behind them.

"I need to talk to him." I touched Sebastian's shoulder, which rippled against my touch. "I need answers."

Astor made a face. "I didn't realize you two were a thing."

"We're not." I scowled. "Sebastian, can you give us a few minutes alone?"

Sebastian tilted his head, his eyes darkening. "If you hurt her, I'll show you true pain."

"I would never," Astor exclaimed, his frown deepening. "I haven't told anyone about her being a sorceress."

"He won't," I told Sebastian. "I'll shout if I need you. But, please, I need my privacy. You told me I wasn't a prisoner here."

After an intense ten-second glaring contest, Sebastian relented. "Five minutes, and I'm coming back. It's him I don't trust." He shot Astor, who stood in the open doorway of the front entrance, a final warning stare before leaving.

I stormed over to him, my fists balled.

"I'm sorry," he began.

"What am I supposed to do with that?" I stared into the eyes of the man I'd whispered declarations of love to since I knew what it was. "My mom is gone, Astor!" My voice rose an octave. "Draven is being used as a blood bag, enslaved, or dead. I know you two didn't get on, but he was your brother-in-arms. Don't you care? What about all the protectors in the guild who died? I listened to them scream as vampires drained their blood. They were so confused about how the sangaree knew how to get past any barriers. I bet it crossed some of their minds before they died that one of their own betrayed them!"

Tears brimmed in his eyes. Usually, it would be enough, like drawing first blood in a battle, but I wanted to keep going. I wanted him to hurt like I was, like the families of all the people he betrayed undoubtedly were.

"They're gone, Astor," I shouted, my voice shaking. "They're all dead, and I'm here, trapped in a city full of vampires, while you date the daughter of a woman who wants me dead. The whole fucking order, Nightshade or whatever, is hunting me. They want to kill me! How could you go from loving me to not caring if I live or die?" A cry bubbled up my throat, escaping into a sob as I tried to control the quaking in my upper body.

He stepped forward, standing only a couple of inches in front of me before I could blink the tears away. His icy fingertips gently caressed my cheek, but I pushed him back. I wasn't crying because I was sad. My tears stemmed from anger.

I'd never felt rage like this, and it was very unlike me, but when I looked at the man who even after all this, held a small part of my heart, I wanted to set fire to the world. That love only fueled the hatred into something dangerous.

"Olivia." His tone softened, a croak joining to his following sentence as he swallowed thickly. "You won't believe me, but I never meant to hurt you. I wanted to come since I saw you in the den, but I had to find a way to sneak away from Gwen."

I stepped back, dismissing his bullshit sentiments. "What about my mom? Did you mean to hurt her?"

"They told me they wouldn't harm her and said the vampire king would take care of her."

"You believed them?" I looked at him incredulously. "Since when did you become so damn gullible?" I shook my head then placed another foot between us. "I don't know you at all."

"It's not like that. Look, your mom confided in me about certain things, and Draven knew too. The whole guild did. That's why I knew they wouldn't hurt your mom."

"What things?"

"Do you truly think Sebastian"—he spat his name—"is taking care of you out of the goodness of his own heart? His reputation precedes him, Olivia."

"I'm not stupid. I know he wants something, but he is my only option here because of the situation you put me in."

He glanced down, then his gaze slowly climbed back to meet mine. "I haven't told the order that you're here," he said slowly. "I even got Gwen to believe you are an old friend, nothing more."

"Am I supposed to be grateful?"

"I do still love you. I won't tell them."

I scoffed, then let a laugh slowly grow. "If this is how you treat the people you supposedly love, then you're far more fucked up than I ever realized." Rage blinded everything, but I tried to calm my breathing enough to follow my train of thought. "You said my mom confided something in you. What was it?"

"Your father, he's a vampire."

"That's the big reveal? I already know."

"You know who he is?"

"Well, no." I mulled over what Sebastian had told me. "But I know he's here, in the city."

His lips pinched together. "That's not the only thing. But, before I tell you, I want you to know I never planned on handing you over, but you're right. The leaders of Nightshade want you dead. They hid that from me, but I soon caught on." He tried to hold my hand, but I backed away, giving him pause. "I will keep your secret of where you are because despite what you think, I care about you."

"That only makes it worse, Astor. It makes this so much harder. You stole everything from me, including my grief. Now I don't know what to do with myself because I'm still mourning you, but now it's different, and it's mixed with hate. I never wanted to feel that way about you." Tears fell thick and fast. "You were meant to be the one who could heal my heart, not break it," I said, rubbing my nose against the back of my sleeve. "So go ahead, keep my location a secret. It's the least you can do because I can't imagine how it must feel to walk around with the heaviness bearing from what you have done. When you take away people's lives like that, it comes with a price." I bared my teeth. "One you will pay, sooner or later."

"You once told me everyone is redeemable." His pleading eyes searched mine.

"That was before you showed me what a monster really looks like."

His jaw clenched, the taut muscles under his loose top stiffening as he inhaled slowly. "I just didn't want to die."

That hit me like a punch to the gut, but I ignored the spark of desire to hold him, to tell him it was okay. For the death of me, that need to comfort him was still there, and I despised him for ruining it. "Tell me the truth, Astor," I finally ordered, knowing I'd said all that could be said. "What's the big secret?"

A whoosh of air spindled cold into my left side. I blinked, turned, and saw Sebastian at my side. "It's time for you to go."

"Not yet," I argued. "He was about to tell me something."

Something dark churned in Sebastian's eyes, and intrusiveness swam to the surface of those bottomless pits. Astor's breath caught when his expression hardened. "He's lying to win your forgiveness. Don't listen to a word from this coward."

Astor looked from Sebastian to me, then exhaled sharply. "I should go."

"No." My eyes widened. I stepped out of the door as he turned. "Astor, tell me."

"Sebastian's right. I was lying."

"I don't believe you," I shouted. He gave me one last look, then disappeared into the early morning blackness. I turned on my heel, a scowl lacing my words. "You!" I slammed a finger into Sebastian's chest. "He wasn't lying. I can always tell when he is."

"Because you know him so well?" His amused scowl only made his face all that more punchable.

"You're all keeping something from me. What he said confirmed it. I swear, I will find out the truth."

He pointed into the night. "*He* doesn't care about you. Some things are better left in the shadows, Olivia. Trust me."

"Fuck you, Sebastian." I attempted to push him into the doorway. He didn't move, but it felt good to let my anger out. "I'm going to my room. I suggest you leave me alone, or I'll find a way to use my powers and make you."

I stormed up the staircase, pausing at the top to look over my shoulder, but Sebastian was already gone. I stared down into the foyer for a long minute, lost in my thoughts before I climbed the rest of the steps.

Then, finally, I reached the second level and came face to face with a man with white shoulder-length hair and violet, dream-like eyes.

"You—" He brushed a lock of my hair out of my face, and I stumbled back. "Are a beautiful little secret."

My brows furrowed as the willowy man closed the distance between us, his nose almost touching mine. Was he a member of Nightshade? No, he had to be one of the guests.

"Sebastian didn't say he was keeping a sorceress here." He touched my arm, turning over my bracelet-less wrist. I never put it back on. "Naughty Sebastian, keeping secrets from his king. Never mind, I won't tell on him." His thin lips curled into a cruel smile. "If he won't tell on me."

"Please—" He slapped a hand over my mouth, muffling my plea.

"Hush now, sweetheart," he whispered. "If you struggle, it won't end well for you."

My scream rang out against his palm as he lowered his mouth to my neck. My heart raced, and adrenaline spiked. A tingle of magic jolted through me. If only I could do something, anything, to get Sebastian or Erianna's attention, but it was too late.

My eyes closed as his fangs sank into my skin, bringing with them a desperate agony, buckling my knees, choking my cry into a squeal. He held me up, his long arm coiled around my waist, knotting us together. Venom seared heat into me, setting every nerve ending on fire, and my body grew limp. I could feel him suckling against my neck, his lips like a suction on my skin, weakening me while he trembled with excitement.

My barrier lowered as my blood drained, and I could feel everything the vampire did—the most potent emotion reached me first: desire.

He moved his hand from my mouth, but I was too incapacitated to shout, scream, or do anything to alert anyone. So this was how it felt to feel utterly powerless, to have one's mortality stripped from them as if they were nothing more than a thing to feed on.

He pulled back as I reached the brink of passing out. "I see why Sebastian keeps you here. A sorcerer's blood is intoxicating," he said, his voice barely a whisper. He ran his thumb at the tip of my spine as a soft moan left his lips. "You are worth a hundred mortals to the right buyer." He laced his other hand against my cheek. "I will give Sebastian a cut to make it up to him." He lifted me into his arms.

I slumped against him, helpless, as he sped us out the open door and into the heart of the city.

TWELVE

Fear outstretched its arms through every room in the auction building, and only immortals were safe. I tried to block the emotions radiating from the other women in this and the surrounding rooms, but the band of fabric covering my eyes only served to heighten my other senses, making it harder to keep my barrier up against so much terror.

"I'm going to die," a woman whispered. "Oh g-gods," she cried, her voice faltering.

I wanted to tell her she would be okay, but I'd only be lying. I didn't need to see the woman—who was at the other end of the room, judging by the distance of her voice and the sound her shoes made when she scuffed them against the ground—to know she was shaking uncontrollably. All that horror quaking through her only elevated my own.

The door opened, hitting the back wall, a sound I'd gotten used to in the two hours since I'd been brought here. The woman screamed as I assumed her band was removed. "Your f-fangs," she spluttered as she was pulled to standing. She and I were the only two left in this room. When I'd arrived, there were four of us, but a vampire came in and took two of them half an hour ago, and they never returned.

"Please," she screamed, "no. Help." I wasn't sure if it was the gods she was asking or me, but there was nothing any of us could do. My chest tightened as she was pulled from the room, kicking back against what sounded like a chair from the way it fell and hit the floor.

Once the door was closed, I wrestled against the ropes around my wrists. They'd placed a necklace on me before shoving me in here, one that acted similarly to the bracelet Sebastian had given me. The only difference was I couldn't remove it myself. They didn't know I was terrible with magic anyway, but I would have loved the ability to try.

Sebastian had to have noticed I was gone by now, or Erianna and Zach. Did they need me enough to come and save me from here? Would they even know where to look? I had concluded that the white-haired vampire who had bitten me was the elusive auction owner to whom Sebastian referred. No, Sebastian had to come; he wouldn't have bothered getting me from Baldoria if I wasn't worth something to him. I could only hope he'd figure out where I was, but as the minutes ticked by, that hope slowly dwindled.

Tears soaked the fabric, slicking it against my cheeks as I cried again. The emotions lifted a little with the women gone, but I could still feel everyone else's from the adjoining rooms. I could taste their dread and panic, and it was nauseating. Mainly because there was nothing I could do to help them, much less myself.

Only fifteen minutes passed when the door opened again. Footsteps stomped across the room, scuffing to a stop in front of me. I didn't scream or cry like the others. I knew better than to beg these parasites for mercy. They wouldn't understand the word if it was spelled out in blood for them.

"Darling." I knew that voice to be the white-haired vampire guy. "I saved you for last. You're our big finale."

"How kind of you," I spat, anger rolling through my bones.

He let out a clipped laugh. "I would keep you for myself if I couldn't make so much stagma from you." His tone was gentler than I expected, and my muscles tensed. "Alas"—he brushed a finger over the area where he'd bitten me"—I must keep you clean for our bidders. Such a shame, the things you and I could have done."

"Sebastian's going to kill you for this," I snapped with the only threat that might mean anything.

He untied the blindfold, and my eyes blurred open to a red room. "He may want to, but he knows better than to hurt me. All who have tried so far have ended up dead."

"It's good to know your ego is in check."

He turned my chair until I was facing him and smiled, creasing the corners of his pale cheeks. "You are so beautiful. It's a shame that vile mouth of yours taints it." He ran his fingers through my red curls. "Your hair is like royalty, so vibrant." His eyes lit up when he grinned, showing his fangs. He let my strands fall back to join the rest. "It reminds me of blood." My nose scrunched as he brought his face inches away from mine, his pale eyes searching mine.

The corner of my eye twitched. If this was going to be my fate anyway, I wasn't going to give him the satisfaction of seeing me afraid. So instead, I lulled him closer, softening my expression. He blinked slowly, and I could feel the desire building inside of him, tasting like honey and spice.

His hot breath hit my mouth as he inched closer, and I fought back the urge to gag and closed my eyes. The moment his lips touched mine, I snapped my teeth against his skin, piercing through his bottom lip. His blood spilled onto my tongue, dribbling out over my chin.

"Bitch!" he spluttered, stumbling back against the wall.

I smiled a bloodied grin. "Now you know how it feels being bitten, you evil fuck."

He wrapped his fingers around my throat, digging his fingers into my windpipe. Blood poured through the gaping hole in his face, but unfortunately, it healed within a few seconds. Regardless, I basked in those few seconds of pain and embarrassment he felt.

"You'll regret that." He grabbed a fistful of my hair with his free hand, jolting my head back.

Throbbing pulsed into my soul as I struggled to catch my breath. "Better I be dead," I croaked, "than in that auction."

His forehead wrinkled as his light eyebrows pulled together. "You're lucky you're worth so much." He released my hair, and a few strands remained tangled around his bony fingers.

"I don't think you understand the definition of lucky," I said breathlessly.

His nostrils flared. "I hope whoever buys you gives you what you deserve."

My bravery slipped away as his words hit deep. I was about to be sold to one of them. As his fingers gripped into my arm, a move I was sure would leave a bruise, I glared at him. He untied the rope around my wrists, and I rubbed the red marks, rolling out the aching in my arms from having them pulled back for the past hour.

"I will make you pay for this," I promised, rage roiling my words.

He scoffed, wiping his own blood from his chin. "It's amusing that you think you have a future to do that."

I gritted my teeth. If I made it out alive, I would ensure I kept that promise.

He dragged me from the room, and I didn't bother fighting back. I needed to save my energy for when it really counted. If there was any moment of escape, I couldn't miss the opportunity because I was weak.

It was hard to see anything in the dim, yellow light of the hallways, but I could see the glossy doors leading to more rooms like the one we'd just left. I'd become accustomed to the feeling of dread filling the building, so I didn't bat an eyelid as more of it radiated from behind the doors. Instead, I focused on steadying my breathing, doing my best to ignore the emotions of what felt like a hundred mortals like myself.

A part of me wondered if Draven had been brought here or to an auction like it. I liked to think he wouldn't have gone down without a fight. Still, as each day passed, the sickening thought became more real.: Draven would, statistically, already be dead if he hadn't been killed immediately. But, unlike my mom and me, who were worth more alive, he was merely a thing to eat, and the best I could hope for was that he was enslaved somewhere. But was that really any better?

The cold air sank through my pores, numbing my cheeks as we walked up ancient, stone steps to the main event. Loud drumbeats resonated around the walls. Three rows of chairs sat in a semicircle, seating thirty or so vampires in front of a large stage. Blue velvet curtains had been pulled back, revealing their twisted source of entertainment.

Drummers played as I was led up to the stage. A woman wept into her palms as she was dragged from the stage, and I noticed on a whiteboard the words *Thirty-two years old*.

I watched her flinging around as her dark hair spilled from a messy bun. One of the soul vampires took her, its long talons curling around her wrist. "Please, I have kids at home," she begged through wretched sobs. She had a family back home, and suddenly the fight instinct kicked in. I focused on the creature pulling her from the room, praying to feel a shred of compassion or kindness, but it only had a lust to devour coiling around its center. That's when I realized she wasn't going to be enslaved. It was going to kill her, and soon.

"Don't hurt her," I found myself shouting, but not even one of them flinched. I closed my eyes, fighting to feel even a spark of power, but the necklace numbed it, pushing my magic deeper every time I willed it to come to the surface.

"Shut it," the auctioneer snapped into my ear. A man cleaned the board as if the woman had never existed, replacing it with information about me. He wrote the words *Sorceress, Virgin, Age nineteen.*

They'd gotten the virgin part wrong, but the rest was true. I supposed it made me more enticing to the bidders, which forced bile up my esophagus, burning my throat as it dawned on me. Being a prisoner or drinking from us wasn't the only thing they could do to us.

"In case you decide to open that vile mouth of yours again," the white-haired vampire said and pulled out the same fabric which had been strapped around my mouth before.

"No, get o—" My next words were muffled as he tied it a little too tightly. His grip tightened against me when he finished and sped me up the few steps to the stage.

I made sure to wear my most hateful glare as I was led out onto the center stage. The drums slowed to a lower, spacious tempo, amplifying the room's ambiance. The orange lights turned to a deep shade of crimson, casting an eerie glow over an already terrifying audience.

"This beautiful specimen comes from Baldoria." The man's voice silenced the chatter. "She is pure." he promised. I shook my head, hoping any looking at me would know that was a lie. "She is submissive too." Another lie. "Her blood tastes like euphoria, better than any drug, and you can have her use her magic to assist your needs if you wish. She wears an expensive, rare necklace around her neck that prevents her from using her powers unless it is removed by one of us. This will come with your purchase."

One sangaree, a handsome man with dark eyes, wearing a leather jacket, sat slumped in one of the front seats. His gaze trickled over me, tilting his head as if that would somehow improve his view. He stretched his fingers over the arms of his chair as a cruel smile slowly spread over his face. Next to him, a muscular female sangaree watched the auctioneer, her eyes greedy.

The auction owner's snow-white hair shone down in a lock of silk down his back as he faced the bidders, telling them more delicious details of me, his words dripping like honey from his blood-soaked lips, lips I had bitten through less than ten minutes ago. The memory flickered some power to my center because I had, if only for a second, bested one of them. I made sure to stare directly at every single one of them, refusing to let my fear resign me into the prisoner they wanted me to be.

"Ten thousand stagma," he announced, starting the auction.

I recalled my mom bringing home two thin silver coins to show me. She said they were the currency of Sanmorte and they were rare, but she'd found them on a raid of vampires hiding in some private club up north. She was often called upon by other guild branches to assist them. Her reputation preceded her, and I only hoped it helped her now that she was in their castle.

I wondered if she had already escaped, and a small, childish piece of me hoped somehow, she was on her way to save me.

It was impossible. She didn't even know I had been taken. If she, by some miracle, had gotten away, she'd have gone back to Baldoria. I wondered how she would react to my death. We'd done everything together since I was born, and she'd been my best friend since I could remember.

Aiden had once said my mom lived for two things: me and her work. Now, all she'd have left is one. My imagination formed a scene in my mind of my mom howling, crying when she saw I was gone too. I could feel her grief, and it was worse than mine had ever been. The daydream was so real I almost forgot where I was until I opened my eyes. Several vampires stood, holding little paddles as they bid for me.

A tear trickled from one eye. I desperately wanted to wipe it away, so they couldn't see what they were doing and how desperate I really was because I didn't want to die. Not here.

Sanmorte was far worse than any of us could have known. I only prayed that the secret of their being able to make vampires remained as such because I couldn't fathom the thought of more people coming here, wanting to become monsters like them, and most ending up somewhere like this.

"Two hundred and forty thousand stagma," one man said. He was handsomely dressed in a tailored suit, wearing a royal-blue necktie.

The room fell silent. The smell of clover smoke reached my nose as one of the sangaree lit a cigar, puffing out smoke hoops into the middle of the room. It waved like an illusory dance under the red light.

"Any more bids?"

The man who'd bid on me looked around, his presence serving to make a few nervous. I could feel it in the air.

"Sold to 4162."

I noticed the number on a white sticker on his paddle. I'd attended an auction like this before, except it was my mom who was bidding on our new house. The comparison was almost humorous. *Almost.*

Another sangaree I hadn't noticed before, standing behind me, pulled me up to stand and walked me down to the blond-haired, immaculate vampire. He barely looked at me as he took my arm, leading me from the room. Before we reached the closed door to leave, I glanced over my shoulder, my eyes narrowing as I looked at the auction owner, hate and promise in my eyes.

He'd better hope I didn't make it out alive because if I did, I would make sure he was the first person I destroyed. At this point, I was gaining a nice list of people I wanted to kill.

The vampire's icy grasp tightened as he walked us out the door and toward a private room. I struggled against him, but he was too strong. "I'm going to enjoy you before I take you home," he said matter-of-factly. He moved my hair over one shoulder so it tumbled down my chest, then laced a finger over the back of my neck, making little circles on my skin. "I paid a lot for you," he said slowly, and I waited for him to tell me to behave. "So I expect you to put up a fight. I hate my prey being so willing."

I ran cold, panic seizing me as I clicked on why I couldn't feel any emotion coming from him. I hadn't noticed due to feeling everyone else's before leaving the room, but his touch should have amplified our connection. Instead, he was devoid of feeling. He was relying on me to make him feel something, anything.

Gods, he was the worst of the worst, a psychopath—and I was his property.

THIRTEEN

"Please, take a seat," the vampire offered with a level of eloquence I didn't expect. The private room housed a queen-sized four-post bed draped in the finest silks. Hanging over the bed was a long, white see-through voile giving the illusion of privacy and intimacy.

A small table, enough for two people, sat between two cherry-wood chairs. I sat on the plush, velvet cushion of the chair, my eyes drifting to the standing sofa tucked away under an erotic painting of a man and woman tangled in lust on the back wall. I noticed there were no windows, and the lighting was a deep yellow.

"Please." He gestured to the bowl of fresh strawberries and cream next to a bottle of champagne. "Eat, drink."

"I thought you wanted me to fight you?" I asked carefully, breathing in the smell of fresh polish and linen.

"Naturally," he said casually, crossing one leg over the other, creasing his perfectly ironed trousers. "But I do not want you to give up easily. From a century of experience, I have learned that a mortal treated with a balance of fear and being treated well makes for the best pets."

My stomach churned as I turned my nose up at the strawberries. "I'm not hungry."

He pushed the bowl across to me. "I insist."

"If I refuse?"

"I'll take you to the bed now."

Slowly, I took a strawberry between my fingers, making a face as I brought it to my lips. The creature watched me like a cat watches its prey, running his hand over his trimmed, dark beard. I pressed the smooth edge of the strawberry against my mouth and took a bite. A burst of sweetness coated my tongue, accompanied by a sour tang. I took another bite of the juicy fruit and finished it with a dollop of cool cream.

"How does it taste?" His wanting eyes followed my fingers as I licked the juices.

I shrugged, not wanting to give him anything he may enjoy, but at the same time, wanting to stall him for as long as possible. I glanced at the bed and the uncertainty and inevitably of what this room meant. "What's your name?"

"Hamza."

"I'm Olivia."

"How average."

I clicked my tongue. He didn't even know my name when he bid for me. We really were just objects to them. "What is it you do, Hamza?" I asked. Right now, as I opened myself to his feelings, he was calm, a little intrigued, and I wanted to keep it that way, for as long as possible anyway.

"I work at the castle." He tilted his head, his gaze trickling over the visible top half of my body from across the table. "You remind me of someone. That hair of yours, it's so unique. Most redheads I've met have auburn tones, but yours, it's the color of blood." His eyes brightened. "Very rare, coveted even."

"Who do I remind you of?"

His lips curved up. "No one I'd want to sleep with."

My lips trembled. "Do you come here often?"

He waved a hand lazily. "Occasionally, when they have something worth buying. I got the message of a sorceress being sold here less than an hour ago. It was worth the trip." He reached across the table, placing a manicured hand over mine.

Instinctively, I slipped mine out from under his, putting it on my lap.

"They say a sorcerer's blood is unlike anything a normal mortal can offer. Liquid euphoria," he enunciated, "I have tasted it once before, but even with two of your people at court, we are denied such pleasures." His nostrils flared, annoyance rippling from his aura. "The king has a soft spot for your kind. He loves magic and desires an heir. So, naturally, only a sorceress like yourself could tempt him."

My heart raced. Was that why my mom was there, to be used for breeding? "You say there are two sorcerers at court. Is at least one of them a woman?"

A laugh bubbled from his mouth. "Aren't you a curious little thing?"

"Maybe I am," I said, deadpan.

He looked down at the table, let out a small sigh, then his gaze climbed back to mine. "Conversation time is over."

I could feel his want from here. "I'm still hungry," I lied, moving my hands toward the bowl of strawberries.

"You had your chance to eat. I'll allow you another meal after."

Goose bumps spread over my arms, and every impulse in my body urged me to run as he stood, but I wouldn't make it to the door before he'd catch me. They were faster than anything I'd seen before. "I'm not feeling well."

He slid out of his navy-blue blazer and folded it over the back of his chair, then tugged at his silver cufflinks. "Remove your dress."

This wasn't happening. I flinched when he scraped the chair under the table, my shoulders tightening. Beads of sweat formed on my upper lip. He wanted me to try to fight. Challenge burned in his eyes, waiting, watching. I was the mouse, he was the cat, and his show of elegance and mortality was an act, a mask he enjoyed wearing to hide the evil underneath. Until he didn't want to anymore.

"Remove your dress," he ordered again, his tone sharpened.

I expelled a scant breath, my fingers trembling. "No."

His fangs showed when he grinned. "You will remove your dress, or I will tear it to ribbons."

I clutched at my chest, holding the fabric under my curled fingertips. Then, stumbling backward, I knocked my calf into the leg of my chair, sending a shot of pain up into my thigh.

He walked to me, his head curving as his expression darkened and eyes rimmed red. He reached me and tore the side of my dress, pushing me back against the wall, knocking the breath from my lungs. His fangs glinted as he curled his lips back, then brought his mouth down to the side of my neck. A whimper escaped my lips as they sank through my skin, bringing with them an agony I'd known twice before.

His hand ran up the inside of my thigh as I felt the blood leave my body, slurped between his lips. It took every ounce of strength I had to bring my knee up and into his groin.

He stumbled back, reaching for his dick, gritting his teeth. I pushed back, kicking up again and landing another hit against his growing length. He let out a low growl, a sadistic smile building as I ran for the door. I slammed against the wood panels, grasping for the doorknob, turning it in my sweaty palms. The door cracked open, spilling in light from the hallway.

Gasping, I took off running. I was shocked at how far I made it until a hand gripped my wrist, jolting me backward. The touch felt different; his rage pierced into me, a difference from the starkness I'd felt from Hamza this whole time.

"Stand behind me."

I pressed my palms to my eyes, relief pouring through me. I'd never thought I'd be so happy to hear Sebastian's voice.

"They sold me in the auction," I explained shakily.

He looked me up and down, his expression darkening when he saw the blood and torn fabric dangling from my dress. "Who did this to you?"

I pointed at the half-open door. Sebastian's eyes widened, revealing the white around his blue irises. His veins strained from his muscles, darkening blue under his skin.

"You!" he barked, kicking the door until it splintered, cracking down the center.

"You're interrupting us, Sebastian" was all the man said, with a small smile. I shouldn't have been surprised they knew each other.

"Hamza." Warning guided his tone as he took a threatening step closer to him. "I should kill you."

"Careful, Sebastian. You may be one of the king's favorites, but I'm at his side every day. I can make things happen, even to you and your friends."

Sebastian's fist tightened, turning his knuckles white. "Is that a threat?"

Hamza arched a perfectly groomed eyebrow. "Does the king know you're hiding a sorceress?"

"I'm not hiding anyone. It doesn't matter anyway. She's my business."

"We both know Sargon wouldn't see it that way."

I stood a step behind Sebastian, not moving my gaze from Hamza, observing every calculated move as he rounded the table between us with precision. His focus was all on Sebastian now. I wanted to warn him of Hamza's emotions or lack thereof, but Sebastian pushed me back as I tried to step to his side. "I could just rip out your heart."

"I have a century on you, boy," Hamza spat. "Besides, even if you could kill me, you would be discovered, and your life would be over. Is it worth it over a sorceress?"

He let out a low growl, his arms tensing, bulging the muscles under his rolled-up sleeves.

"Are you going to tell him?"

"How you stole my property?"

"She's not your property!"

"Was she already yours? I thought the great Sebastian doesn't keep mortals enslaved. That it is beneath him."

I could feel the anger rolling off Sebastian. It was enough to set my adrenaline into overdrive.

Hamza spoke again, taunting in his voice. "Unless she's your wife or property, then you have no hold over her. She's mine. I paid a lot of stagma for her. So if you want to contest it, you can take it up with the court."

Silence danced around us. Hamza enjoyed this too much, watching Sebastian walk the fine line between wanting to kill him and knowing he couldn't. I stepped past him, my fingers gently pressing into his forearm.

"Who's saying we're not engaged?"

Hamza blinked twice, confusion radiating from him. "This is ridiculous." He regarded me this time. "This a ploy, to save you. Sebastian wouldn't marry. He's always despised the concept."

I clasped my hands together, trying to control the shaking in my fingers. "Why do you think Seb is so angry?" It felt wrong using his nickname, but it was a necessary evil. "We haven't announced anything yet, but yes, he asked me to be his wife. Maybe he didn't want to be married, but that was before he met me."

Surprise rippled through the room, most of it coming from Sebastian.

Hamza scoffed a laugh. "Even if this is real, you didn't ask permission from the court." A trail of saliva trickled over his bottom lip.

My eyes widened. This was my chance to go there and find my mom. "We were coming to the castle this week to ask for it."

Hamza scowled, and Sebastian remained unusually quiet. "Well, well." Hamza backed away, a smirk playing on his lips. "It seems as if you found your one." He glanced down at my stomach. "That or you want an heir. Such a rarity." He paused, coveting me with his eyes. "You should keep a better watch of your bride."

"Oh, I will."

Relief flooded me. He was, at the very least, going along with it for now. Hamza moved to open the door. "I'll talk to Achais, let him know of our misunderstanding. I won't be paying for her, and I expect compensation for my trouble here." He paused at my side for a second longer before disappearing.

Once the door clicked shut, we waited a solid minute, ensuring he was gone before speaking.

"I'm sorry," I blurted out.

"I should tear his fucking head off."

"Calm down, please." I swallowed thickly.

Sebastian's expression hardened. He didn't even look at me. "I shouldn't have let you wander off like you did."

"I only went to my room."

"You didn't put the bracelet back on," he scolded.

"Sorry."

He let out a long exhale and closed his eyes. "No matter. What's done is done."

"What does that mean?"

"It means, for better or worse, you've placed a target on your head. You're now my bride-to-be, and our culture takes marriage seriously. Engagements aren't made often."

I swallowed thickly, a lump forming in my throat. "I only said what I needed to, to get us out of this. We're not actually engaged."

"There were other ways I could have handled that."

"Such as?" I wasn't going to be ridiculed for saving us. "Killing him wasn't an option. He's too important, he said so, and if he wasn't, I get the feeling you wouldn't have left him standing as long as you did."

The muscle in his jaw feathered.

I pressed my fingers against the bite mark, a sob laying thick in my throat. "I won't apologize for doing something."

He turned me to face him, his hands on my shoulders, his touch gentler than expected. "You don't have to be. What did he do to you?"

"He bit me, and he was going to try to…" I trailed off. "You arrived just in time."

"You put up a fight of your own." His gaze darted to the tear in my dress.

"Here, you have no need for this anymore." He reached his hands around me, caressing the back of my neck. I flinched as he gently removed the necklace and pocketed it.

I rubbed where the necklace had rubbed my skin. "When did you realize I was missing?"

"Not long ago. I went to three auctions before here. I didn't think he'd have the balls to take you to this one. He didn't even try to be subtle."

I touched his chest as his anger built, reaching its peak. I splayed my fingers over his shirt, feeling his heartbeat under my palm. Finally, his rage withered away until his glossy gaze deepened into mine.

"What was that?"

I quickly pulled my hand away. "Sometimes, I can change someone's vibration. You were angry, and it was just—"

"Instinct," he finished, not looking away from me. "You're different from how I thought you'd be."

"I didn't know you had much time to think I would be like anything."

His expression faltered. "You should know something now that you've set our engagement into motion."

I moved back, putting a few extra inches between us. "What?" Here it was, the real *why* of why he was holding me here, or at least I hoped.

"I can't take you back to Baldoria. It's not safe for you there."

"I know, and I wouldn't leave without my mom or Draven anyway."

"Things have changed. Before, we had a plan"—he rubbed his forehead, smoothing out the wrinkles which had formed—"to take down Nightshade first, but now, with us having to fake being together and going to the castle, you're safer knowing than being kept in the dark."

I pressed my sweaty palms together, fidgeting with the ring around my finger.

"Your mother is no stranger to Sanmorte."

"I assumed as much, considering you told me my dad is a vampire."

"Your mother's true name is Ravena." He paused. "And she was once queen."

I blinked twice, my jaw slacking. Clearly, I hadn't heard that correctly. A small laugh escaped my lips, and I clasped my hand over my mouth.

"You are the daughter of the vampire king."

Okay, this really was a fucking joke.

"There's been a lot of speculation about the lost heir of Sanmorte hiding in Baldoria. I didn't believe it myself until I saw you for the first time."

No. No. I shook my head, stepping backward until my back hit a wall. "I'm not."

"I know this is a shock."

I laughed again, although none of this was funny. "A shock?" Another laugh. "It's impossible. I can't be. I mean, you said the Nightshade people want me dead. Why would they want that if I'm the heir or whatever?" I searched for anything to confirm he was lying.

"The king's brother does not want you found. He wants the throne for himself; that's why he sent them after you. They were caught with your mom, which is why Kalon handed her over to Sargon. He pretended it was his plan all along."

"My mom would have told me if that was true."

"Would she?" he questioned. "Being the heir to the most desired throne in the world isn't the safest position. She left in the first place because he wanted to turn you into one of us. You can't be both vampire and sorceress. He would have taken your powers, and she didn't want that, so she left and integrated you into a mortal society, placing herself in a guild which she knew would protect you and her secret."

My world crumbled beneath my feet, cold seeping into my core, tingling my skin. "The guild knew?"

"Yes."

"Then Astor knows," I said shakily after letting out a deep breath.

"Yes. He knew exactly who to go to and used her official title."

My mind flitted with questions, but only one statement stood out. "He didn't give me away."

"Even traitors can care for someone," he drawled, his lips turning into a hard line.

"No." I shook my head again, slipping back into disbelief. "There's no way."

"You process this however you need to, but it doesn't change the truth. You're the lost princess of Sanmorte, the only heir to its throne, and I have no reason to lie about it."

Moving slowly, I lifted my hand to my neck, slowly stroking my throat as the realization weighed heavy in my soul. "Why did you keep this from me?"

"For your own good. I didn't know how you'd react at first or what you would try to do. We needed a plan."

As my stomach dipped, I cast my gaze to my feet, wondering how I'd missed this. "You mean to work out how best to use me to gain the most for yourself?"

His lips parted, but no words came out. That told me everything.

I placed a hand on my hip, tears welling in my eyes. "You're just as bad as Astor and Nightshade."

"Careful."

"Or what?" I challenged as shock turned into anger.

He didn't answer.

"I'm leaving," I snapped, trembling as I felt my heart pounding.

"You should know something else too, before you try to go off on your own."

"What?" My fists clenched briefly. "Am I also the secret cousin of a goblin prince?"

"No," he said, deadpan. "Your real name isn't Olivia. Your mom changed it, along with her own."

I inhaled deeply, heaving out my chest. I couldn't take any more surprises. "What is it?"

"Seraphina."

Shred by shred, I felt my identity slip away. "I want to get out of here," I shouted, the room suddenly feeling too small. "Take me back," I demanded, needing to be away from this place.

So we walked outside, onto the bustling streets of the city of nightmares, and he cradled my head against his chest as we spun into the air, his wings extending out, flapping wind, circling leaves around us. The last thing I wanted was to be in his arms, but in a world of darkness, he was my only ally.

SHADOW KISSED   182

His confession swam in my thoughts as I nestled into the vampire who was only using me for what I could give him as we flew over the city, a place which should have been mine, once upon a time.

Lost princess. Heir to the throne. Daughter of the vampire king.

FOURTEEN

I sat upright, rubbing the sleep out of my eyes, dragging the skin underneath, which was raw. Sunlight arrowed through the crack in the drapes, shining a warm light onto the floorboards. I stepped out into it, basking in the warmth on my skin, but felt no joy from it. The emptiness had returned—a place beyond sadness.

After the adrenaline left me shaking when we'd arrived back last night, I found myself plunged into a nightmare-fueled sleep, waking up constantly while trying to figure out how my life had ended up this way.

Everything I knew was a lie, and I couldn't find much to live for now that I'd survived the auction. If it wasn't for my mom being locked away, I wouldn't bother even getting out of bed. Most of the night, I prayed behind closed eyes for the gods to take my soul, so all this would be over and I'd be safe. I assumed Draven would be there waiting for me because from what I saw yesterday, there was only a little hope he had survived this kingdom until now.

"Knock knock," Erianna said as she stepped in, startling me. "I brought you coffee."

She placed the mug of swirling brown on the nightstand and flipped her black braids over her shoulder. "Seb told me you know about your father."

I slumped back on my bed, pushing myself against the cold wall, happy to feel anything, even if it was a splash of discomfort. "Yes."

"How do you feel?"

"Not overly surprised. My life's already terrible, so why not throw in the fact that everyone I know has lied to me."

She sat on the chair, her gaze fixated on mine. "You've been through a lot. I'm prepared to go and kill Achais for taking you, then I'll go after Hamza."

I knew it was all words. Hamza, I was confident, was untouchable. Still, I appreciated the sentiment. "Don't bother."

Worry lines deepened around her mouth. "Olivia…"

"Why not use my real name? Seraphina, or whatever." I didn't know why I was being so harsh. She was the only person who I still somewhat liked.

"I wanted to tell you the truth, but you were already struggling with your mom being gone and searching for your friend, and then your ex-boyfriend, that this felt like too much."

Tears brimmed in my eyes. "Draven's probably dead." Hearing the words out loud cut deeper than a knife. She didn't answer, which only grew the ache in my chest. "I wish I was too."

She stood, fast enough to give me whiplash, and was holding my hands before I could take my next breath. "Don't go there." Her deep, earthy eyes glossed over. "I know how you feel and that pain that just won't go away, but I promise you, life is so much more than the way you feel right now."

"Everything hurts, and it all just feels pointless. What do I have to wake up for?"

She rubbed my arm, her calluses rough against my skin. "I know how you feel, trust me. We live in a world shrouded in secrets and lies, but it's okay." A glisten swam in her irises. "It's why we're here. Without all that suffering, our existence here wouldn't be necessary, and we may as well already be dead, with the gods and live amongst the stars, but we're not. We're here, and that's because we have so much left to learn, to grow."

I looked down at my blanket, nestling in it for warmth. "I wish I could see it that way."

"You will, one day. For now, everything is going to feel like darkness. The price to pay for being here is pain." She paused, glancing up at the ceiling as if she could see another world I couldn't. "If I'm honest with you, I'd rather be here, with all the imperfection and suffering than all-knowing and perfect where there's no hurt. I love being alive, well, some form of that at least, and while it may be agony sometimes, it's so gratifying. I love walking out the door in the morning, never knowing what might happen. If I was gone from here, I would miss the bad times too because it makes me love harder. I never take a thing for granted because death exists, and in its aching grasp, I feel everything. I live for that, Olivia, to feel deeply, and I know you do too. So be angry, scream at the sky and cry yourself to sleep, but don't you dare wish for death. Not yet, not when there's a world of wonder out there for your soul to experience."

I wanted to believe her words, to let them make me feel better, but I couldn't allow myself to have hope. Not when my heart felt so heavy, and every shard of trust I had in the people I loved was broken. "That's your world, Erianna, not mine."

"It's everyone's world."

"There's a difference. You have purpose and friends here. I have no one." Tears fell in thick droplets before I could stop them. "I can't even use my powers properly. I'm worthless."

"No." She shook her head, sandwiching my hands between hers. "You're afraid and hurt, but not worthless. Do you know why I like you?"

I shook my head.

"You have a fight, and hope, inside of you. I saw it from the moment I met you, and I know what that can turn into. So give yourself a chance before you give up. You might surprise yourself."

"I don't even know anything about my life, really. Sebastian brought me here last night, and I haven't spoken to him since."

"Go talk to him," she urged. "You can still go to the castle. He told me of your plan, and don't get me wrong, I feel bad for you having to pretend to be his betrothed."

I almost smiled, but depression snatched it away first. "I don't know."

"Why not? Find your mom, then you can be pissed at her, and as for Draven, he may still be alive. They have mortals at the castle too. They use them as servants, guards, and for food. Plus, Hamza's there, and you can always get revenge."

"I don't know."

"Go talk to Sebastian. He'll tell you everything now you know who you really are. Also, I prefer Olivia to Seraphina."

I took the coffee, sipping it as it soothed my scratchy throat. "Thank you for being kind."

"Always, and when you said you have no one here, you were wrong. You have me. We may not know each other that well yet, but you can call me a friend. I promise I will not lie to you again."

"I believe you."

"You know"—she moved back, giving me space—"you and Seb are more similar than either of you would ever believe."

"I'm nothing like him."

"Hmm." She smiled at the floor. "Get dressed and come down for some food. Seb had some sandwiches made. I know he's not the easiest to understand, but he's trying."

"Thanks, Erianna."

I faltered when I reached the bottom step and saw Astor's girlfriend standing in the open front door with Sebastian. Great, another thing to ruin an already terrible day.

"Don't embarrass yourself, Gwen." Sebastian leaned coolly against the doorframe. "I've told you before, I'm not interested."

She flushed red, which I didn't even think was possible for a vampire. "I'm not here for you." She scowled, turning her head in my direction. "Astor came by to speak to her. I want to know why."

He looked over his shoulder at me, but I glared directly at her. "Why don't you ask your boyfriend that?" I said between gritted teeth as I walked to join them.

She ran her hand through her platinum-blonde waves, and her glacier-blue eyes shone under the afternoon sun, emitting a red-orange hue behind her. "Because I didn't believe his answer. He's hiding something, and I want to know what."

Sebastian answered, bringing her attention back to him. "You're always so paranoid."

"Don't taunt me." Her voice rose an octave, and her posture straightened. "I came here as a courtesy before getting the order involved."

Sebastian stiffened. They were the last people we wanted in our business. She didn't know that I was Ravena's daughter, and while I should have been grateful to Astor for not outing me, I couldn't be. He still gave up all his friends and my mom. I only hoped whatever tatters of loyalty he had left for me remained until I got my mom back and got out of here.

I took a step forward. "Astor and I used to date," I said, stating the obvious. "He came to apologize to me for letting me think he was dead and to tell me that he's with you now. That this is his new life and to leave him to it."

The jealousy swarming in her eyes calmed. Had I leashed the monster?

"That's what he said too." She lifted an eyebrow, observing me. "So just stay away from him."

"Don't worry. I will."

She snapped back to Sebastian, shaking her head. "Now that's taken care of, my mom wants to know why you've been avoiding her calls."

The hairs on the back of my neck stood erect. He'd said Gwendolyn was the daughter of the head of Nightshade, the woman who wanted me dead and probably knew what I looked like through pictures and research.

"I've been busy," he said nonchalantly. "I'll get back to her when I'm ready."

Gwen rolled her expressive, blue eyes. "Are you going to hold a grudge forever, Seb?"

"Don't push me, Gwen."

She turned, looking me up and down. "I'll tell her you've found a new plaything, and that's why you've been distracted. Don't keep her waiting too long. You know how she hates it."

"Goodbye, Gwen," he said, closing the door on her.

"Do you know her well?" I asked. "Should I be worried about her mom?"

"No. Gwen, despite everything, won't put me in danger."

"Why not?"

"Gwen was there when I was turned. She was the first person to show me how to survive as a vampire when her mom forced me to change. Mostly because her mom also forced her to change once she turned twenty, so she knows how it feels." His expression darkened. "Gwen may be jealous, paranoid, and spoiled, but she's not her mother. Velda's worse. She's intelligent and takes what she wants."

His eyes glazed over as he looked up, lost in a memory of a life torn away from him.

"I'm sorry she did that to you."

He swallowed thickly before he returned to his usual self—on the surface anyway. "She will pay for it one day. Besides"—he forced a small smile—"I met Erianna and Zach shortly after. They saved me in many ways."

"What about your family and friends? Have you been back to see them?" I asked, assuming he'd had to come here after being turned in another kingdom.

"I don't have any family to go back to," he admitted, the line on his forehead creasing deeply. "My life wasn't the only thing Velda took."

"How did you cope?"

"I could ask you the same question. You've lost everyone close to you too."

The reminder hit me like a brick wall, catching the breath in my throat. "I'm not coping."

He paused, searching my expression. I looked over his sharp features, landing on the dimple which only appeared when he smiled or frowned. "How did you manage?"

"I surrendered," he said, stilling me.

"Isn't that just a fancier word for giving up?"

"You think surrender is weakness?" he asked, tilting my head up with two fingers.

"Yes," I choked out. "What else could it be?"

"Power."

My eyebrows furrowed. "How?"

He took a step back, shoving his hands in his deep pockets, and walked toward the dining room. I followed. "When you release control, no one can force your hand. I realized a long time ago I couldn't force the will of the world, and in that, I found faith. I realized I could do anything, be anything, and decided anything that happened to me was meant to be. I believe, with everything I am, that I'm going to make it out of this alive with some shred of happiness, and that belief made me more powerful than I ever could have imagined."

"So I should surrender?"

"That doesn't mean being okay with everything," he said. "It might not work for you, and that's okay. I'm just telling you what helped me."

"I can't do that," I said slowly.

"I gave in to my anger, to the grief, knowing that I couldn't change what happened, and accepted that my family was gone. It gave me a second chance to become so much more. I took all those broken pieces of me and stuck them back together."

I understood where he was coming from, but I wasn't there yet. My surrender wasn't empowering. It was me giving up. Something I'd come closer and closer to since I found out about my dad and what should have been my destiny. The scene unfolded in my head, of a younger me growing up here instead of in Baldoria. Maybe I would have siblings, or my mom would have turned. So, I imagined her as a vampire, the color gone from her tanned face, her teeth pointed, ready to bite.

"Have you come to a decision?" he asked, snapping me out of my dreamlike state. I couldn't help it. Even my mom had to explain to people at the guild how sometimes I went off in my head. My daydreams were as tangible as reality, and occasionally, I'd caught myself wondering which version had been more real.

"Sorry?" I blinked twice, noticing we were already standing by the table in the dining area. I took a seat, staring hazily over triangles of sandwiches and pitchers of freshly squeezed juice. "I should go to the castle, but I don't know if I want to."

He picked up an apple and rolled it from one hand to the other. Not to eat, but as something to play with, like Gwen believed I was. "It's okay to be angry with her," he offered as if he could read my mind. "Your mom, I mean. She did lie to you, even if it was to protect you. You're not betraying her by being upset. It's very…" He tilted his head at me. "Mortal of you."

I wasn't sure whether to take that as a compliment or not. "You also lied to me."

"Yes."

I shrugged. "It makes me trust you less."

He placed the apple down, placing all his focus on me, which somehow made me feel far more vulnerable than it should have. "I'm not going to apologize for not telling you while you were acting unpredictably. If I told you the truth, I couldn't have known what you'd do with that information. You were already processing being here, your father being a vampire, and your mom and friend being gone." He turned his back to me, looking to the arched, undraped window. "Then there was the betrayal by the ex."

I took a turkey sandwich and slowly chewed on the crust.

He looked my way. "I know you're not a flight risk now. At least, you're not stupid enough to try to leave. Not now that you know what this city can do to you, I'll be honest."

"That'd be a nice start."

His shoulders tensed. "I want you to become queen of Sanmorte," he said, his expression dead serious, and I burst into laughter.

FIFTEEN

"It wasn't a joke," Sebastian stated, his expression deadly serious. "I want you to take Sargon's place as the reigning monarch."

I spaced. What did he mean that *wasn't* a joke? "You're insane."

"I know it sounds crazy."

I scoffed a laugh. "Yes, it does, and it's out of the question. I'd never, in a million years, want to become a vampire, let alone rule a kingdom of them."

"You could change things here."

"I don't care about Sanmorte. Anyway, I thought you were a favorite of the king?" I questioned, not able to bring myself to refer to the king as my dad yet. "Why would you need me to be queen? Wouldn't that mean he has to die? Some friend you are."

"Or we can force him to retire," he added, but uncertainty filled his expression. "There are certain abilities which come with having the throne."

I didn't believe that the king of vampires would choose to retire. He would have to die if I were going to become queen. Fortunately, that notion was just as ridiculous. I would never want to become queen, especially one of such a horrid kingdom, and choose to give my powers up.

"One"—I put a finger in the air, leaning forward, my torso pushing against the table—"I will never become queen. Two, why would you want that?"

"Like I said, the crown comes with a particular set of abilities."

"Such as?" I asked, not because I was considering it, but to know what Sebastian really wanted.

He leaned back in his chair. "It's a wide collection. One of which is the ability to turn any vampire into ash using a cane carved from the bones of the first immortals to be killed."

"Lovely."

He continued. "The king doesn't use it often, if ever. He prefers to make a spectacle of those who would go against him during executions."

"How so?"

"Normally, he drags the charged out into the court grounds and cuts off their heads in front of a crowd."

"How very ancient. It sounds like he hasn't come into the century yet."

"Sanmorte is behind the modern world in so many ways, and Sargon and many others at court prefer that."

"So." I moved my plate away from me and grabbed a drink instead. "You want the bone-cane for yourself."

He laughed. "It's called the Cane of Cineris, although bone-cane sounds so much better."

"Why do you want it?"

"That's not the gift I'm after. There are several, one of which is the blood of the goddess, Vaneria."

My brows furrowed as I sipped on orange juice, which tasted surprisingly good. "Why would you want the blood of the goddess of hearts?"

"It is said that her blood can return the mortality to any immortal."

My jaw slacked, and I curled my fingers, my nails biting into my palm. "Okay." I didn't really know what to say. I wanted to laugh, but his expression told me he wasn't joking. Even a little vulnerability cracked through. "I didn't think that was possible."

"The king has the power to grant it, but he won't. I've asked him before." He drummed his fingers against his leg. "He believes immortality is a gift not to be wasted."

"So he could, in theory, turn himself mortal?"

"Yes. Vaneria gave it as a gift before she ascended for any new king, queen, prince, or princess who claimed their place. To become a ruler of Sanmorte, you must become immortal, which, to the gods, was seen as a great sacrifice. While there was not enough blood to turn back an entire race of vampires, she could offer enough for each new heir so that when they chose to finish their reign and hand the throne to their successor, they may become mortal once more."

"Then the king is keeping it for himself? That doesn't seem surprising. It is his gift after all."

"He will never take it," Sebastian said coolly. The afternoon sun lowered in the sky, pouring warmth onto the table and over my hands. "There has been much discussion around his retirement, and he has declared on more than one occasion that if he chooses to end his reign, then he will remain immortal and eventually die as one too. He's not afraid of the underworld. In fact, he thinks it's the perfect place to go in death, a guaranteed afterlife filled with all the vampires he's ever met. Why would he die as a mortal? He would die and leave behind everyone he cares about."

"If that's true, then he should give it to you. The king," I added.

"He won't do it. His gifts are precious to him and represent the power he holds. His brother, Kalon, is also crowned prince and is next in line for the throne. After you," he added. "He too has these gifts but would never give one to me. He's far crueler than Sargon and despises me."

"What other gifts did the gods give him?"

"He doesn't feel bloodlust like we do, so if he doesn't drink, he won't desiccate and die. He can enjoy mortal food too, delights in showing off his ability to consume both. Only the reigning monarch has this power, so not even Kalon knows it."

"The gods really must have believed in the monarchy."

He nodded, leaning his chair back, his dark hair showing hues of deep brown under the sunlight.

"The first king was crowned by them. As you know, there are four gods: Laveniuess, Jaiunere, Vaneria, and Salenia."

I nodded, and he continued.

"They saw it as their responsibility to bring structure and law to Sanmorte, as it was their sister who had brought such a curse onto the world. So the three of them, while Salenia was in the underworld she created, found a ruler of a kingdom who had succeeded in bringing order to the chaotic mortals from that time. They called him the chosen one and asked him to sacrifice his mortality and kingdom to rule Sanmorte, with the promise of a beautiful afterlife and the chance to become mortal once again one day. He already has a son and daughter, but his wife had died from disease not long before. The king agreed, and his children were also turned, prepared to one day take upon the burden of the monarchy."

Hearing all their history unfold, things hidden in books that had been long banned in Baldoria, was far more fascinating than I could have ever thought. As I listened, stories unfolded in my mind, and my writer's brain itched to tell them of the first king and his children. "Am I from his bloodline?"

"Yes. Fortunately, his bloodline has not run dry, for if it did, the king could choose a successor. His son married a sorcerer, and they had two sons, naming them Sargon and Kalon."

"How far back was this?"

"A millennium ago. The first king ruled for four centuries, his son for five, and the daughter helped him, remaining as princess until she decided to consume the goddess's blood and become mortal too. Sargon was then crowned king as the eldest son and ruled for a century before having you. The first king achieved some level of peace between Sanmorte and the rest of the world, forming treaties and finding a balance between the need for vampires to feed and how they would do it."

"What happened?" I asked as the blood dens and auctions swam into my mind.

"There's always corruption and a dark underbelly to any society. Blood dens have been around for hundreds of years, but they remained hidden, and those who ran them felt the wrath of the king if found. When Sargon took the throne, he kept to the laws at first, but slowly, he was corrupted by greed, power, and desire. He believes vampires are superior and should embrace their true natures. When your mom left him, taking you with her, he changed for the worse, and all of that underbelly became normal, or so I've heard. Zach and Erianna have told me stories."

"So his heartbreak made Sanmorte worse?" I closed my eyes for a minute, finding solace in the darkness as I imagined him, the man I'd never met but always wanted to, lost, betrayed, and saddened by her absence.

"Yes. Your mom is the rightful queen, but in name only. Because she was not immortal, she never received any of the gifts or powers which came with the crown. She had no actual power, but marriage is sacred in this culture and divorce doesn't exist. One of the few reasons why I would never want it," he added with a grin. "So Sargon couldn't remarry without knowing if she was dead or alive. He loved her dearly, and he was left without an heir or wife and no options to find another."

"How do you know all of this?" I asked, considering that he had only been a vampire for three years, which in the measure of immortality was no time at all.

"I make it my business to learn everything about those in power."

"So noble," I snapped.

"It's not difficult to find out. Those at court have little to do than to gossip. Sargon has also told me things about his life. He once said I remind him of his young self. That's why I'm his favorite. The king enjoys my ambition and humor."

"Someone has to."

"You, however, are nothing like him."

"No?"

"You care about others more than yourself."

The comment took me by surprise. "You think I'm caring?"

"Yes."

I hid my smile, mostly because I didn't want to enjoy being in his company. Still, after Astor's betrayal and all the lies, he wasn't the worst person in the world anymore, although he was still using me to get what he wanted. "So my mom hurt him," I stated, urging him to continue.

"Yes." He sat in the chair, leaning back, tapping a finger against his knee. "He loved her more than it was possible to love a person, if you're to believe Sargon and those close to him. From what I've concluded, he was controlling and paranoid of losing her. He suffocated her with that same love, and when you came along, he became a monster, obsessed with making sure no one took you from him. He thought there were people at court conspiring against him to take his crown and kill you so you couldn't inherit it after. It drove him to decide the one thing he promised your mom he would never do."

"At twenty-one, he declared he would turn you into a vampire once you became an adult. Until then, he was going to send you away, to lock you up away from the castle where no one could hurt you."

My eyes widened as I imagined myself as Rapunzel, trapped in a tower somewhere waiting for my freedom. But instead of a prince on a horse, there was my dad, with fangs and red eyes. I shook my head as if to scatter my thoughts. "How did my mom get away?"

"Well, he wasn't entirely wrong. Someone tried to hurt you when you had just turned one. No one knows who, although apparently Sargon tortured half the kingdom trying to find out. They found poison in your bottle. One of your tasters died. It was prolonged. You must have refused your feed that night because the poison took three hours to kill the taster."

I shuddered.

"The story is infamous at the castle."

Hearing my own history of a life I knew nothing about until yesterday was strange. "Then what?"

"Sargon threatened to turn your mother. She loved being a sorceress, so she refused, but he insisted, throwing her into a ceremony to become shadow kissed."

"Huh?" I questioned, leaning forward.

"It's a fancier way of saying *'to become a vampire.'* They hold a big celebration when it's someone important, and they are reborn. Before preparations, she used her powers to break out of the castle, with you in her arms."

I couldn't help but admire her for it while also feeling a little bad for the king. "He must've been pissed."

"That's an understatement. Someone helped you both get to Baldoria, a vampire loyal to her, and he was found and killed not long after."

I glanced down at what was left of my sandwich. The entire story was awful, but it sounded like something out of a fairytale and not my reality. Not even in my notebooks of half-written scenes could I have created something so insane.

"I didn't know they were married," I said, finding it weird to hear my mom referred to as anyone's wife, but it should have been obvious.

"They had to be." He paused, then changed the topic back. "Like I said, he changed after that. Many prefer the way Sanmorte is ruled now. Mortals are treated with no dignity or respect, and the aniccipere are given free rein."

My stomach churned as I pictured the man who helped give me life. I'd always wanted a father and longed to meet him until I eventually gave up asking who he was. Now, I wish I'd never found out.

"Sebastian," I said slowly, my words aching. For the first time since coming here, I might have felt slightly bad for him. "I don't want to become queen. I appreciate you telling me the truth, and it is kind of amazing to know my bloodline was chosen by the gods." That was the only part that filled me up a little. "But I don't want this."

"Even if you become the princess, you would still have the ability," he explained. "You just need to take your place in the royal bloodline. Becoming queen would be easier without Sargon in the way, and you really could make changes with that power. You'd only need the right advisor to help you understand the inner workings of Sanmorte politics."

"Don't you realize what you're asking?" I asked incredulously. "For me to take your place as a vampire and to give up the chance to ever become mortal again."

He shuddered. "No, that's not what I meant."

"Yes, it is. I'm sorry, but I won't give up being mortal. If this is your big plan for me and the only reason you're helping, then you may as well hand me over to him now. Maybe ask him for your mortality in exchange." I stood, my hands shaking. The only reason he hadn't handed me over was to ensure I would give him what he wanted first. This was his way of striking a deal, but there was no chance I'd allow anyone to turn me into a vampire with no way of going back.

"If you don't want this, then I will take you back to Baldoria tonight. It won't be safe, and you'll have to go on the run. But I won't hand you over, and I will not force you to stay here. I may be many things, but I'm not a monster." I scratched the side of my neck, and he continued. "I just want you to consider what you're giving up. You've spent your whole life being lied to and feeling powerless. Don't pretend otherwise. I've seen it, and you don't even feel confident enough in your powers to use them. You wouldn't miss them."

Ouch.

But it was true.

"You could save your mom and put a stop to the blood dens and auctions. Just think about it. It's not an accident that you've returned to Sanmorte just a year and a half before you turn twenty-one. Some destinies belong to the shadows, Olivia, and yours always has. If you decide to follow it, all I ask is to grant me the mortality your father refuses. If you do, I will help you, in any way, to get it and retrieve your mother too."

I turned on my heel, heading to the door. "This is a lot. I can't just…. I need time to think," I spluttered, my thoughts racing as the history of a place I was chosen to inherit played out in my mind. What he was asking for me was no small feat, and although he'd finally been honest with me about what he desired from all this, I didn't expect to hurt this much.

SIXTEEN

I stared at my star-kissed gown, billowing out at my knees, as Erianna and I prepared to leave for the royal castle. Erianna was right. I could still have the life I wanted on my terms. Only, she didn't know that I was lying to them all to have it.

Sebastian had been more than open to believing that I was on board with their plan to sneak me into the castle under the guise of his wife-to-be and place me on the throne as queen. We'd gone over the details this morning after I explained I'd thought about it overnight and was willing to accept if only to protect my mom and hopefully Draven, if gods willing, he was still alive.

Despite my mom hiding the truth from me, I wasn't mad, not after spending the night thinking about how she was just trying to protect me from them. She'd dedicated her life to the cause, and now it was my turn to save her.

Agreeing to become queen was more manageable than saying I'd agree to become the princess, so Sebastian wouldn't immediately tell Sargon who I was.

However, Erianna confided in me that the king would likely arrest them all for not telling him who I was straight away, so the plot to make me queen instead worked in everyone's favor, especially mine. It allowed me to conceal my identity while ensuring their help to find my mom, and Draven if he was there, then escape before anything irreversible could happen.

Pressing my fingers to my neck, thinking about the alternative future where I could have become one of them floated into my mind, consuming me in a blood-hazed daydream.

Erianna snapped her fingers, and I shook my head as if to scatter my thoughts. "You'll need to make them believe it," she said for the seventh time between this morning and sun-kissed dusk. "They're allowing you and Sebastian to visit the castle to ask for the king's permission."

I rolled my eyes. "How archaic."

"You can't have that attitude there," she warned, worry lines deepening around her Cupid's bow lips. "But yes, I agree."

"Why are they allowing you to come?"

"I'm hired by his majesty to hunt criminals in the city and bring them in for questioning, so my appearance at the royal court is hardly suspicious. I go there every so often to brush up on my combat skills." Her fingers flexed to the dagger in her waistband, and everything fell into place. She fit the role of hunter well, with her sharp reflexes and take-no-shit attitude.

"What about Zach and Anna?"

"Zach's welcome at court whenever he likes. He's been a part of the king's military for eighty years. He has special dispensation to remain in the city." Unzipping a bag, a dress was revealed, looking as if it belonged to the night with its sheer, flowing whites running over a deep, navy blue with silver embroidery. "You'll wear this tomorrow when you meet Sargon."

My head spun. Tomorrow I would meet my dad for the first time and possibly see my mom for the first time in weeks. It felt so unreal. I had to pinch myself to ensure this wasn't some melatonin-induced fever dream. "It's pretty."

"Sebastian knows the best dressmakers in the city."

"Of course he does."

I was glad she was coming with me, and although she was loyal to Sebastian, I hoped she would help me when the time came for me to escape. He was her friend, but she was mine too. "Why are you helping Sebastian? It's not like you're getting anything out of this."

Her dark brows pulled together, and she placed a hand on her hip. "What makes you think I want anything? He's my family, Olivia. I vowed to protect him when I found him broken and ready to give up. I've seen the goodness in his heart, although I'm sure he likes to pretend it's not there. If there's a chance for his happiness, I'm going to fight to get it for him."

I forced a small smile, and she returned to packing my suitcase, but uneasiness crawled over my skin. Perhaps she wouldn't help me escape then. "What about my happiness?"

"I care about that too." She stopped what she was doing. "You're embracing your destiny, and while that's scary, I admire your bravery to take it on. Sacrificing yourself to the good of others is most noble, and I will be honored to serve you as my queen. You can make a real difference here. I can't pretend it won't be a relief to not have Sargon on the throne and knowing Kalon won't rule."

"But won't he need to continue the bloodline? I mean, I won't be able to have children once I'm a vampire."

"You can choose a successor whenever you decide to retire the crown. They don't have to be your blood."

I swallowed hard, trying to remove the lump in my throat.

"The castle's magnificent," she said as she zipped the bags.

She wanted me to save this kingdom, but I was no savior, not even if I wanted to be. I'd have to be authoritative and influential, which I wasn't, not to mention I had zero interest in becoming immortal.

"I can't wait to see it." I pulled a jacket around me and rubbed my forearms.

"I'll have this dress sent to your hotel room, so you can wear it in the morning."

I hated lying to her, but I justified that she had lied to me too, not long ago. Still, it hurt my chest to do so. Dishonesty wasn't in my blood, and each lie darkened me a little. "Great."

"Here's the ring." She handed me a little black box. Carefully, I clicked back the lid, my heart swelling a little. I'd always thought this moment would be with Astor, or at the least, with the person I'd marry. I touched the white gold metal curling up to a point, housing a blue diamond that glittered under the light, feeling only sadness.

"Shouldn't Sebastian be on one knee for this?" I teased, trying to lighten my own spirits.

"I hate this." She winced. "One day, you will find your true mate and wear a ring which means something."

They really did take marriage seriously. "It's stunning."

"I picked it out."

I slowly pulled off my promise ring for the first time since Astor had put it on my finger, vowing to replace it with an engagement ring one day. "It's time to leave the past behind," I said as I placed Astor's ring on the nightstand, leaving behind a piece of my heart with it. I glanced out the window, spotting a car parked out the front. "That's the first car I've seen since being here," I marveled. "Sebastian wasn't joking when he said Sanmorte is behind modern times."

"They're not as necessary, considering we can fly, but even we can't transport this many bags."

Through the glass pane, I watched Zach close the trunk to the black vehicle, then speed to the other side. "How does Zach feel about this? I mean, I'm not his favorite person."

"He hates the idea of you leading the monarchy less than Sargon or Kalon."

"That's something, I guess," I contended, "although I'm certain he would pick someone else if he had the chance."

"There is no one else."

Sitting on my bed, dangling my feet over the edge, I thought about the escape I hoped for from the castle, knowing Zach would try to stop me, even if by chance Erianna didn't. I would have to keep him away from us as much as possible. I hoped with Anna coming, he would be a little distracted by her presence.

"If it isn't my future queen," Zach said from the door, as if saying his name one too many times had summoned him. He played with the top button of his silver shirt that matched his silky hair, surprisingly fashionable when paired with his black pants and brown leather boots. "I've packed mine and Anna's bags. Do you need help?"

"You can take these two down." She pushed a suitcase to him, and he caught it with mind-spinning speed.

Sebastian cleared his throat as he appeared out of nowhere, his grim expression lowering the room's energy. "I need you to take Olivia away from here for a few hours."

"Why?"

"Velda's coming here. News of our engagement has reached Nightshade." His gaze swiftly brushed past me and back to Erianna. "She's one of the few people who could know what Olivia looks like."

Zach chimed in, leaning back against the wall. "Look at her hair. It's not a big jump to guess she's the king's lost heir."

"About that." Erianna pulled out two boxes of hair dye from her bag. "I'm sorry." She shoved them into my hands.

"There are plenty of people with red hair!" I placed the boxes on the dresser. "I'm not coloring my hair."

Sebastian shoved his hands in his pockets. "Not that kind of red, and the king and his brother both have the exact same color, as did the king before him. There are others, I'm sure, with that color, and people have even dyed their hair to appear 'royal,' so it wouldn't immediately give you away, but you are also a sorceress and at the right age. It's too coincidental, and someone could look too closely."

"Hamza's already seen me."

"We can tell him you changed your hair back to its natural color. I won't risk anything. There's too much on the line."

I bit the inside of my lip, touching the ends of my red strands. He wasn't willing to risk his precious gift of mortality, he meant, and he didn't care what I had to sacrifice to get it. I blew out a tense breath, reminding myself how I was also lying to his face, and we were both being unfair to each other in different ways.

"I guess I can dye it." My hair was something I always cherished, mainly because it was so different from everyone else's.

"You can change it back after." Erianna's thick lips curved into a pitiful smile. "Once Sargon has been removed."

"Yes, once I'm queen, it won't matter." My heart raced, a reaction I prayed they'd all put down to nerves rather than my body's response to lying.

Zach was the only one who regarded me with hooded eyes crowned in suspicion, but he shook it off, wanting to believe this as much as the others. Footsteps creaked up the stairs behind the door, and Anna appeared inside my room, moving to Zach's side, and all his worries slid away in her presence.

Her light-brown hair curled into a tight knot at the back of her head, with a couple of curls falling at the front to frame her heart-shaped face. Her jade-green eyes found Zach's, a low smile building as if he was the most beautiful thing in the world.

I remembered feeling that way once when I was with Astor. I missed it, which was the opposite of how I wanted to feel. Still, with each passing day, that love lessened, tainted by the realization that the Astor I adored never existed. It was a version of him I loved because the man I knew would have never put himself before his friends, lied to his family, or hurt me. Dying, I decided, could bring out the very best or worst in a person. When confronted with death, Astor chose his life as more important than everyone else's.

"She's off again," Erianna teased.

I blinked twice, shaking my head. Even they had noticed it. "Sorry."

"Don't be." Sebastian smiled, deepening his dimples. His eyes brightened, and I couldn't help but smile back. It was annoyingly infectious, especially when I hated him for being so selfish. "Erianna will take you to the Lake of Laveniuess while Velda is here. Take some time to strengthen your powers. You'll need to practice with them."

"Why, if I'm just going to become a vampire at the end of this all anyway?" I questioned.

Zach rolled his eyes up. "Because having magic is helpful, especially when you can use it." His words bit through the room.

Erianna placed her hand on my shoulder. I noticed she'd painted her long nails a deep shade of yellow. "We will evaluate our options of how to remove Sargon from his throne and avoid an uprising once we're at court, but having your powers could be helpful. Especially if it comes down to a fight." She squeezed gently. "There's a reason vampires try to capture your people. They're afraid of you."

"We scare you?"

"Not me," she said with a wink, "but vampires in general. Your mom managed to escape the castle, something no mortal has ever achieved. If she wasn't a sorceress, it wouldn't have been possible."

A strange feeling circled in my stomach. "Then you don't know my mom."

Erianna grinned. "I did."

My eyes widened. "What?"

"I've met her when you were a baby. It was only once, but even then, she was a badass."

"That's so...."

"Unnerving?" Sebastian interrupted. "Erianna looks far younger than she is."

She rolled her eyes at him, and he smirked.

"Weird," I finished. "Okay, I'll go. At least I don't have to wear that bracelet now."

"Good." Sebastian moved toward the door. "Velda arrives in an hour. Zach, you will come with me."

He nodded, swaying his white ponytail, which was separated into sections with black bands. "Anna, sweetheart, you should stay in your room."

"I will. I know what Velda's like…" Her soft voice trailed off as it was lost in the dominant tones of those around her. Erianna spoke over her, assuming she'd finished her sentence, and Sebastian mentioned something. I made sure to look directly at Anna to show her I was at least listening, annoyed at the rest of the room. None of them, I was sure, did it on purpose, but it didn't make a difference. Anna's small lips curled at the corners, her cheeks blushing.

They left the room together, and Erianna followed, halting at the door. "I'll get you a jacket. The lake is cold," she called behind her as she sped away.

The door clicked shut, and Sebastian stared over at me, turning to leave himself.

I inhaled sharply, the words I wanted to say since he'd entered playing on my lips. "Why bother entertaining Velda after everything she's done to you?"

"She's an important person at court."

"So? Tell her to fuck off. I can't believe someone like you would allow her to come close to your home."

Power burned behind his eyes, begging to be unleashed. "Let me assure you," he stated, standing, "if I could kill her without threatening everything I've built, she would already be dead."

"Why do you care? You're willing to give it all up to be mortal again." A spark of guilt erupted in my stomach, but I reminded myself that I didn't owe him anything. "Where is it you plan on going once you get what you want?"

He caressed his chin with two fingers, sitting back on the chair next to my bed. "I haven't thought much about it."

"Why?"

"Because until now, I never thought it was possible. I didn't dare to dream."

A ghost of a smile crossed my lips. "So the big bad Sebastian does have dreams."

"We all do, even the villains." A daring glint darkened the blue in his eyes. "We had a big family growing up. We lived on a farm."

I could not see the well-groomed, tattooed court favorite growing up mucking out stables. "So you'd want to go back to farming?"

He shot me an incredulous look, then laughed. "No, but I would like to continue to be a royal advisor or work in politics. It's the only thing I'll miss about being here, apart from Erianna and Zach, although they will come and see me. They've assured me so."

My chest tightened. "Why do you want to become mortal? I mean, you have it all here."

"I miss the rush of fighting for life every day. Immortality makes everything seem a little meaningless. What's there to achieve if I can live forever?"

"I suppose if you ever wanted children, you couldn't."

He shrugged. "I've not thought much about it."

"Although you can always find a sorceress," I joked, but an awkward silence befell us both.

"Marriage and children have never been something I've desired, but I would like to travel," he said as a light-heartedness sculpted his expression.

There were nineteen kingdoms in our world and many islands inhabited by tribes and small communities. He wasn't the only one who'd wanted to see it all.

"Astor used to want to travel too," I replied. "I suppose in a way, he did."

"Yeah, well fuck him."

I sat on the end of my bed, crossing my legs. "He was kind once."

He rubbed a finger over the black markings running up the side of his neck from his arms, like thick thorns. "Sounds like you've been wearing rose-tinted glasses."

"How so?" My face flooded with heat. "He really was a good boyfriend."

"People don't just change like that." He snapped his fingers. "Let me ask you something. If you were dying, would you give up everyone you cared about to save yourself?"

A lump formed in my throat. "Of course not."

"I understand people do crazy, desperate things out of fear, but his selfishness didn't just appear overnight. I can see he loves you, or at the very least, he believes he does, but not enough. Maybe you're one of the few things he holds onto, and I count on that so he doesn't reveal who you are to the order. But even you weren't enough to stop him from becoming like us. Whether you want to admit it or not, your relationship with him couldn't have been perfect. You're, what, nineteen?"

"Yes."

"Isn't it possible that you don't really know what love is?"

I scoffed. "And you do?"

"I don't pretend to."

I puffed out my cheeks. "I know what love is, okay. Astor made me feel safe. He took care of me."

His eyes narrowed. "You don't seem like someone who needs taking care of."

I rubbed the side of my arm. "I was never really good at using my powers, and Astor knew that. Everyone else kept pushing me to try harder when I couldn't do it. But he accepted that I couldn't and didn't push me when I stopped going to lessons."

"It sounds like he didn't challenge you at all."

"He was gentle. There's a difference."

"Perhaps," he said slowly but didn't look at me. "I need to prepare for Velda's visit."

His face was unreadable, and curiosity lowered my barrier, allowing the anger he felt to flow in. It was muted under the suffocating sadness, which I presumed was brought on from Velda's visit.

"Sebastian." I spoke gently, caressing his name. "One day, when this is all over, I'll make sure Velda pays for what she did to your family."

"Why would you do that?"

"I may be many things, but I'm not a monster." I repeated his words back to him. Although I wasn't sure how I'd achieve such a task.

He paused in the doorway. "You won't need to. One of my last acts before I leave will be to kill her." We stared at each other for a few seconds before he spoke. "Erianna's back. Enjoy your time in the lake. You weren't made a sorceress for no reason; magic is a part of you. Embrace it."

With that, he was gone, and Erianna appeared at the door, holding a thick leather jacket. "It's wool-lined inside." She whipped her head back. "What were you and Sebastian talking about for that long?"

"Nothing important. Mostly about what Sebastian would want after becoming mortal."

Her eyebrows raised. "I'm surprised he opened up at all."

That made me feel even worse. "What about you?" I asked the question which had been circling my mind since this all came out. "Wouldn't you want to become mortal?" It wasn't possible if there was enough blood for only one dose, but I was curious why she was so willing for Sebastian to take it.

"Not really. Zach and I have been alive for far too long to know how to fit into that world again."

"You've never wanted a family?"

"I have one." She smiled, looking at the door. I knew she meant Sebastian and Zach, but I couldn't help but wonder if she was lonely. Sometimes, when she didn't think anyone was looking, I could see her smile waver, and a sadness swam in her brown eyes. "Let's go to the lake before Velda arrives." She spat her name and threw me the jacket. "Follow me to the roof. I'll fly us there."

SEVENTEEN

"It's pointless," I declared, throwing my arms up in the air. The magic pulsated beneath my skin, but every time I tried to welcome it as a part of myself and cast a small spell, doubt trickled in, and nothing happened. "I'll never be good enough."

Erianna's face crumpled, whereas Zach just rolled his eyes from the wall he leaned against.

"It'll happen," Erianna promised and sat cross-legged on the armchair. "In time."

"We don't have time."

Zach cut in, tucking a lock of silver hair behind his ear. "We will make time. Your powers will be helpful if we're backed into a corner."

I threw myself back on the bed, letting out a long groan. "I can feel Laveniuess's energy, but it's like it's blocked by something. I spent an hour freezing my ass off bathing in that lake, and for what?"

"Velda's gone, so that's one good thing," Erianna said.

"I suppose." I let out a heavy exhale.

"It's a good thing you're not dramatic or anything," Zach said, deadpan.

"Excuse me for having emotions, unlike some people," I said, shooting him an extra hateful glare.

Erianna leaned forward, her necklaces spangling together. "Enough." She suppressed a smirk, then shook her head, her eyes rolling up. "Laveniuess's energy will remain in your veins for weeks, so it's not too late, and Zach's right, we will make time when we're at the castle."

I rubbed my temples. "It's just happening so fast."

"I know, but we couldn't delay the trip. Once news of your engagement reached the castle, the clock started. The king is already upset about Sebastian not asking permission first."

"So stupid," I mumbled. "I suppose I should get ready." The woman on the box of hair dye from my nightstand taunted me, smiling, fangs exposed, as she flicked back dark-brown curls. Grabbing the box, my mouth twisted as I prepared to say goodbye to my red hair. "I've never done this before."

"Why do you think I'm here, honey?" She stood and took the dye from my hands. "Come. Let's make you look like the wife-to-be of a court official. I have the perfect dress, and makeup picked out to go with your new hair."

"I have to start now? I thought we don't arrive at the castle until tomorrow?"

Zach rushed to the window, running his hand over the thin layer of dust on the ledge. "You'll begin the ruse as soon as you're at the hotel." He gazed out over the spires and roofs of the city. "Most of society's elite stay there. It's where many dignitaries stop to rest between visits to the city and the castle."

"Okay." I eyed Erianna, who seemed just as uncomfortable with makeovers as me. Although I used to love doing them a few years ago, I stopped bothering once I was with Astor. He hated me wearing makeup, and I didn't exactly go out anywhere to bother dressing up. "Let's put on some music while we get ready."

Erianna smiled. "I can't recall the last time I listened to music for fun."

"I've never had this, like a girlfriend to do these things with. It was always Draven or Astor, and neither seemed particularly interested in makeup."

She laughed. "Neither have I, nor do I care much for it, but I don't see why I can't make this fun."

A sense of normalcy settled over me, and I couldn't help but feel a swelling of excitement building. Was this what I was missing out on all these years? Real friends to hang out with?

Draven and I mostly watched TV or talked about his work, and Astor and I just talked, cuddled, or got takeout.

"That's my cue to go." Zach headed out the door. "Anna's waiting for me."

"Bye," I said a little too cheerily, happy for him to leave.

Once he was gone, I joined Erianna, who sat me on a chair at the bathroom vanity and prepped the dye. "One day, I'm sure you will both be good friends," she predicted out of the blue.

"I know you can't mean Zach."

"He can be a lot of fun once you get to really know him. It takes him time to warm up to people and open his heart. He guards it heavily."

"Luckily for him, I don't want anything to do with his heart."

She scoffed a laugh. "No, but he does value the few friendships he has. He's good to Anna, and before her, he was with Levian for fifty years."

"Levian?" I inquired.

"He was Zach's soulmate, but he was killed."

"Zach's bisexual?"

She shrugged. "I don't think gender means much to him. He falls in love with the person's soul, and as for Levian, they were perfect for each other. Finding your soulmate is rare, but once you do, it's like being with the person who completes, understands, and challenges you, unlike anyone else. I've heard it can be quite the tug-of-war. It definitely was with Zach and Levian."

"How do you know you've found your soulmate?" I asked. Normally, I'd never believed in such things, but I couldn't ignore that I was sitting with an immortal in a kingdom of vampires, so being open-minded wasn't really a choice.

"You just feel it. Vampires feel it more. They can sense it in each other. Levian and Zach didn't know they were until Levian was turned."

My eyes widened. Perhaps Draven was right, and soulmates did exist. If so, was mine out there? Knowing my luck, I doubted it, but still, I couldn't help but feel intrigued. "How did he die?"

"A hunter found him."

My eyebrows knitted into a frown. "Hunter? Like you?"

"No." She cast her eyes down as she started layering on the hair color. It filled the room with a polarizing odor that burned the back of my throat, watering my eyes. "There are mortal vampire hunters."

"Like the guild?"

"Sort of, but most are rogue and highly trained. Levian visited his brother, who was still mortal and living in Baldoria. A hunter found him and ripped out his heart. For a while after, I wondered if Zach still had one too. He became cold, callous, distant, but decades later he met Anna. While they may not be soulmates, she makes him happy. It's all I could hope for."

Pity pinched through me. "Being immortal sounds like a tragedy."

"It can be," she admitted, clipping sections back of my hair as she slacked my red with white cream, which quickly turned dark. "It has its perks too. I guess it's all about perspective. When one is alive for as long as Zach and me, you're bound to experience a lot of heartaches."

"Have you?"

Her fingers flexed, and she paused. "Of course." She didn't elaborate, but when I looked at her reflection in the mirror in front of us, a story swam in her eyes. "You remind me of my sister."

I blinked twice. "Oh? I didn't know you had one."

"I did."

Goose bumps rippled over my arms. "I'm sorry."

"It was a long time ago." She finished painting my hair and stepped back. "Let's leave it for half an hour. Do you want something to eat?"

I nodded, and she removed her gloves and left the room, leaving me locked in the pasts of the people I lived with, curious of their tragedy, feeling things they might have as I imagined

Zach losing his soulmate, Erianna, without her sister, and Sebastian alone with no family. Finally, I started to understand why they'd created a new one with each other.

***

I could hardly recognize myself as I stared at my reflection. Erianna had tied my dark hair into a loose updo, allowing a few curls to fall from the bun and frame my face.

Voices trickled under the bathroom door from the bedroom. I stepped out, spotting Sebastian leaning against my dresser and Zach and Anna over by the door. Erianna waited on my bed, sipping on a cup of blood.

Sebastian straightened the collar of his shirt. "We can fly the next morning," he explained to Zach, finishing a conversation I wasn't there for. "It'll look better if we get their firs—" He turned, spotting me. His stare intensified as he looked me up and down.

I fiddled with the neckline of my dress, feeling self-conscious. "Is it bad?"

He cleared his throat, blinking twice. "No—uh, you look beautiful."

"Don't sound too surprised." Erianna winked in my direction.

I curled a lock of brunette hair around my finger that hung down the side of my face. "I'm not sure about the hair, though."

"Stop playing with it." Erianna batted my hand away. "You look amazing. Really gorgeous, and I love that lipstick on you."

"You chose it." I'd never worn deep peach shades, but it looked surprisingly nice, especially with the darker shade of lip liner.

Erianna smiled. "Zach, Anna, and I are going to drive to the castle. Sebastian will fly you. It'll be expected," she added. "All eyes will be on you."

"Why? They don't know who I am."

Sebastian's eyes fell on my lips, then climbed to meet mine. "You underestimate how important *I* am."

Erianna rolled her eyes. "Try not to kill each other while I'm gone. We'll see you at the castle." She kissed my cheek, handing me her blade as she whispered in my ear, "Sebastian will protect you, but just in case you need it. It's infused with a rare herb that'll slow us down."

I gripped the hilt, watching as she walked with mortal speed out the door. Then, examining the cool, sharpened blade, I ran my finger up and over the grooves of the hilt.

"She must like you to give you that." He marveled when she left the room. "We'll leave for the hotel now. I already have things you'll need for overnight waiting for us there, along with the dress Erianna picked out for you to meet the king in."

My eyebrows raised. "How rich are you?"

"Enough not to have to worry about money." He moved back the drapes. "We should leave before the sun sets."

Turning around to check my belongings, I realized I didn't have any of my own. Everything that had been brought for me was already in the car with Erianna, Zach, and Anna. So with no belongings, I followed Sebastian out onto the roof.

I stared out at the sun, low in the sky, soaking the obsidian, gothic city in red. "Hold on tight," he said, wrapping a jacket around me. He lifted me up into his arms as if I weighed nothing at all and flapped his wings outward, sweeping them against the gusts of wind and into the sky.

I pressed my chin against his arm, nestling my head into his chest, trying to ignore the iciness numbing my fingers. My breath fogged, even as I pulled his jacket tighter for warmth as we flew into the horizon.

EIGHTEEN

His grip tightened as he landed us in front of a hotel. Leaning my head back, I gaped up at the seven-story building of white stone, which glistened like crystal under the setting sun. The sky pinkened, striking purple and red under the thin, misty clouds. Indigo pinched the distance, bringing darkness to this world.

I steadied myself, heating my hands against my breath. "There are no aniccipere," I stated as I watched sangaree speeding in and out of the double glass doors to the foyer and onto the grounds. They stretched out in the bowl carved out from the smoky mountains surrounding us on all sides. A thin mist enveloped the ragged edges of the mountain jutting out, and the streams of water running between them. "Wow."

"Welcome to Black Mountain Retreat, and you are correct. You won't find aniccipere here. They're not excluded, but as this is an invitation-only establishment."

"Ah, so the sangaree rule all the wealthy parts of Sanmorte."

"Naturally." He walked me through the doors into a bright foyer with tall, vaulted ceilings and a large, crystal chandelier that reflected off the marble floor.

"Mr. Vangard." A woman greeted him at the front desk. "Your room is ready."

"Excellent."

I arched an eyebrow. *Vangard.* I hadn't heard his last name before.

She pushed a keycard across the mahogany surface. "Will you be requiring any champagne tonight?"

"No, but we will also need mortal food."

She eyed my neck, and I pulled the strings on the jacket, hiding my bare skin from view. "Very well."

My chest heaved as we walked to the elevators. "She didn't like me."

"She didn't know how to act," he responded. "She, like every other vampire in here, can sense your magic. It speaks to our immortal blood. The traces of the elixir originally given to Vener when he was made immortal was made from the blood of gods. As you are descendants, it also runs in your blood. So we're not too different."

"We're not cursed, or immortal."

"No, but there are similarities. While you are made from gods and mortals, we are a creation of theirs. Once mortal, now something else entirely, but still, our blood recognizes yours."

"Good to know," I said, feeling vulnerable as vampires stared at me with zero subtlety. Sebastian tugged me to his hip, entwining his arm with mine. I wasn't sure if it was for show or to make me feel better.

We finally reached our floor, and Sebastian stretched his arms, rolling his neck back until I heard something pop. All that flying must have taken its toll, even for a vampire. He walked inside and immediately headed to the minibar, which I was shocked to find stocked with bottles of blood. He casually poured a glass, as if it were nothing but wine, and gulped it down. I looked away, for his privacy more than my disgust, and found the bedroom beyond the suite.

My lips parted. "There's only one bed."

"It's a king-size," he said as if that made it any better.

"Will I be staying in another room?"

He finished his blood. "This is our room."

"I am *not* sharing a bed with you."

"We're engaged now, well, pretending to be. We need to play the part, and this hotel is used by nobles and dignitaries."

"Can't you just fly us all the way to the castle then?"

"Even I need a break now and then."

I swallowed thickly. "Perhaps you can sleep on the sofa."

"With these wings? No." He paused. "You're welcome to sleep on the floor if you prefer, but I wouldn't recommend it. There's no heating in these hotels."

I hesitated, as the floor looked appealing right about now. Then, with a tense breath, I found a small suitcase with my name on it. I shoved it against the closet, not trying to be quiet so he could see I was not happy with our arrangement. "When are they sending food?" I asked, my tone laced with annoyance.

"It won't be long. I'm going for a shower."

I searched for something sarcastic to say, but nothing good enough entered my mind. The whole arrangement pissed me off, but I guessed he was right. We did have to act like an engaged couple, and if this place was what he said it was, then having two rooms would seem suspicious to any who would typically go to the castle.

Sebastian closed the bathroom door, and I noticed a white robe hanging from the back of the closet door. I pulled it on, cuddling against the soft fabric. I hadn't long closed the window and thrown myself on the bed when there was a knock on the door, and I was handed a plate of beef, gravy, potatoes, and green beans. There were no menu options, not that I expected one in a kingdom where mortals were thought about so little.

Still, I was starving and ate the whole plate, pausing for a little breath between bites. I'd barely finished when the door opened, steam pillaring out into the bedroom.

Sebastian walked out of the bathroom with just a towel wrapped around his waist. Droplets of water clung to his toned abs, carved by years of training. My gaze trickled over the sharp contours to the two V-shaped muscles running from his hips down to below the towel line.

I danced my finger up to my clavicle, running my hands over my skin, tilting my head when I realized I was staring. Then, quickly clearing my throat, I averted my eyes, catching a smirk as he turned to the mirror above the vanity.

My face flooded with heat, and I touched my bottom lip. That was embarrassing, although was it totally wrong to stare? Just because he was conventionally handsome didn't mean anything. I was only looking, in the same way I'd watch the protectors work out at the guild, although a part of me wondered how it would feel to be curled up against him, wrapped in those muscular, tattooed arms.

I shook my head. Gods, it had been too long since I'd had any intimacy, and I was clearly losing my mind that I was even thinking of or considering a vampire. Being in this kingdom was messing with my head.

He dried his hair, and dark strands curled against his forehead. "See anything you like?" He glanced at me in the mirror, his lip lifting at the corner.

"I was just thinking that I need a shower too."

He bit his bottom lip, licking over it after. "How are you feeling about tomorrow?"

"Nervous," I admitted, bouncing my knee.

He turned, showing off his tattooed back. At the bottom right was a wide scar running toward his spine. Pinching my lips together, I flinched. "What's that on your back?"

"The scar or the tattoos?"

"The scar."

"It's nothing."

I raised a fist to my mouth, staring at the scar, wondering how it looked before it healed. "Sure doesn't look like nothing."

"It's my death mark," he said casually. "Because it was made as I was becoming a vampire, it's the only blemish left."

A lump formed in my throat. I'd never seen a single blemish or scar on any vampire. They were perfect, and every inch of him was, except for this. "Were you stabbed or something?"

He shrugged. My chest heaved, but I decided to let it go, running the back of my neck. He wasn't the most forthcoming.

"What time do we leave tomorrow?" I asked, changing the subject, catching myself glancing at it every few seconds.

"We have an appointment with the king at two in the afternoon, so we should fly out at ten."

"What about our bags?" I eyed the small suitcase Sebastian had arranged to be brought here for me.

"We leave them. They only have necessities for one night. We can ask for anything we need outside of what's been taken when at court."

"So wasteful," I mumbled, and I saw him look at me in my peripheral vision. "I didn't ask, but how did the meeting with Velda go?"

He pulled on a short-sleeved top then searched in his suitcase until he found a pair of gray sweatpants. At least he wouldn't be sleeping naked. My mind wandered again, and I mentally kicked myself.

"She didn't suspect a thing."

"That's not what I asked."

He shrugged. "It was fine."

I looked up. "Seeing her must hurt you."

"You should take that shower. I'm going to bed soon."

I pursed my lips, rolling my eyes at his inability to open up about her. Talking about the deep pain inside helped sometimes.

I knew that and missed having my mom or Astor to open up to. Well, the old version of Astor anyway. Not the new, monstrous update of him. I grabbed a towel and closed the door on Sebastian, who waited until I was gone to fully undress.

I lay next to him, stiff as a board, not daring to move. Night had come too quickly, bringing with it the promise of a new day, one that had my stomach in knots.

Sebastian switched the lamp off, shrouding us in darkness. In the end, I'd decided the bed was comfier than the floor.

The bed dipped as the covers tugged his direction. In the pale moonlight, which swept through the voiles, I could just make out the silhouette of his bare chest and muscular shoulders. I turned, draping the blanket over my arms and breasts up to my neck. I hadn't shared a bed with anyone since Astor. It felt strange, mainly because I'd vowed never to sleep next to another ever again when I found out he died. Except he didn't, and what I had with Sebastian wasn't real.

Life had taken so many unexpected turns in the past month. First, I could never have thought to find myself in another kingdom, a princess, fake-engaged to a vampire, while trying to find my mom, who's been captured by her ex-husband. It sounded so unbelievable that I would have laughed at the very concept if I wasn't living it.

Curling against the sheets, I moved onto my left side, kicking one leg out of the blanket, enjoying the warmth under the covers with the cold on my foot and calf. Astor unwantedly entered my thoughts again, spiking anxiety through me. Would he tell anyone the truth once his belief he still loved me wore away? I was certain Gwen wasn't the type to give up until she got to the bottom of something, and she didn't come across as stupid to me. She knew there was more to what we were saying.

I was tossing and turning again when Sebastian let out a long exhale. "It's like trying to sleep next to a tornado."

"I can't sleep."

"Have you tried?"

"Not really, but it's pointless. My mind is spinning."

He moved slowly to face me. "Come on then, what's up?"

"You mean you actually want to listen to me for once?"

"For once?" He let out a low chuckle. "I don't think you realize how much you talk."

I scowled at him, hoping he could see.

He propped his head against his palm. "If it means we can get some sleep before the sun comes up, then I'm all ears."

I turned onto my back, staring up at the shadows of the room cast against the moonlit ceiling. "I can't stop thinking about Astor."

"Just what every man wants to hear when he's sharing a bed with a woman."

I knew he was joking, but I couldn't bring myself to laugh. "I haven't shared a room with anyone since him. It's like he stole an entire chapter of my life. So much of who I was revolved around him. Every day he would come back from the guild, most evenings, he'd stay with me. My mom used to joke he'd have to start paying rent because he stayed over so often. Without him, I don't know what to do half the time. I'm still grieving someone who isn't even dead," I admitted.

He paused. "I don't know how that feels, but your life should have never revolved around another person."

"It just happened. I was supposed to start a writing course, but I gave it up because else I would have had to move, and Astor needed me. He had a lot of problems with the people he worked with." I smiled at the memory of Draven and him arguing. It felt so normal to place myself back in that time. "He didn't get along with my best friend."

"When was the last time you wrote anything?"

I closed my eyes, trying to recall. "Before Astor died, I would write during the day when he was working. It was an escape. I only wrote for myself. I never intended for anyone to read it."

"What did you write?"

"Fantasy, love stories, and poetry. But I haven't felt like writing since then."

"It'll come back," he said.

"Yeah, maybe."

A long pause had me listening to every breath in the room. "You're better than him, Olivia, and he knows that. You'll find yourself again. It will just take time. He wanted you to depend on him before. It's why he never challenged you to grow."

"You can't know that!" I defended.

"I'm taking a stab in the dark, but going by what you've said about him, I doubt I'm wrong."

"If that's true, then why did he leave me alone?" I hated how cracked my voice sounded when the emotions slipped through.

"Because he wasn't strong enough to be what you needed. It was for the best, trust me. You're destined for far more than Astor."

I wanted to believe that, but I couldn't just let go of the chapter of my life. Not just yet. "I'm going to try to sleep now."

"Goodnight, love." He rolled on his side, and I pulled the covers tight against myself.

My arm brushed against the edge of his wing as he rested on his side. "Sorry," I whispered as I tried to make myself comfortable.

The room was freezing cold, and the warmth in the blanket slowly dissipated. These rooms weren't built for mortals. But, while he was usually cold, his body seemed to radiate heat as he lay still. I deduced that they still had blood pumping around their body, and his wings were warmer than the rest of him. Slowly, so as not to bother him, I inched closer to his wings, feeling the heat from them, even if they were tucked behind his back.

Flickers of touch ran between us as I turned, and he rolled over too. His breaths grew longer and more pronounced as his head leaned closer to mine.

I didn't dare speak. His eyes were closed, from what I could tell anyway. I shivered, moving half an inch closer, curling deeper into the blanket.

"Are you cold?" His voice jolted me.

I breathed in the icy air. "Yes. I don't remember it being as chilly back at the house."

"We're farther north." He extended an arm, his touch lightly brushing against my hip. I flinched, and he paused. "You can move up against me. I won't bite."

"You're cold too."

"Not always," he drawled. "Not when I'm resting. I just live in a cold climate with no need to keep myself warm. I'm not cold-blooded."

I shuffled back against him, against all my better judgments. But I was far too cold to argue. His arm curled around my stomach as I turned my back to him, and he pulled me closer against his torso.

Together, our bodies generated heat which stayed trapped under the covers. The shivering subsided, and the muscles in his arm tensed. I shifted my hips against him, entwining my legs with his, wanting to steal all his warmth.

His breath whispered against the top of my ear. "You might want to stop rocking against me, unless you're willing to do something about it."

Tingling fluttered in my stomach. He had to be joking, but I wasn't so sure. "No, no. Gods, I'm sorry," I apologized, moving an inch away from him, leaving a gap between us. I glanced up and back, and I swore I saw him half grin before turning over.

I lightly touched his wings, staying close to them as I fell asleep, and to my surprise, he let me snuggle up against them. Sleep consumed me, lulling me into a place where my nightmares felt far too real, filled with a hundred scenarios of meeting the vampire king—my father. In less than fifteen hours, I would be face to face with him for the first time in eighteen years.

NINETEEN

Sebastian tucked his wings behind his back as we landed inside the large, stone walls of the royal castle. We stood upon the ancient cobbles of the walkway going all the way around the court. Moss clung to the gray-blue stone, the same color as the few forest-green trees beyond the wrought-iron gates.

Fog covered the area as we walked under the dove-gray sky with the sun hidden beyond clouds and mountain peaks. Tucking my fingers underneath the fake-fur coat Sebastian had brought up for me this morning, I found I wasn't as cold as I thought I'd be, although my breath sent mist from my lips.

"It's huge." I marveled, craning my neck as I looked up at the arched windows emitting a yellow-orange hue, moving my gaze to the tall towers and spires which disappeared into a layer of mist. "I'm nervous," I whispered as he walked us to the open double-wood doors.

He took my arm, pausing before we walked inside. So far, there were no sangaree guests outside, only two guards, both of whom acknowledged Sebastian and nodded for us to proceed.

Everything was said in the light squeeze to my hand and a half smile from him. Last night and our midnight encounter, I decided to call it. It had been awkward, and I expected him to act as much when we woke, but he pretended as if nothing happened. In fact, he wore an amused smile as he got ready and drank his breakfast.

The high, hand-painted ceilings were the first thing I noticed, as they portrayed scenes from a thousand years of vampire history. Oranges mixed with browns, reds, and golds swirled together to create figures from a time our world forgot. We kept to the ornate red rug outstretched over uneven stone slabs.

I stole a glance out the window and stared at the view. It was hard to believe minutes before we had flown over through those mountains.

How was I going to escape from here? I saw now why my mom had a vampire help her escape. This place was built for flying, except for one long, narrow road winding between the mountains and running up to the gate. A sea of trees stretched between the walls and the obsidian-black mountains and snowy crevices.

Sebastian nodded as we walked past the most beautiful vampires I'd ever seen. Women wore dresses that appeared as if they had been spun from the stars and moon in their shimmering colors. One had blonde hair, which fell in waves around her shoulders as she walked with three other ladies and a man, who was wearing a suit which even outdid Sebastian's three-piece.

I stared around, noticing that Sebastian somehow managed to look casual, even in a suit. His rolled-up sleeves and top-unbuttoned shirt showed off his tattoos. His blazer was folded over his free arm, and his smile as he greeted his people was enough to charm a kingdom out of its empire. No wonder he'd risen so quickly with the way he spoke, his body language and expressions. It was enough to make any person feel like the center of attention when he focused on them, and he was comfortable in his surroundings, as if he belonged here.

Many looked at me, of course, with a curiosity I had not seen in the city. Perhaps they were more used to sorcerers here. Finally, I spotted a mortal woman on the arm of a man, dressed as if she was one of them, and got my answer. Everything was an illusion, a place where the true barbarity of the kingdom was hidden behind eloquence and decadence.

We walked into an open room with tables lined for a banquet, except there was no food, only goblets, and I didn't need to look to know what was inside of them. "We're almost there," he said as if he could sense my anxiety.

The tail of my dress floated out behind me as I hurried down a second corridor, finally ending up in a hallway of paintings and doors. "The king is beyond these doors, love," he said, lowering his night-blue gaze to meet mine. Could they hear us from here? I only nodded, and he brought his lips to my ear, his hot breath hitting the lobe. "We can do this," he said, his voice barely a whisper.

I noted the dusty, musky smell lingering in the air from lifetimes using the decor and carpets with little updating. He opened the doors, and my stomach knotted. I followed him, pausing for a second before, as the sudden urge to run came over me.

This wasn't just the king. This was my dad. The man who had given me life and loved too much, according to Sebastian. He was mad, terrifying, the leader of a world where mortals like me were imprisoned, enslaved, and looked upon as nothing. I almost forgot about Hamza until I saw him standing at the side of the small room. His eyes found me, watching like a snake as I matched my pace to Sebastian. He halted before a long, marble desk. Behind it sat the man who'd consumed my thoughts ever since I learned who he was.

A fire crackled near the two windows, hissing embers between logs and sending a charcoaled, smoky smell into the air.

"Sebastian," the king said in greeting, his smile far more vibrant than I could have guessed.

I saw now why my hair would have given him pause. The king's hair was a perfect match to mine, only confirming what I already knew: he was my father. His locks fell in a slight wave down to his shoulders, which were draped with gray fur and clasped by a gold circle. The crown sat halfway down his head, stopping midway on his forehead. The antique gold housed glittering rubies and ornate designs. Thick brows lifted when he noticed me, forming lines above the bridge of his nose. "You must be the beautiful sorceress I keep hearing so much about."

My breaths quickened as he walked around his desk, closing the distance between us. He took my hand in his surprisingly warm grasp and lifted it to his lips. He placed a kiss against the knuckle above the engagement ring Erianna had picked out and lowered my arm. "I am King Sargon of Sanmorte."

I couldn't speak. Closing my eyes for a moment, I searched my mind for words, anything to say back. There were many greetings. Even a grunt would've sufficed right now or a nod. Had I forgotten how to nod?

Sebastian cleared his throat. "Excuse Olivia. She's a little shy."

Sargon leaned back against the desk, picking a piece of lint off his embroidered sleeve. He turned his attention to Sebastian while I continued to look at him, taking in every line on his deceivingly youthful face. He appeared to be in his late thirties, although I knew his age far surpassed that.

"I have been awaiting your arrival. You did not tell me you met this lovely young woman," he probed, looking from me to him. Hamza said the king would be angry that Sebastian hid a sorceress from him. I watched Hamza from the side of the room. A slight sneer curled against his lips, and I found my voice.

"Excuse me, Your Majesty, but that would have been my doing. I was brought here from an eastern town of Baldoria some time ago, and Sebastian found me in a blood den." I paused for effect, glancing in Hamza's direction, and was glad to see the smile on his face erased. "They placed a strange jewelry on me so I couldn't use my powers, and when Sebastian found me and—" I gazed up at him with the most adoration I could muster. "W— well, I fell for him. He didn't know what I was until much later. I'm grateful he's accepted me for who I am."

Sargon arched an eyebrow, regarding me carefully. "Accepted?" He scoffed a laugh, slapping a hand on Sebastian's shoulder. "I would say he lucked out, finding a sorceress. I can see why he made you his so quickly." He eyed the ring, and a shiver snaked down my back. "You can sire an heir now, Sebastian. A child to one day take your place as Master of Travel when you want to retire, that is," he added.

Sebastian laughed with ease, his fingers now entwined with mine. "We both know you can't get rid of me that easily. But, like you, I doubt I'll ever retire."

"Good," Sargon said, a slow smile building. "Of course, you have my approval."

It took a moment before I realized he was talking about our engagement. "Thank you."

The corners of his eyes softened when he looked at me. "I'd do anything for Sebastian here. He's my eyes and ears of the city. Hamza was there recently, actually." He waved a hand in Hamza's direction, and Sebastian's jaw tightened.

"Next time you should stop by. I'd love to host you for a night," Sebastian said, somehow making it sound threatening. Fortunately, Sargon didn't notice.

As I watched the king move, I suddenly had the desire to blurt out who I really was. But whether it was some biological response to being in front of my father after all these years, or just some stupid want to get this over and done with, I had to stop myself from speaking.

He had my mom, I reminded myself. Somewhere, in this castle, she was locked away. She hadn't escaped with me for no reason. Things must have been horrible here for her to do that and hide me for this long. If I told him who I really was, Sebastian would be punished for keeping me from him, and I would undoubtedly be turned into one of them come my twenty-first birthday, fulfilling a destiny I didn't want.

"Sebastian," my father said, snapping me from my thoughts. "You will join me for dinner this evening. We have business to discuss."

He nodded, and I noticed my lack of invitation. "Of course, my king."

Hamza opened the door, reading the unspoken signal it was time for us to go. Sebastian dipped his head in a bow and turned to the door. I curtseyed clumsily because I hadn't practiced, then followed Sebastian out. Before reaching the door, I stole a look over my shoulder at my dad, and my heart ballooned. I knew he was dangerous, or so everyone said, and I could never tell him who I really was, but I was weirdly glad he was looking at me too. I wanted to believe he recognized his blood in mine, that he could see the daughter he'd lost and loved, but I knew it had nothing to do with that and everything to do with the magic in my veins. He loved sorcerers, and I was one of them.

Once we were outside, Sebastian pulled me into an empty room with a dusty four-post bed at the end of the corridor. "How are you feeling?"

I let out the breath I'd been holding. "He wasn't what I expected."

"Even demons can appear mortal, love."

"I know." I looked down at my feet, my heart pounding. "I wasn't invited to dinner."

His brows knitted together. "Naturally, you will be coming with me tonight," he assured. "It's common courtesy to just invite the man. It's expected that their partner will join them."

"In my society, women are equal and would expect an invitation too."

"I know. I was a part of modern society only a few years ago."

I'd forgotten about that.

"Yes, of course," I said and paused, trying to ignore the fluttering in my stomach when I thought about my dad being nothing like I thought he was, and suddenly, my other parent forced her way into my thoughts. "Can we look for my mom yet?"

"Not right now. All eyes are on us as recent visitors to the castle. One of us making a detour would raise suspicions."

I wetted my lips. "What should we do?"

"We go to our room, get settled, and wait for Erianna, Zach, and Anna to arrive. Then, we get ready for dinner."

"Okay," I said breathily, then gasped on seeing the open door. Hamza stood, glaring through the crack. Stumbling back, I fell against Sebastian, who placed his hand on my back, his frown deepening.

"You!" Sebastian growled, the muscles in his arms tensing.

"If it isn't the happy couple." Hamza tilted his head to the side, regarding me as prey. "You colored your hair."

Fuck!

"I dyed it red before to look more royal," I blurted. "Sebastian suggested I go back to my natural color."

Sebastian's intense stare never left Hamza. Pressing my fingers against his shoulder, I felt his muscle feather, his skin flushing red. "Get out of here," he scathed.

"It's a shame. I preferred it before." He bit his bottom lip, and Sebastian stepped forward, planting one foot in front of the other, ready to lunge.

"You didn't tell the king you'd already met Olivia. Unless you'd rather he didn't know. What were you supposed to be doing in the city?" Sebastian inquired. "The king wouldn't have allowed his top advisor to leave the castle without good reason. You must've lied to him so you could go to the auction."

Hamza hesitated. "I was going to question myself how she was supposedly in a blood den for all those months and was taken from an eastern town of Baldoria, when everyone knows any sorceress is to be brought straight to the castle." He put a finger in the air. "Unless she was actually brought here in the recent attacks by Nightshade, along with Ravena."

My heart leaped when he spoke her name. Sebastian's fists balled. "We have no reason to lie."

"I would hope not." He examined his cuticles, a grin spreading over that smug face. "Because if you are, I will find out, and, well, we both know how Sargon feels about disloyalty." He peered around Sebastian, locking eyes with me. "Enjoy your stay, Olivia."

He left, and Sebastian took a step forward. I didn't need to lower my barrier to know how he felt. Instinctively, I reached forward, pressing my fingers against his arm. Under my feather touch, I sensed the familiar tightness from his anger swirling throughout his body. Closing my eyes, I held my breath, allowing the emotion to flow into me. He changed the way he looked at me when I peeled back my eyelids, watching as the hatred melted away from him. His jaw slacked, and after a moment, he flinched away from me.

"Stop."

"What?"

"Trying to take my anger away."

I licked my dry lips and pulled my hand back, rolling my neck against the heaviness of his anger in my own bones. "I'm only trying to help."

"My anger fuels me. It gives me the strength I need to protect you and myself." He took a step toward the open door. "Leave me to my emotions."

I followed him out. "You know, you can be a real ass sometimes."

He didn't respond. Instead, we walked in thick silence all the way to our shared room, where low lighting, melting candles, and a bed big enough for four people sat. He tossed his jacket onto the silk sheets then walked into the bathroom.

An odd question popped into my head, and I broke the silence. "Do vampires need to urinate?" I'd always thought they didn't.

"Where do you think the blood goes? Evaporates?"

I shrugged. "I don't know. I thought maybe it was absorbed or something."

A ghost of a smile danced over his lips, but it was gone before I could tell. "Absorbing blood. That's a new one," he said and shut the door.

The sky darkened as night came early. I rushed to the four arched windows side by side, across the wall from our bed, and stared out at the endless silhouettes of mountains, trees, and sky. I'd gotten us trapped here, in a place almost impossible to escape, and the only hope I had was to win Erianna to our cause and find my mom.

If I could find a way to use my own magic, that would be even better. I heard the shower turn on from the bathroom and closed my eyes. Power thrummed in my fingertips, tingling up into my wrists. I cleared my mind as best I could.

Sebastian believed I could do it, for whatever reason, and perhaps he was right. I'd always thought I was damaged somehow, and that's why my powers didn't work. I recalled Laveniuess's lake and what Sebastian and I had spoken about. Laveniuess believed embracing the darkest parts of ourselves was the key to becoming the best version of who we are. His energy was still inside me from my last visit to the lake.

Maybe what I really needed was to embrace the shadows I hid from. With a deep breath, I acknowledged the fear that came with feeling others' emotions and how I was afraid of not being enough. As the thoughts circled, the magic untangled, becoming easier to manipulate with each breath.

I lowered the barrier, allowing the emotions and energy of the surrounding rooms. The pain Sebastian felt resonated in the room, matching my own. They danced together in the darkness, only recognizing each other. I allowed the grief to fill me up, knowing it was okay to be scared.

Magic spiraled through me, rolling in waves as my heart rate elevated and adrenaline spiked. I smiled until I heard the crack of the window and glass splaying outward, all over the floor. I steadied myself as the rest of the shards disappeared into the walkway below, and Sebastian flew into the room, naked, and pulled me back.

TWENTY

"What happened?" His wide eyes searched mine. Slashes covered my hands, blood speckled my arms and my dress.

"I did it," I announced, shaking my head. "I think I just used my powers." I looked at my hands and over to the window. "Shit, I'm sorry."

"Don't be." He sat me down, and I couldn't help but see him in all his nakedness in my peripheral vision, my fist pressing into my thigh when I saw his enormous length. Unexpectedly, warmth gathered between my legs as I imagined him on top of me.

"See something you like?" he teased, and I let out a strangled laugh. "I'll put something on. Wouldn't want to distract you."

I touched the heat creeping up the back of my neck. "I-it doesn't, I mean, why would I..." I rubbed my forehead as I stumbled for the right words. What the hell was I doing?

He sped away, grabbed a towel, and wrapped it around his waist. I shook my head, scattering those unwanted thoughts. I refocused my attention to the window, glad for the cold air that whooshed inside, cooling me.

"How did you do it?" he asked from the bathroom.

"I used Laveniuess's energy to heighten my own by opening myself up," I said, looking at the floor which glittered with glass.

"How do you mean?"

"Normally, I refrain from lowering the barrier I'd learned to build to protect myself from feeling everyone's emotions, except on rare occasions, but this time I let it all in. Even when I lower it, I'm cautious, mostly because I know how quickly everyone else's energy can affect my own, but it was different this time. Laveniuess was guiding me."

He sat at my side, taking my hand. "That's good, but next time you practice your magic, we can do it outside."

I licked my lips. "I'm sorry about the blood."

"Why? I'm able to control myself." He lifted my finger to his lips and gently kissed away a drop of blood. "Here." I squirmed as he grabbed a shard of glass and cut it into his wrist. He'd lost his fucking mind. "Drink."

I flinched back. "No."

"You won't turn into a vampire on a small amount. It'll heal you quicker than if you don't. You don't want to be walking around this castle smelling of blood."

"I thought you could all control yourselves."

"We can, but most don't want to."

I rubbed the back of my neck, feeling the sting of the air against my cuts. Hesitantly, I eyed the cut and saw it was already healing. He reopened it with the glass, and I cringed. "I'm not doing that again," he said, and I leaned in closer.

My lips surrounded the wound, and his blood seeped into my mouth. I tried not to gag as the thick, metallic liquid hit the back of my throat. There was something different about his blood when compared to the times I'd quickly sucked the blood from a paper cut on my fingers. His had a cloying aftertaste that clung to my teeth. I pulled back, wiping my mouth with the back of my hand. I couldn't look him in the eyes. That was, by far, the weirdest thing I'd ever shared with another person.

"They're healing already."

The gashes slowly closed, the skin knitting together in front of my eyes like magic. "That's so strange."

"You should get used to it. You'll heal without my blood soon enough."

I forced a smile but let out a heavy breath. He was speaking of my becoming a vampire, something I had no plans on doing, but I couldn't let him know that. It was the only reason he was helping me.

"I should shower," I exclaimed, looking at the dry blood. "What should we do about the window?"

"I'll have someone come and sort it. We might need to move to another room. Go take your shower." He gestured to the bathroom. He hadn't even finished his own, but he was already drying his hair before I could say anything. I stepped into the bathroom, feeling my magic tingling under the surface. Despite the window and blood, I couldn't help but smile. For the first time in years, I could use my powers properly.

Perhaps, I wasn't as broken as I'd thought.

***

Dressed in burgundy, matching Sebastian's suit, we made our way to dine with the king. "He doesn't seem that bad," I admitted as we walked down ancient stone steps. "Sargon, I mean."

His stoic expression gave nothing away. "If you're thinking about changing your mind, let me know now."

"No, I'm not," I assured. "I just don't see the mad king from the stories."

"You've only met him once." Our footsteps echoed around us. "Against the judgments of Zach and Erianna, who despise him, I don't actually hate the man. But, apart from denying me what I've asked for and putting aside his more salacious tastes, he's not the worst king Sanmorte could have." He side-eyed me. "Nor is he the best. His brother, Kalon, is far worse."

I recalled our conversations at the house. "That's who Nightshade serves."

"Yes." His jaw hardened. "He and Sargon are close, and he trusts his brother, for some reason."

"Doesn't the king know about Nightshade?"

"Yes, but he has his own order protecting him too— Midnight Lotus. Sargon doesn't know Kalon has been making moves against him for the best part of a century."

"So he wants the crown."

"Yes, and that's why he sent the order to find you and your mom. His plan was to kill you and capture your mom, giving her as a gift to his brother, hoping it would be enough to make him forget about his daughter." He paused. "About you."

"Was it?"

"I've no idea."

"How do you know all this?"

He stopped us under the dim light of a lamp at the beginning of a long corridor, placing his hand against the wall. "I make it my business to have eyes and ears everywhere, including inside Nightshade. It's how I knew they were going after you." He looked around us and lowered his voice. "You'll meet Kalon at dinner. Keep your wits about you. While Sargon may have claimed the power and inherited the charm and charisma from his mother, Kalon came out on top for intelligence. Everything that happens at court has Kalon's hands in it. He schemes, unlike anyone I've met, and has a wicked intuition."

My eyes widened, and I shuffled backward. I didn't want to be around him if he was so dangerous, and suddenly the thought of being here felt like a dark cloud hanging over my head. "How can we make any move against my father if Kalon's in the way? Surely, he'll try to kill me once it's revealed who I am?" I questioned, then quickly remembered that none of that would matter if my plan worked because I'd be far from here. I hoped. I chewed on my nails, my gaze darting around us.

"We need to get rid of Kalon first."

"You left that out when discussing your plans with me! How do you expect us to take on two of the most ancient, powerful vampires in Sanmorte? You're a three-year-old vampire, and I'm a fucking teenager, Sebastian."

"You're a sorceress," he pointed out. "As you proved this afternoon, your powers are strong. Besides, when we find your mom, we can use her. She's the only one who's ever won against Sargon, and don't forget about Erianna and Zach."

"They have an army," I exclaimed, then quickly lowered my tone. "It doesn't matter, as long as we find my mom first."

"I promised you we would. So tomorrow, it's my priority to find out where she's being held."

I nodded and walked without him. He quickly caught up to me and placed a hand on my lower back. I flinched away, but as a door opened, I realized we were already at the private dining room. I wasn't sure why I'd thought we would eat in the large banquet room with everyone else. This made more sense. A guard stepped aside as Hamza pushed past us, his eyes rimmed red with rage. He moved on down the corridor, not even looking back at us.

"He looks upset," I said, but Sebastian didn't answer.

"My king." Sebastian swept into a low bow.

Sargon stood at the head of the table. "You're late."

I checked the time from the clock on the wall. "We were told seven. It's ten to."

Sebastian cleared his throat. "It's customary to arrive an hour before."

"You didn't tell me." I scowled but quickly smiled on seeing Sargon's expression. "I apologize, Your Majesty." The words felt odd coming from my lips. "It was my fault. I couldn't find the right dress."

The lines around his mouth softened, and he extended his hand, closing the distance between us in half a breath. "It was worth the wait, sweet one. You look beautiful." I took his hand, and he brought my fingers to his lips, kissing them as he'd done yesterday. That must've been how he greeted ladies here. Then he embraced Sebastian, slapping him on the back with a very unroyal demeanor. "Please, sit. This is my brother, Kalon," he said to me and gestured toward a willowy man with a groomed, black goatee, amber eyes, and red hair to match his brother's, but his was cut short. He watched me, reminding me of a predator as I took my seat. There was a coldness in Kalon's stare, which my father didn't possess. It was calculating as he evaluated our every move, making me feel more vulnerable than ever.

"It's a pleasure to meet you."

"My brother tells me you call yourself Olivia."

I ran cold, realizing this was the man who'd sent an entire order after us. So he had to know the fake name of the king's daughter, and here I was, using it, like an idiot. I think Sebastian had the same thought as he looked at Kalon, worry fleeting in his eyes. "Yes. I know it's such a common name." I laughed, then wondered if that was too obvious.

"It's a beautiful name," he said, half raising his goblet to his lips, "and not as common as one may think." He took a sip of blood, licking any traces away before lowering his goblet. "Excuse me for prying, but I can feel your magic from here. It's—" He inhaled deeply. "Intoxicating. Now, sorceresses, they are uncommon."

My heart palpitated, and to distract myself, I spun my ring around my finger over and over, glad to see he couldn't see it under the table. "Not as uncommon as one may think," I repeated his words back to him, but they meant nothing because they weren't true.

Sebastian sat upright, sipping from his cup.

Sargon spoke this time, his voice slicing through the air. "Food." He stood as a platter was brought inside. As I assumed it was customary, I stood with him and was correct. Kalon seemed bothered by the small gesture, and I pondered how much he must hate being second to his brother, especially because Sebastian said he was intelligent and clearly interested in the crown. Did he think himself more politically affluent than Sargon?

Kalon saw me staring, and a cruel smile ticked up one side of his lip. It was gone before anyone else could notice. How many sorceresses were called Olivia, who happened to be in Sanmorte not long after Nightshade attacked us? Did I look too much like my father, even without the hair? Suddenly I was too aware of my facial features and wanted to hide. Sebastian said Kalon had wicked intuition. We were screwed, and I don't think even Sebastian had thought too deeply into this. He was at least a shade paler than when we sat down.

A platter of sliced beef, chicken, and some other meats paired with roasted and mashed potato and enough vegetables to keep a farm in business was placed in front of me. I took a serving onto my plate, the only one at the table, and carefully lowered my barrier. Then, as I forked half a potato, I focused my mind on Kalon, shutting out the numbed grief radiating from Sebastian and curiosity from Sargon.

It started as a pinch, then turned dark and heavy. Then, tentatively, I reached out further, not looking away from Kalon as I reached for his mind, and as I was about to touch his emotions, to embrace and feel them as my own, I was shut out and forced back.

The hairs on the back of my neck stood erect. I glanced at Sebastian, who seemed none the wiser to what just happened.

Kalon had to be an empath, like me. How else could he shut me out like that? I thought only sorcerers could have gifts like that, but then I had heard of plenty of mortals who said they possessed the same abilities, maybe not to use it with magic, but to feel what others felt. Was Kalon one of them? Did it carry over when he became a vampire?

He gave me a knowing look, and I froze. He knew who I was. He must have felt my anxiety and fear the second I walked in, and I had no idea. I needed to alert Sebastian, but there was no way to say that something was wrong without alerting Sargon.

I zoned back into the conversation, unaware I had even zoned out in the first place. Sargon and Sebastian discussed politics and business in the city, while Kalon listened, not saying a word.

We were totally screwed.

TWENTY-ONE

I barely ate but forced enough down my throat to appear grateful for him providing me food when they didn't eat it. Then, Sargon demanded Sebastian join him in the throne room for dancing and evening entertainment, and I didn't want to be left alone, so I joined them.

At Sebastian's side, I squeezed his hand, shooting him a pleading look. Unfortunately, Sargon remained three steps ahead of us, so all communication had to be non-verbal.

He shrugged me off, seemingly annoyed at my obviousness. Kalon walked a step ahead of us, glancing back once and smiling.

He knows he knows he knows, I screamed in my head, hoping Sebastian could somehow become telepathic. "Darling," I finally said, earning a raised eyebrow from Sebastian. "I'm feeling a little dizzy. Can you show me where our room is again? This castle is so big."

Sargon paused, looking behind us. Sebastian wrapped his arm around me. "I will join you shortly. I'm going to escort Olivia back to our room."

Sargon's eyes focused on me. "I hope you feel better soon. I'd love for us to get to know each other better, with your wedding coming up soon."

Kalon stepped back, standing beside me. "I don't see why young love should wait. We can have a wedding here, at the castle. Sebastian's always felt at home here, and we can all attend."

Sargon clasped his hands together. "An excellent idea. We shall begin arrangements."

I touched my forehead, feeling beads of sweat gathering. "That sounds perfect, thank you, Your Majesty. Excuse me, I apologize."

Sebastian bowed and then walked me away from the king, his guards, and Kalon. Once we were far enough, I pulled him into an empty parlor room with a bench. Then, closing the door, I leaned over, placing my hand on my knees. "We're in danger!"

"I made an oversight with your name," he admitted. "It's salvageable."

My fingers trembled as I rested my back against the closed door, feeling a lump form in my throat.

"He knows, Sebastian." My shoulders tightened as an uneasiness crept through me. I ran my fingers through my hair, feeling beads of sweat forming over my eyebrows. "He's an empath, like me. When I tried sensing his emotions, he blocked me, and he gave me this look, like he could see right through me, and smiled when no one was looking."

Hugging my arms around my core, I squeezed, feeling like I'd swallowed a bag of rocks. Every part of me wanted to run, nervous to still be stuck inside these stone walls. Licking my lips, I gazed at Sebastian, my eyes bulging. Why wasn't he saying anything?

He tapped his finger against his chin, looking up in thought, slowly sitting on a bench pushed against a wall. "We can't know for sure."

My breath hitched as I closed the distance between us. He had to understand how much danger we were in. "I do. Trust me, he knows who I am. If the name and what I am didn't give me away, then my emotions did. I even look a bit like Sargon." My words stumbled over each other as I struggled to get them out fast enough.

He loosed a heavy sigh. "Then we're out of time. We need to act now."

"And what? Kill him?" Goose bumps spread over my arms, raising the hairs and pricking cold on my skin. I recalled the feeling of Kalon blocking my gift, seeing the knowing in his eyes as I tried to touch his emotions, and shuddered. "He's too powerful."

"We don't have another choice."

I pressed my fingers against my temples, shaking my head slowly. "Yes, we do. We can find my mom and get out of here tonight."

His lips formed into a hard line. "Erianna and Zach will be arriving tonight or by the morning. We can't leave them here."

I pointed a finger at his chest, tears welling in my eyes. "You promised to protect me."

"I am, but we have a deal too."

My heart raced, raising the hairs on the back of my neck. "I don't want to die here," I admitted, my chest tightening from the idea of being buried here, this castle being the last place I saw before I left this world. Shaking my hands at my side, I paced in a circle.

"I will not let that happen. You will become queen."

"Fuck you and becoming queen." I balled my fists, halting my pacing to glare at him. "I will not let myself get killed for your mortality."

"It goes beyond that now."

I held my breath, storming over to the window. "What do we do then?"

He stood. "We go downstairs, we dance, and we get close to Kalon, watch his every movement. So now we know he's a threat. We can monitor him."

"He probably has eyes on us." I stared, my chin trembling.

"Then we need to give him one hell of a show." He strode to my side, cupping my shoulder. "I'm not going to let him kill you. I promise."

"No." I wiped my nose on the back of my sleeve. "Gods forbid someone murders your tool to get your mortality back." Bitterness threaded my tone. "Take me down there, then."

"As soon as Erianna and Zach arrive, we'll be better off. They can help."

I thought about Erianna and the blade I'd left in my room. After tonight, I wouldn't let it out of my sight. Not with Kalon waiting in the shadows.

We reached the banquet room. Sargon waved us over, and Sebastian smiled as if he didn't have a care in the world. I did my best to emulate that. In the shadowy corner of the room, tents were erected, with doors made from a thin net allowing visibility inside, enough to see the erotic writhing of bodies together inside.

Beyond them, mortal women danced, dressed in fabrics that barely covered their breasts and stomachs. Their jewelry looked more expensive than anything I could ever afford. They were treated well, it seemed, as they moved to the beat of the string quartet playing.

Sangaree devoured their victims at the back of the room, laying mortals down on the long, wooden tables and benches, sinking their fangs into their necks. A man and woman couple swapped their victims after they'd taken a drink, holding them up with ease while laughing about something seemingly unrelated. The mortals looked drugged, just like those in the blood den, but they were dressed in fine outfits. They even decorated their food. I pulled Sebastian's sleeve when Sargon pulled my attention to him.

"Young lady." He kissed my hand.

I curtseyed despite my disgust at the room. "Your Majesty."

"I'm glad you're feeling better. May I?" He took my arm without waiting for an answer. "May I have this next dance?"

Sebastian gave me a sharp nod. But, of course, I would not turn down the king. I searched the room for Kalon, but he'd disappeared. Sebastian was looking around too and walked off to the back windows. I gazed at the stained-glass artwork depicting Sargon's coronation, which was probably centuries before I was thought of.

"You're distracted," he said firmly and took my hand in his. Sangaree spread around us, giving us the space to move freely, whereas they all moved close to each other.

"Sorry," I whispered, letting him guide me into a waltz. "I was feeling a little dizzy earlier."

"How are you finding the castle?"

How to answer without lying? "It's interesting."

"Yes. It can be. Coming here alone and being in a den must have been hard. If I'd known you were there, I would have had you brought to the castle immediately and have you serve as a part of my council. But, alas, Sebastian got to you first."

I didn't like his tone. "I'm not anyone's property."

An uneasy laugh trickled from his parted lips. "No, you most certainly are not. Anyone in my council is free to do as they please, as long as they take care of minor tasks for me occasionally."

"It would have been an honor." I paused, peering around him for Sebastian.

Cold pricked in my veins when I spotted him on the back table, drinking from a mortal woman in her late twenties along with another male vampire. They feasted on either side of her neck, allowing blood to soak into the top of her dress.

Sargon whipped his head around, then looked back at me, a cruel smile playing on his Cupid's bow lips, which were far too close to my own. "I do like Sebastian. He's an ambitious man with great tastes. He would often stay here until the early hours drinking from mortals and getting drunk on our best whiskey and champagne. Most of it is brought in from Baldoria, actually."

Nausea overwhelmed me. "I'm sorry, I feel a little sick."

There was no pause in his movements as he twirled me around. "This is your world now. I know he's caught your eye, and I would never dream of taking what is his, but know this: you have a choice. He can't offer you a measure of safety unless he turns you into one of us. With me, I can ensure your safety. No man or woman in this castle would touch you without my consent. You can remain a sorceress, keep your magic, and have a life of luxury." Lips grazing my ear, he murmured, "Do think about it, Olivia. You can marry him or not, but either way, you will be welcome to join my council here." He stepped back, inclining his head.

I forced a smile and curtseyed. "I will consider it," I said because any other reply felt dangerous.

"Speaking of sorceresses, my wife has arrived. Excuse me."

I tilted my head. I had no idea he'd gotten remarried, although it made sense. No one should be alone for that long. Even if my mom insisted on it. I thought about Aiden and his flirtations with her. He was probably dead now.

His wife turned. Raven-black curls coiled down from a tight updo, bouncing as she moved.

"No!" I gasped. Her porcelain-like skin and bright eyes were too perfect. Even the scar over her lip was gone. "Mom." The word shakily left my lips, echoing in my mind.

"Don't react." Sebastian was at my side, a whisper dancing into my ear as he pulled me away.

My mom looked over, spotting me. Her eyes widened.

"People are looking. Dance with me." He pulled me to the side of the dance floor, holding me in his arms as I tried my best not to buckle under the crushing realization. "You're okay." He lifted me higher. "Put your weight on me."

I swallowed thickly as he pulled me closer until there was no distance between us. "My mom."

"She's alive," he said, although his darkening expression told me he wasn't happy about it either. "That's all that matters."

He curled me around, and I thought about everything we had gone through. She taught me how to ride a bike, paint, learn my ABCs, and times tables. She waited in line in the store for four hours to get me the newborn doll I wanted for Christmas one year, and on my sixteenth birthday, she took me to a bookstore to meet my favorite author at a signing. There was no way she was gone. I needed her, but I could only see a monster when I looked at her.

"She's not alive," I exclaimed, a cry bubbling up my throat. "She's a vampire." I wiped a tear and panicked as more came thick and fast. My chest heaved, and Sebastian cradled my head against his chest, shielding my tears from the rest of the room.

"Not here, love." He tucked a lock of hair behind my ear for the benefit of the king, I assumed. We had to appear in love, dancing, and they couldn't see I was crying.

I sniffed, pulling back, and he pressed his cold fingers against my cheek. "What are you doing?"

"Cooling the redness," he said stiffly, looking around. "Smile. Sargon is looking at us."

I was giving us away. "Has he noticed?"

He smiled in their direction and leaned down, whispering a kiss against my cheek. "Think of anything else."

"Like how you were sharing your drink with someone over there?" I made a face.

He twirled me, then caught me at dizzying speed. "I have to drink."

"Not like that."

"Sorry to have disappointed you," he said with a smirk. "There's enough chatter and music in this room. They can't hear us."

"Sargon must have turned her. She loved being a sorceress. This is awful. She doesn't look the same, like some airbrushed version of herself."

"She's here. Be calm, please. Don't give us away, Olivia." Sebastian looked over my shoulder. "Ravena."

"You must be Sebastian." My mom's voice carried between us.

I stood upright, and Sebastian held me still.

"Thank you for taking care of her, but I've got it from here."

Sebastian glanced in Sargon's direction, then smiled at Ravena, pretending to be introducing us. He gave my mom my hand and backed away. Another lady asked to dance with him, and he took her out onto the floor, never moving his eyes from me.

"What are you doing here?" My mom grabbed my hands, squeezing them tight. "I wish I could hug you, honey."

The sentiment took me by surprise. I wasn't sure what I had expected, but her being her normal self wasn't it. "You're a vampire."

She walked me to the window, looking out. "Whisper," she breathed. "Although it's loud in here, use caution. The king is watching us."

"You mean my dad," I hushed.

The corner of her mouth twitched down. "You know."

"That I'm a vampire princess, yes. Sebastian took me from the guild. They killed almost everyone else."

Her face crumpled, but she quickly regained her composure. "Draven is here," she whispered. "I have only been allowed out since yesterday but haven't found a moment to speak to him."

I swallowed thickly, placing my hand against my chest. "He's alive."

"We'll get him out of this too. He's enslaved."

My stomach dipped, and I wrung my hands, trying not to let my tears fall. "I hoped he wouldn't be. Do you have a plan?"

"I didn't," she admitted. "I was hoping my being here would be a distraction enough that Sargon wouldn't look for you, but here you are."

"He doesn't know who I am," I said and chewed on my nails.

"I guessed as much. Walk with me." She snapped her fingers at her side and headed for the drinks table. "We have to part ways before he becomes suspicious. What room are you in?"

"The uh—" I searched my memory. "Red suite in the west wing."

"I'll find you. Do not come looking for me. Stay with your friend."

I nodded, unable to contain my shaking as I watched her leave, returning to the king's side. I hurried across the room, stumbling over a discarded necklace. I found Sebastian looking over and gestured for him to join me. I couldn't help but glance back at her and pinched my eyes shut when I saw her.

Sebastian's hand landed on my shoulder, and I leaned into him. "She's going to come to our room, and Draven's here, somewhere."

Kalon returned at Sargon's side, watching us, whispering something to the king. Sebastian cupped my cheek. "Keep it together, love." He brought his lips close to mine. It would appear as if we were sharing an intimate moment to anyone else in the room. Whereas he was just trying to make sure I didn't break down, but I was past that now. The thought of Draven being here, being alive, was enough to keep me standing.

"I'm okay," I promised as his breath tingled against me.

"Good." He ran a thumb over the side of my neck.

It may have all been for show, but I melted into his touch, enjoying the feeling, even though it was pretend, of being cared for by anyone right now. Then I left the room, leaving a longing look after my mom, wishing more than anything she could hold me and take me away from all of this. But when I watched her move with such grace and speed, I was reminded that she belonged here now, in Sanmorte, as one of them.

TWENTY-TWO

I'd collapsed from exhaustion before I could find Draven last night. Sebastian shuffled against the sheets when I moved, opening my eyes to the dimly lit room. Someone had repaired our window, so we didn't have to move rooms, and the glass was all gone. Dappled light reached around the cracks in the long drapes, sending slithers of light up the carpet and over to the bed.

I felt differently this morning, perhaps because I'd finally found my mom and Draven after all my searching, but only one of them was unsavable.

Even if I wanted to, I couldn't bring her back to Baldoria with me if I had any chance of making my escape. She'd be executed immediately once the guild found out what she'd become, and if out of some loyalty they didn't, she'd at least be imprisoned.

There was little choice. The kingdoms weren't kind to vampires, and I couldn't blame them. She had to stay here, in Sanmorte, or die. There was no third option. My heart felt a little heavier as I climbed out of bed, careful not to wake Sebastian. My toes hit a line of sunlight on the carpet, warming them. If I couldn't help her, then I could at least save Draven. He was the only thing I had to hold on to because thinking about permanently leaving my mom here and living a life without her was too much grief to bear. My soul was already too weary of processing anything more. So, for now, I would live in the present. With Kalon knowing my true identity, I couldn't return to Baldoria anyway, not when Nightshade would hunt me.

Where would I go?

I could either stay here and come clean, become a vampire, and lose the powers I'd just started to control, along with my mortality, or flee with Draven, somehow, to another kingdom far from here, where Nightshade would have a hard time reaching me.

My options weren't great.

"You're up early." Sebastian rolled over and yawned. "It's barely—" He checked his watch on the nightstand. "Eight."

"I want to be awake before all the bloodsuckers are."

"Well, aren't you a ray of sunshine in the morning," he said, stretching his arms. "Erianna and Zach should be here soon anyway, so I'll get up."

"I'm going to find Draven."

"I could lay here and point out all the reasons why that's a terrible idea, but you're not stupid." He added, "I hope."

"I'm going to wear a cloak."

"Yes. Kalon and his followers will be trumped by a simple traveling cloak."

I rolled my eyes. "They're probably not even awake."

He sat upright, running his hand through his tousled hair. He somehow managed to look even sexier in the mornings, with bed hair and a roughened look.

I shook my head, pushing that thought somewhere into a nope box in my mind.

"Olivia, Kalon is dangerous. He will have people looking out for you around the clock, and I guarantee you, the moment you're alone, they will take you and kill you before Sargon finds out who you are. The king knowing your identity is the last thing Kalon wants."

"Then come with me."

"We should wait for Erianna and Zach. They can help you look for him safely, and they can fight. The guards here are highly trained in all forms of combat."

I thought back to my lessons at fifteen and how every time anyone had tried to teach me how to fight, I'd always end up on my ass. "My mom said she would come to find me. Did she? I shouldn't have fallen asleep."

His shoulders slumped. "She didn't come by here last night, but with Sargon's men watching her more closely than ever, it could take a day or two for her to sneak away and see you."

"Why can't you come with me to find Draven again?" I questioned, realizing he'd changed the subject on me. "Unless you're doubting your own ability to protect me against Kalon's men?"

Challenge glinted in his eyes. "Don't play with me, Olivia."

"Then help me, or I'm going alone."

"You're going to get yourself killed!"

I shrugged. "Then give me some of your blood. After all, if I'm killed, I'll become a vampire, and I can take my place as the princess and give you your mortality back. That's all you want, right?"

"Are you upset with me for that?"

"What if I don't want this anymore? I don't hate the king enough to kill him. He's still my dad, and it's just not who I am." I wrestled with my morality as I walked toward the bathroom door. "If I become princess, I'll always have a target on my back, and I've only just found my powers. I enjoy being a sorceress. I don't want to become like you."

He climbed out of bed, wearing only a pair of gray sweatpants, showing the white band of his underwear. "You made me a promise." His nostrils flared as he closed the distance between us, and for the first time, I was seeing how it felt being on the wrong side of him—no longer as his ally, but instead an enemy. "We had a deal."

"People break deals all the time." I stood firm, but my heart was racing. He didn't know I had no plans to keep to his deal all along, but now I couldn't even pretend. Not with Kalon after me. "I'm sorry."

He scoffed, his jaw tightening. "You're sorry?" he mocked. "I gave you my word I would protect you. I put my fucking name on the line to bring you here, to fake being engaged so you could become queen." He searched my face, then shook his head, stepping back. "I was giving you everything you wanted."

"No." I balled my fist. "It was everything you wanted. I was forced to go along with your plan."

He changed his direction mid-stride, running one hand through his hair. "I should have never trusted you."

"This has nothing to do with trust," I exclaimed. "Don't act like the victim in this. It doesn't suit you."

"Don't you get it?" He threw his hands in the air, his eyes wild. "If it comes out that I knew who you were, I will lose a lot more than the promise of mortality. I'll lose my life. If I help you escape before anyone finds out, Kalon will come after me. He'll know I know where you are. I'll never be safe again. My name, my reputation here, it will all go up in fucking flames because you couldn't keep to your end of the deal." Tension ran thick in his voice. "What's the plan then? Find Draven and run off into the night? In case you couldn't tell, you're surrounded by hundreds of miles of forests and mountains, and even if by some miracle you managed to get past those, you'll still be in Sanmorte, as a mortal."

"My mom..."

"Will get herself killed trying to help you."

I blinked back tears as everything unraveled.

Sebastian took a step closer.

"What are you going to do, Sebastian?"

Power reached from my chest into my fingers, daring me to hurt him if he came any closer, but he didn't.

"There's nothing left for anyone to hurt me with." The words ached, falling from my breathless lips. I lowered my barrier, feeling the sting of betrayal and rage that reached into his core.

I hurt him. Badly. Which only made him more dangerous.

"I've already lost everything," I said because it was true. "My mom is a vampire, and after all these years after waiting to find out who my dad is, I can never have a relationship with him." My mind flooded with memories of my life before this, when everything changed. I'd taken them for granted, my mom,

Draven, and Astor. I'd become so used to reading my stories to my mom in the evening while drinking cocoa. I'd gotten used to being with Draven in the backyard, who persevered in trying to teach me combat, even though I was terrible. Then cuddling up with Astor, who held me so tight that I sometimes wondered if he was afraid I'd disappear. They were my world, and when I wasn't with them, I was writing. Or taking long, hot baths, and watching reruns of my favorite programs.

The echoes of my former life slipped away. The transformation of who I was becoming, and everything that had been taken from me, burned a hole so deep I was afraid it could never be filled. My voice cracked when I opened my mouth again, the words biting into me, relentless.

"The love of my life turned out to be a liar who cared more about himself than me, and my best friend is a slave and will never be the same again." My voice cracked. "There's not much left for anyone to take, and you stand here and talk to me as if I owe you something. I don't have to give you a damn thing because I never asked for you to save me, and sometimes..." I hesitated, my chest heaving. "Sometimes I wish you'd let them kill me."

He gave me a pained look, his eyebrows drawing together, deepening the line appearing on his forehead. He reached out to touch me but stopped midair as I stumbled back.

"Don't," I warned. "I'm not in the mood for some emotionless bullshit about how I need to just keep going and keep to some deal I made when I thought my mom could still be saved."

"I wasn't going to say that." He paused, his posture mirroring mine.

Silence hung between us as we stared each other down, neither looking away. His anger dissipated slowly, turning into pity.

"Don't you dare."

"What?"

"Pity me. You have no idea how any of this feels."

"I do." He let out a tense breath, his muscles slackening. "My mom—" He struggled with the words as if this were the first he was speaking them out loud. "She was a good woman."

The cold sank through my skin, chilling my bones. I rolled my neck to combat the shiver dancing in my spine. I wanted to stay mad at him, to yell at him to go fuck himself, but his words hit somewhere deeper than they should. "Were you there? When she—"

He nodded. "She threw herself in front of me. All movie style," he joked, but the sadness pinched deep in his eyes.

It was never going away. That kind of grief never left.

"I thought I could at least save my siblings." He winced at the memory. "We lived in a border town in another kingdom, and Velda and others from Nightshade came in the night. They tore my mom and dad apart. I should've fought them, but I wanted to protect the rest of my family."

My mouth dried, and I raised my fingers to my throat, watching him through glossed eyes.

"They were so scared, begging through tears to spare us, but they didn't care." Tears swam in those deep-blue eyes I'd only seen show hardness before now. "When I woke up, I found them dead. I fought, but I was nothing against them. The men who drained them of blood did... other things too. I wanted to die. Then, I guess for whatever reason, Velda changed me."

"I'm sorry," I said, my hands shaking as I imagined the whole scene in my head. Tears of my own threatened to break through when I looked at him. I could feel everything he did, and it stole my breath away.

"My sister and brothers were taken to Sanmorte. They didn't survive more than a few weeks in the blood den. Some aniccipere got hungry. That's the only reason I agreed to come here, to help what remained of my family, but by the time I got to them, it was already too late. Gwen helped me after that." He looked up, lost in the memory of people who no longer existed. "She wanted me, but I couldn't look at her without seeing Velda, and I wasn't interested in finding anything that resembled love after that. There was no space in my heart."

"You said Zach and Erianna saved you."

"They did. I ran from Nightshade and gave up, but they found me and made me keep going."

I knew firsthand how persuasive Erianna could be. "I'm glad she did."

"I don't think you mean that." He let out a watery laugh, and I walked to him slowly. He shoved his hands in his pockets. "Now you know, so trust me when I tell you I know how you feel. But I'm still here, fighting, and you must as well because your mom may be a vampire, and your best friend is enslaved, but they're still alive. I'm not the only one who has lost everything. Probably half the vampires in Sanmorte have no family."

That hit hard, pushing my tears over the edge. I noticed one trickle down his cheek. Instinctively, I reached up, wiping it away. He sniffed, looking away. He looked so broken when he cried. I placed my hand on his chest, not to take away his pain, but to share it. "I guess the gods had a sense of humor when bringing us together."

"If you believe everything happens for a reason," he countered.

"It makes it easier to have faith." I rubbed the side of my neck. "Why is getting your mortality back so important?" I dared to ask. After all, he didn't have a family to go back to. Not that I'd ever say that out loud.

"Because." He turned to face the window. "I'm one of them now, and when I look in the mirror, all I see is a murderer."

"You're not a killer."

"No?" He balled his fists, turning so I could see the darkness in his eyes. "You don't think I haven't killed anyone? I'm just as bad as they were, and if I don't get away from this place, I'll end up worse than the people who murdered my family."

I shook my head. "I don't believe that. You're not a bad person."

"I am, Olivia, and the moment you try to convince yourself that I'm not is the moment you'll lose. You have to show some teeth in this kingdom and take what you want because no one will help you. It's not in our nature to show kindness."

"My mom will," I stated.

"You have to help yourself. Find your power and take your place on the throne. Don't you see? You can make sure no one hurts you again. You can punish Astor, Gwen, and anyone else who's crossed you."

I took a step back. "If you believe that's what I really want, then you don't know me at all. You say you have to look out for yourself, but Erianna and Zach are here, for you. So you're not as alone as you tell yourself you are. Also," I added, "there are many mortals who are far more monstrous than the vampires I've met. Mortality won't take away those dark parts of yourself, but if you want to keep believing you're a bad person, that you're somehow worse than the people who tore apart your family, that's because you want to believe it."

I felt bad saying it, but I had to because it was true. "You're not a monster, Sebastian. You're just like me—a little broken."

He sat on the edge of the bed, placing his head in his palms. "I don't see how either of us is getting out of this alive."

A lump formed in my throat. "I know you're upset with me."

"It's more than that. I threw away everything to help you. This was supposed to be my chance at a new life."

"What about me and what I want?"

He let out a long exhale. "I guess I didn't really see you as a person when the plan was formulated. When I met you, I tried to keep my distance, emotionally, but now, it's all too real."

"I'm glad you see me as a person," I joked. "Honestly"—I glanced over at the draped window—"I don't know what to do either."

A knock resonated through the room. Sebastian jumped to his feet, speeding to the door before I got a chance to process what was happening. He placed a finger against his lips. "Who is it?"

A whisper muffled from behind the door, a sound only Sebastian could hear. His expression softened when he pulled down the handle, and Draven walked in, looking like something from out of a horror movie.

TWENTY-THREE

"I was hoping it wasn't true," Draven said when I threw my arms around him, resting my head against his shoulder. "Your mom told me you were here and where to find you. I couldn't believe it was her at first."

I released him, eyeing the bite marks all over his neck and wrists. "I know." I gave him a bitter smile. "She's one of them, but she seems herself."

"Except for the blood-drinking part."

Sebastian cleared his throat. "Did she say anything else to you?"

Draven looked over my head at Sebastian, his frown deepening. "No." He glanced back at me. "This must be your betrothed."

"No." I laughed. "We're faking it. It's a whole thing. I have so much to tell you, but first, I need to, um, talk to Sebastian." I looked over my shoulder, worried about what he would do now I'd spoken of breaking our deal. I couldn't focus on Draven as much as I wanted to if I couldn't count on Sebastian's help. "Give me five minutes. There are some butter cookies over there that they left me." I pointed at my nightstand. "Help yourself. I don't care for them anyway."

I watched him devour one and sighed. How the tables had turned from him trying to get me to eat. He looked so thin, and his muscles were wasting away. Draven looked like a shadow of his former self. Dark circles hung under his eyes, darkening his too-pale face.

Sebastian followed me into the bathroom. I closed the door, sighing heavily. "What are you going to do?"

He gripped the vanity. "What can I do?"

I licked my lips. "We can re-strategize. There has to be a way for us all to win."

"No." His expression turned stony. "I'm going downstairs to find Erianna, Zach, and Anna, who should be here by now. In the meantime, I will keep up our facade, but you need to decide what your plan is because we can't continue as if nothing happened while you scheme behind my back."

I fell silent.

"If you want to escape, then you need to find a way to do that," he said slowly, "because myself, Erianna, or Zach will not risk our lives for you to run away and leave us to clean up this mess. I won't have them hurt because you changed your mind."

I nodded gently, knowing I was truly alone in all this. Not that I could blame him. "I don't know what other options there are."

"You can stick to our original plan, and we can dethrone Sargon. If you don't have it in your heart to kill him, then we can do it."

The coldness of his tone cut through the air between us. "I can't."

"You could tell him the truth of who you are, but we will be punished for keeping you from him, and your list of enemies will include far more than just Kalon."

"So my only good option is to plot to kill my father."

"He did it to his own." He shrugged. "He has lived for centuries, Olivia. You're not cutting his life short. He has had far more time here than anyone else."

"He cares for you," I said pointedly. "You would betray him so easily."

He shook his head. "He likes me. There's a difference. Don't think he wouldn't hesitate to do the same to me if he were in my position. I would take it if there was another way out of this, but this is the cleanest way. Sanmorte needs change anyway, and being a vampire doesn't have to be as bad as you think it is."

"Says the man who will do anything to become mortal."

"You're a far better person than I am, Olivia. If anyone can keep their morality as a vampire, it's you."

I flushed red. "If I escape, will you tell Sargon who I am?"

He paused, looking at himself in the mirror. "No, but I won't be able to stop Kalon from hunting you."

"How do you know the king will punish you for hiding me? I'm sure I could talk to him. If he's been looking for me for this long, then surely he'd welcome what I have to say."

"Don't be naïve. You don't know him like I do. He hates being lied to. Disloyalty will get anyone in this castle killed faster than breaking any of the few laws we have. He'll suspect a plot. The madness you can't see, it's there, mixed with a dark paranoia that bubbles just beneath the surface. Do you truly believe your mom chose to become a sangaree?"

My eyebrows knitted together. "No."

"I'm sure he made it seem like she had a choice, but I doubt whatever other option he gave her was a thousand times worse."

Just like the options I was facing, I pondered. I rubbed my forehead, ironing out the deep lines which formed. "I want to talk to Draven first."

"Whatever you decide, give us the courtesy of the truth so Erianna, Zach, and I may decide how to proceed. If you escape, we need to be prepared."

He didn't so much as look back when he sped out of the bathroom. He grabbed a shirt from the closet, pants and shoes, and looked at Draven. "Don't leave this room. Kalon's looking for her, and he will kill her."

I joined Draven on the four-legged sofa in front of an unlit fireplace at the far end of the room while Sebastian dressed, then left without so much as saying another word. Once he was gone, I inhaled sharply. "Your neck." I leaned over, brushing a touch over the scabs. "I should have asked him to give you some of his blood to heal you."

He winced. "I wouldn't drink it if he offered."

His tan was all but gone. He usually spent his days training in the outside areas of the guild, where the sun beat down in Ismore. Now he was in some gothic-horror castle trapped in the ancient ages, being fed on for fun. "I'm sorry this happened to you."

"I hate that you're here," he countered, his brown eyes narrowing. "How did you end up with that vampire?"

"He saved me right after you were taken." The memory of watching Draven being flown away in the arms of a vampire intruded into my thoughts. "Took me to the City of Nightmares, which is a delightful place," I joked. Luckily, he'd always preferred dark humor. "So I found out why the sangaree attacked us. They were after my mom and me."

He leaned forward, chewing on the last cookie from the packet. "Yes."

"Well, you know why. Apparently, everyone did except for me," I berated but softened my tone when I saw how beaten and broken he was. "Astor gave us up."

He clenched his jaw. "I had my suspicions, but I hoped I was wrong. The way he died; it was far too clean."

"I've seen him," I admitted. "He's a part of the order, Nightshade, which came after us."

His fists clenched, and I was surprised to see he had any strength left. "I already told him off."

"That's far nicer than what I have planned for him."

I touched his fist. "Draven, we have far bigger fish to fry. I want to get you out of here, but Kalon, he's after me."

"I know all about the king's brother." His mouth twisted in disgust. "Why is he after you?"

"He knows who I am. He's an empath too, although a bad one. I don't think he can manipulate people's energies like me, but he can certainly feel them. He blocked me from feeling his emotions."

"Interesting. Perhaps it's hereditary."

I hadn't thought of that. Slowly, I tapped a finger against my chin. "Then that only doubly proves to him who I am. As you can see, I dyed my hair, but it wasn't enough. He knows my name is Olivia, and I'm a sorceress."

"He would have known that when coming after you and your mom in Baldoria."

"Exactly." I blew out a tense breath. "I made a deal with Sebastian that I would dethrone my father and become queen."

Draven leaned back, his eyebrows shooting up his forehead. "I hope that's some fucking joke."

"I didn't plan on keeping to that deal. At the time, I'd only wanted to find a way into the castle, but now my mom's a vampire and… Well, look outside. How will we escape? Even if we do, with Kalon knowing who I am, he will never stop hunting me."

"Then we kill him first."

I gave him a look. "How much luck have you had killing anyone since you've been enslaved here?"

He winced on the word. "Your friend can help."

"He won't because he knows I'm leaning toward escaping, which ruins his life and Erianna's and Zach's."

He arched an eyebrow.

"His friends," I explained. "If my mom helps us, she'll be hurt because she can't come with us. You know she'll never be welcome amongst mortals."

He tapped a finger against his knee. "I assume your plan to become queen"—he rolled his eyes up—"means you'll be losing your mortality too."

"I'd have no other choice."

His expression hardened. "Absolutely not."

"I have little choice. If we try to escape, I will lose my mom, we'll probably die, let's face it, and I will hurt my friends." I blinked twice, realizing I'd included Sebastian and Zach in that word, and almost laughed at myself. Zach was far from being my friend, and Sebastian, well, he was only using me to get what he wanted. Even if I wanted to believe differently.

Draven stood, his posture poised to fight. "I won't let that become your fate."

"I will not have my mom, nor Erianna and especially you, get hurt because I was selfish. If I run and try to save myself, then I'm no better than Astor." The words stilled me, mostly because I hadn't let myself think about them before now.

"You're nothing like him."

"That's why I have to choose this."

He gritted his teeth, looking around for an answer that didn't exist. "Can't you just tell him who you are? Go to the king. Look, I know the whole story. They told us all at the guild, including that weasel Astor. It was our job to protect you from them, but from what I'd heard, your father wanted you back more than anything else. So he won't hurt you."

"He'll hurt Sebastian and the others."

He shook his head. "Don't let that stop you. Come on, Olivia, they're vampires. They don't care about you."

"I can't just throw them into the fire after they protected me."

"I would do it for you."

I touched his hand, and his anger melted away. "I know, but I can take care of myself." I stepped back, moving over to the window. "I broke this yesterday with my powers."

"You've been practicing?"

"Yes, and I know I can get better."

"Good." He paused, looking up. "Look, if you tell the king you're his daughter, he might let you stay a sorceress."

"Like he let my mom stay as one?"

"She hurt him. You haven't."

"No. He's paranoid. He won't let that happen. Sebastian told me—"

"You put a lot of faith in the words of a vampire," he snapped, his eyes bulging. "You always did try to see the best in people. I never said anything when you did it to Astor. You couldn't see past the fact that he controlled your life at every turn, and now you're letting a vampire manipulate you."

I crossed my arms, smelling what was left of the butter cookies as I moved back from the sofa. "You have no faith in me."

He hesitated. "You're too sweet, that's all. I don't want you being taken advantage of."

My toes curled inside my slippers. "I can take care of myself. The whole relationship with Astor, it was a mistake, but it taught me a lot. As for Sebastian, I know what he's like. I'm not stupid enough to think he cares for me, or he wants to help me with no gain of his own, but I am aware enough to know when he's lying to me." I closed my eyes, lowering my barrier. Draven's anxiety rippled in, mixed with worry and love. "Just like how I know you care about me. I can feel it radiating from you. You're worried about me, anxious about yourself, and I can tell the feeling is genuine. I can read Sebastian's emotions in the same way."

"So I'm just supposed to trust this vampire?"

"No." I inhaled sharply. "You're supposed to trust me. He has a plan to remove my father from the throne."

"You're okay with that, are you?"

I swallowed thickly. "I have no other choice. I must become queen. It's not like if there was a better alternative, I wouldn't take it, but I can't hurt everyone else because I'm a coward."

"No one would think you're a coward for running."

"I would." I didn't break eye contact. "At least this way, I can protect my mom, and you, Draven. I'll have you sent back to Baldoria as soon as I have the power to."

"I won't allow this."

"Please, don't try to stop me. This is my choice."

His face crumpled. "Olivia…"

"I've already made up my mind." I stepped closer to him, noticing the veins in his bloodshot eyes. "Take a shower. No one is going to look for you in here, and I'll ask Sebastian to have some food sent up for me, so you can eat."

"I can't hide up here. They'll notice I'm missing."

I sighed, wrapping my arms around him, never wanting to let go. He smelled like a mix of ash and charcoal. "I'm going to get you out of here soon. Don't worry."

"I'm not." He held me tighter. "I'm more worried about you. If you change your mind and decide you want to escape, I'll be there at your side. I won't let anything happen to you." He kissed the top of my head, and for the first time in a month, I allowed my anxiety to slip away.

"Don't go yet," I begged, although I knew Erianna, Zach, and Sebastian would come back here soon. "Just stay for a little bit."

He brushed my hair back, and I rested into his arms. I missed my best friend, and as we talked about the castle and the weird things the vampires did, my world centered and I found a semblance of normal amongst all the chaos.

TWENTY-FOUR

Erianna stood in front of me, arms crossed over her armored chest. Zach stood over by the window, leaving Anna to have her bath and a nap. Draven, fortunately, left before Sebastian brought them up to our room. "Don't get mad at her."

"It's okay."

"You're allowed to get scared. What you're offering to do is an enormous sacrifice. Being queen is not a simple task. As they say, heavy is the head that wears the crown."

Sebastian extended his arms out, talking with his hands. "She was going to screw us over."

"I don't believe Olivia would do that."

My stomach dipped. He was right, my original plan did mean hurting them, but I didn't know it at the time. I hadn't thought into anything too profoundly past my escape. Now I was, and with Erianna in front of me, I felt a little better about my choice. Perhaps she could be my advisor, like Hamza was to Sargon. I clasped my clammy hands together, steadying my breathing as the overwhelming weight of my decision pushed down on me. "All that matters now is I'm sticking to the plan." I looked Sebastian directly in the eyes. "I hesitated for a moment. Can you blame me? Get over your tantrum so we can strategize."

I saw Zach smirk in my peripheral vision. It felt unlike him to find anything about me funny, but clearly, the long journey with his beloved had lightened his mood. "She's right," Zach said, sending my eyebrows halfway up my forehead. "We need to come up with a plan. We didn't count Kalon knowing her identity or Ravena being a vampire." He walked over to the sofa by the fire, placing a folder down on the round, wooden table. "Here, I have a list of all the dignitaries at court."

"How did you get that?"

Zach tilted his head, spilling his blond strands down one side of his chest. "I am an officer in the king's army, specialized in archery." He gestured to Erianna. "She captures prisoners and those the king wants brought to the castle."

"Wow," I exclaimed. "I'm surprised he lets you live in the city."

"We are his eyes and ears there. He expects us to report back to him, and he can send for us when he needs us here. Sebastian has a similar arrangement, although he's not often needed here."

"A perk of being the master of travel."

Erianna rolled her eyes. "It's not even a proper title. Sargon created it for you so you can party and not have to work running some blood den."

I sat on the chair across from Zach, crossing my legs. Sebastian sat next to him, whereas Erianna opted to stand. Sunlight glistened off her thin armor, which appeared to be made from blue-purple scales. She wore it like any other clothing, and it hugged her when she moved. She spotted me staring, and I looked away. "Sea serpent scales." She answered my unspoken question. "They're razor-thin but impenetrable. Feel."

She walked to me, and I reached out, touching one. It reminded me of a flower petal, feeling so fragile in my fingers, but when I tried to break it in half, it was hard as stone. "A lot of sea serpents must have died to make this," I thought aloud, imagining small snakes who lived in our rivers and lakes.

She laughed. "Just one died for this shirt. There are far more monsters than just us vampires," she joked. "In the north seas, there are sea monsters twice the size of most ships. When I was first changed, I traveled with pirates. I still have most of my armor from those days."

Sebastian cleared his throat. "You can talk about fashion later. We have a lot to go over."

I scowled. He brushed it off like it was nothing. "Sometimes, I swear you don't even try to have normal conversations, you know, form meaningful relationships."

He scoffed. "You're snarky for someone who just broke my trust."

"For someone who wants something from me, you sure are acting like a dick."

He stood, racing over to me.

We stared at each other for several seconds as fury spilled into his sharp features. "I need to know I can trust you, that you're not just lying to me so you can leave at the last minute."

My fists balled. "I wouldn't do that." Tension rolled between us. I lowered my barrier, mostly out of curiosity, and felt something different pierce through his pain—fear. He'd opened up about his family, and now he was worried I would hurt him too. Under all that rage and grief was a man who felt alone in the world. He didn't even see what he had. I looked from him to Erianna and Zach. While he may have lost his family, he gained another. One I didn't think he appreciated as much as he should have. "I'm not going to hurt you."

His eyebrows furrowed, and his frown faltered. "This... this has nothing to do with being hurt." He half laughed at the idea. "I'm just looking out for myself."

"For Erianna and Zach too, right?"

"Obviously," he said, his tone slick. "What are you implying?"

I didn't look away. It was a game I couldn't escape as he stared what felt like into my soul, with impenetrability that made me nervous.

Zach clicked his tongue, snapping us out of it. "Would you two fuck already," he said, deadpan.

Erianna laugh-snorted, and my face flooded with heat. "I have no interest in him whatsoever," I blurted out, hating how red my face was. Now I really hated Zach, who was back to looking at the papers in his folders.

Sebastian remained silent, and I waited for anyone to say something. "So…" Erianna sat on the ledge of the window, pressing her suppressed smile into a hard line. "How is your friend? I'm glad he's alive."

I shook my head, reorienting myself. "Draven, yes, he's good. I mean, not good." I was stumbling. What the hell? "He has bite marks."

Sebastian looked slightly amused as he looked over Zach's shoulder at the papers, half glancing in our direction.

"You can help him soon enough," she said. "How are you feeling about becoming a vampire?"

"You're the first person to ask me that."

She waved a hand in Sebastian's direction. "I'm not surprised. He probably feels guilty at you becoming like us but can't say anything because he desires his mortality so much." She gave him a look, but he pretended not to hear us. "I know him better than he thinks. Him pretending not to care is easier for him to move ahead with any of this."

I inhaled deeply, wondering if she was right and maybe, somewhere, he did care even a little. I'd caught myself wondering, in the quiet moments between sleep, if in another life he and I might have been friends. I had classed him as much when I spoke about him to Draven, but friends didn't do this to each other. Erianna was one, and I knew I could at least count on her.

"It's okay. I'm used to it."

"Not being thought about?" she questioned.

"No. I've always had people who care about me. I mean, no one has ever really asked how I feel about things. My mom never asked me how I felt about not having my dad or if I wanted to know him at all, and Astor, well, I think he just didn't think about what I wanted half the time. It's my fault. I never really spoke out."

"You should change that." She tipped her finger up against my chin, smiling. "Words have far more power than you know. Use your voice."

"To answer your question about becoming a vampire, I haven't thought much about it. I've spent my life being afraid of you all," I admitted. "I grew up surrounded by guild members, and it's no secret how they feel about the sangaree."

"For the most part, they're right. There are decent vampires, but most are not. They once were when there were laws in place. We're a predatory species, but so are mortals. The difference is we've justified giving into our darker natures, while mortals have not, and those who do are placed in prisons. The laws here are lenient." She looked over her shoulder, out at the mountains. Flurries of snow swirled in the wind, clouding the view. "I've been around a long time and have seen the worst of the worst. When you give anyone, immortal or mortal, the chance to enact their deepest desires from the anonymity of the shadows, the line between monster and person blurs. It's why I serve Laveniuess. I pray to him every day."

A small smile grew. She understood because I felt the same way. I often wrote about him in my notebooks. "I worship him too. That's why I enjoyed being at his birthplace so much," I said, thinking back to bathing in the glacial lake. "He helps us find the balance between dark and light."

"Exactly." Her sharp, brown eyes brightened. "I think, Olivia, we have been waiting for you for a long time. Once you've been shadow kissed, you will find all your senses heightened, including your empathy. That intelligence you possess to look beyond the confines of your mind and see more openly will be what makes you a great ruler. Maybe our best one yet."

Goose bumps spread over my arms. "Please don't do that."

"What? Refer to you as royalty? Because you are. You need to get used to it."

"I can't wrap my head around it sometimes."

"You are descended from an ancient and revered bloodline. Your grandfather was a powerful king, and his father ruled Sanmorte for centuries. Greatness is in your blood."

I cringed away from the idea of myself being any of those things. "I think you overestimate me."

She shook her head. "No, but I'm certain you underestimate yourself."

Sebastian cleared his throat, grabbing our attention. "We have an opportunity. The mortal princess from Asland is coming to strengthen alliances with Sanmorte tonight."

My nose scrunched up. "Wait, royalty from other kingdoms come here?"

Sebastian smirked. "There are far more secret alliances made between kingdoms than they'll have you believe, love." I was only glad his lousy mood had lifted. "Look at these plans for tomorrow night. Hamza and Kalon are in charge of negotiations for the ball in her honor tomorrow."

"A ball?"

Erianna shrugged. "They're old school here. I can't complain. I love dancing."

I would have never guessed it. "I've heard of Asland. Isn't it mostly desert?"

Zach nodded. "She wants to become one of us, but Sargon has been hesitant. The alliance with her father's kingdom is already weak. If we changed her, it would cause a lot of problems. He can't turn her down, however, as she's his main tie to Asland."

"Why does he care about a mortal kingdom?" I asked.

"He's always had plans of taking over more land," Sebastian answered. "We're only one land, and while no one has dared attack us for centuries, the mortals' weapons and technology only grow stronger with each passing year. So he's concerned, and rightly so, about an attack. Mortals are tired of vampires. Most want us wiped off the face of the planet."

"So he wants to invade and take over Asland?"

"Yes." Sebastian shoved his hands in his pockets. "With more space, he can change more people into vampires, strengthening our numbers. It's the same reason he holds the tournaments here."

"Tournaments?"

Erianna answered this time. "Of course, you don't know. Every year, the king holds a big event where enslaved mortals can come and fight for their freedom. They're given different weapons, evaluated on their skills, and made to fight each other until the strongest are left. Sargon then appoints them to our armies. He turns seven of them. It's why he ensures no one is shadow kissed without his approval, even though Nightshade has often turned people behind his back. He likes to decide who is turned, making it desirable so people will fight for it. He wants loyalty and thinks controlling everything around him will bring him that."

"You can't force loyalty."

Zach stood, holding the lists in his thin fingers. "Already, you're sounding like a better ruler than him."

"Thank you," I said slowly, unsure how to take his compliment.

Zach continued. "What if we don't need to kill Kalon? If we can get him to commit a crime instead, it would be enough to have him exiled."

"But I wanted to kill him," Erianna complained.

Zach shook his head. "We both know killing him is almost impossible with his security."

I chimed in. "I bet I can get him alone. He knows who I am and wants me dead. I bet if he had the opportunity, he would."

Sebastian gave me an incredulous look. "While you're at it, you can lie down and put that dagger to your throat for him to slit it with."

"Obviously, I wouldn't actually be alone. You would be there."

"It's too dangerous."

"But—"

"Zach's right. Besides, it would be too suspicious. Sargon wouldn't stop until he found out who was responsible. If we can break the illusion of loyalty Sargon has for his brother, that's a fate worse than death for Kalon."

"What's stopping him from telling the king who I am if he's exiled?"

Erianna jumped off the window ledge, cleaning her dagger against her sleeve. "He won't. As long as there is a chance, however small, that he might be able to take the throne one day, he won't say a thing. He doesn't want two people to contend with for the throne, and as long as you're here, you're a threat, but not enough to make him dangerous. You haven't told Sargon who you are yet, and I bet that's driving Kalon crazy. He'll want to know why."

"But won't he come back to try to kill me?" I contested, much preferring the idea of a dead Kalon.

"He won't be able to get close to the castle once he's exiled. If we can remove him, Hamza, and his military leaders, it'll be easier to take down the king. Once you're crowned queen, we can persuade the court's loyalty to your side. Sebastian's good at planting ideas in people's heads."

Sebastian smiled smugly. "I can send whispers to the right people of your return. I'm careful on who to trust, as you know."

"What about me? What can I do?"

Zach strode over to me. "Strengthen your powers, so you can fight when the time comes. Speak to your mom. Make sure she's on our side."

"She is," I snapped. "She hates my dad and what's become of her."

"Good," he said nonchalantly. "You will have one job, however."

"What's that?"

"Try not to get yourself killed."

Erianna sheathed her blade. "So, Zach, how are we going to get Sargon to exile Kalon?"

Zach smiled, throwing me off guard. "We have him turn the princess. Sebastian can plant proof that Kalon planned it to break the ties with Asland."

"Is it enough to make him exile his own brother?" Sebastian asked. "He's forgiven many of Kalon's treacheries."

"He can't ignore it if it's brought before the entire court," Zach responded.

Erianna headed toward the door. "It seems we have to plan." Her face lit up. "I'll start tracking locations."

Zach nodded curtly. "I'll take care of making sure she's turned."

"Couldn't this start a war?" I questioned. "Between Asland and Sanmorte?"

"Probably," Sebastian replied. "But we have no choice. Besides, you can remedy it soon enough."

I swallowed thickly, thinking about the throne I was destined to inherit, along with all its problems and enemies. "Rest up, love," Sebastian offered. "We have a long day tomorrow."

***

I lay perfectly still that night, thinking about my fate. Panic seized me when I thought about becoming a vampire or ruling a kingdom of them. I wished I could see my mom, but she hadn't come tonight either. Midnight sent a distant clock from the hallway chiming twelve. Unable to sleep, I turned on the dim light on my nightstand. Walls emerged from the shadows of the room. I yawned, stretching my arms and legs. How would it feel to lose my mortality and crave the blood of the people I cared about? Would Draven still want to be my friend? Of course he wouldn't. I'd never be able to see him again. It wouldn't be safe for him to visit a kingdom like this.

I imagined him now, sweeping the fireplaces or being used as a blood bag by some sangaree noble, and shuddered. I'd get him out of here soon, I told myself, calming my racing mind.

I rolled onto my side, and Sebastian let out a slight grunt, moving his head against the soft pillow. I wondered what he was dreaming about, so gentle, his expression softened. I couldn't help but look at him and think about the man who'd watched his family die and believed that he was alone in the world.

I tossed and turned until late into the night. When sleep finally came for me, it pulled me deep into nightmares that weren't too different from my world now.

TWENTY-FIVE

"Mom!" I wrapped my hands around her neck, burying myself in her coconut-scented hair. At that moment, I forgot she was a vampire. She was just my mom. She hushed me as she stroked the back of my hair. I let my emotions pour out on her, and tears of relief soaked my red cheeks. "How did you get away?"

She pulled me at arm's length, examining me from head to toe. She eyed my neck, seeming satisfied to see no recent bite marks. "That doesn't matter. I've found a way out for you." Her eyes glistened with hope, and in them, I found the same woman who evoked fear in the men at the guild.

"H-how?" I stuttered.

"For Draven too. He's going to help you escape. I trust him." She looked around my room, pausing on the pile of Sebastian's clothes he'd left sprawled out on the bed. "Tonight, when the court is distracted, you will be taken out of here under cover of darkness. I've paid two guards I trust to take you and Draven to the forest. There, two horses will be waiting for you. Cars are in short supply here, plus one would be too conspicuous. You'll ride out to the east. There's an abandoned beach by the tower. I've given Draven enough stagma to get you on a boat. The guild will take care of you once you arrive back in Baldoria."

My mind raced as I struggled to keep up with her words. Her manic expression told me she wouldn't take no for an answer. "What about Kalon? He knows."

She let out a tense breath, pacing in a circle. "I did wonder. Don't worry about him. I'll take care of him after you're gone."

I trusted she would, but I also knew what she meant by that. "You'll get yourself killed."

She brushed a thumb over my cheek as she pressed her lips together. "Honey, I'm already dead. All that matters to me is that you're safe."

"I can't leave you here."

"Don't worry about me." Tears threatened to soften her dark eyes. "You have your whole life ahead of you. Here, it'll be taken from you. If Sargon finds out who you are, he'll take your mortality, like he has mine." She placed her hand over where my heart thumped. "I can't allow that. I won't see you turned into one of them."

"It's just...." I fumbled with my ring, turning it around my finger. "My friends."

"Those vampires?" She shook her head. "You will not sacrifice your beautiful, mortal life for those whose fates are already lost to the shadows. You will go, Olivia."

"I-I don't know."

"Draven told me you've been practicing with your powers. He said you broke a window." She squeezed my hands in hers, the wrinkles around her eyes deepening. "I'm proud of you, honey. When you're out of here, you can continue to practice. You've already gone through enough."

I swallowed thickly, my hands shaking in hers. This was my mom, the woman I trusted beyond anything. Yet some strange piece of me said not to go along with her plan. "We have something in place too."

"Does it involve your escape?"

"Well, no."

"Then I'm not interested in hearing it. If those vampires are really your friends, then they'll want you to get out of here too. Go, be with Draven. Honestly, before Astor died, I thought you'd end up with him anyway."

"No." I slipped my hands out from between hers. "He's my friend, and Astor's alive. Well, sort of. He's a vampire and the reason you and I are here." I lowered my head. "He sold us out to Nightshade."

Her voice lowered, venom lacing her tone. "What?" I was worried the vein pulsing in her forehead might burst at any moment. Her hands balled into fists, her lips baring back, showing her teeth and two elongated fangs. "That traitor." She planted her feet apart, looking as if she might attack anything that moved.

"He's kept my identity a secret, but he did tell them the guild's secrets and how to get inside headquarters."

Her tongue darted around her fangs, the whites of her eyes showing as she contemplated a scene I didn't want to see. "I trusted him. We all did." Her voice rose until she was shouting. "You are in danger. Our life was utterly uprooted because he decided to be a coward."

"Mom." I went to touch her, but she stepped back.

"Don't try to take away my anger, Olivia," she warned. "I plan on honing it into a weapon against that traitor."

"He's not even here!" I spluttered. She'd always been a little hot-headed, but never on this level. Turning into a vampire had heightened her emotions and her senses, it appeared. "Astor's in the city."

"Then he's not unreachable." She bared her teeth, storming to the door. "Pack nothing for tonight. Raise no suspicions." She tempered her rage into her escape plan for me. "Draven will come to your room at midnight when the masquerade ball will be in full swing. Go, Olivia, and don't look back. I need to go before I raise suspicions."

She was gone before I could argue her point or calm her down before she went back to the king in such a foul mood. She didn't even say goodbye, but I got the sense she didn't want to be around me while feeling so out of control.

I walked to the window, looking out at the evergreen forest blotting out into the distance, disappearing into the fog surrounding the base of the mountain. My mom had handed me what I wanted on a silver platter, but if I left, it would be without her. I would never know if she was okay or bothered to try to stay alive. There were no doubts in my mind that she would kill Kalon and maybe Astor. Despite all he'd done, I didn't want him dead. Just hurt a little.

Then there was Erianna. She'd been so kind to me, one of the few people who'd tried to understand me and show me any compassion since I arrived. If I left, what would happen to her?

I shook my head, closing the drapes on the horizon. I wouldn't turn my back on the plan now, especially if it meant leaving my mom behind. I was sure she'd end up dead trying to protect me. I loved her more deeply than anyone, and I would not abandon her. Especially when she needed me the most. I had to do this, and it was almost time for me to get ready for the ball.

As if I was given a sign from the gods that I was on the right path, Erianna entered the room, smiling. I checked the clock on the nightstand. It was six o'clock already. "The festivities will begin soon. Do you remember what you need to do?"

I nodded slowly. "Yes. Stay with Sebastian, pretend to be enjoying my time with him, and not arise suspicions."

"Kalon will be watching. If you leave, he'll get suspicious."

"I know."

"Then get dressed. At midnight, the king has a surprise for everyone. I'm pretty sure that means it'll turn into a blood fest with mortals brought in for everyone to feed on. I'd suggest you leave before then."

"If everything goes to plan, won't the princess of Asland be dead?"

"A vampire, yes." She corrected me, even though that's what I meant. "Is everything okay?"

I touched my blotchy cheeks and freshly dried tears from my mom's visit. "Yes." I decided not to tell her about my mom's escape plan. It would only complicate things. "I was thinking about my ex." It was a lie because I'd thought less and less about him recently. His touches had become a distant memory, and the grief I'd felt for him had become a part of me, along with all my other trauma. All of it was changing me into a new version of myself which felt a hundred times stronger than the girl who was always afraid.

"He'll get his one day," Erianna promised and left me alone to get dressed.

I eyed the sparkly, floor-length gown made of material so thin it may as well have been a second skin. "Hopefully, we can keep the attention of a room," I said to the dress. "Because there's no backing out now." Magic tingled in my fingertips, begging to be used. I wasn't in control enough to attempt any spells yet, mostly because I was worried I would destroy another window. However, it was comforting to feel it there, as a part of me, ready to fight.

***

The ballroom was decorated in reds and golds, a decadent display of wealth and power. Women dripped with diamonds and silks as they held up thin masks, not hiding who they were in the slightest. Champagne flowed from mortal servers dressed in tuxedos. A fountain of blood poured, forcing bile up my throat.

It reminded me of the chocolate fountain from my seventh birthday party, but one made from nightmares.

Sebastian came up behind me, placing his hand against my back. I could feel his touch through the thin material. "You are stunning."

My cheeks turned a deep shade of pink as I looked at myself in the reflection of a champagne glass. I took it from the server and drank the whole thing. "Let's get this over with."

He smiled devilishly, grabbing a glass of champagne for himself. "Just what every man wants to hear. Ah." He pointed toward a bald man who looked in his late thirties. His brown skin shimmered as he moved under the low, yellow light. When he neared, I felt something change in me. It was as if I recognized him. "Olivia, this is Azia. The king's sorcerer."

He took my hand and placed a gentle kiss against my ring. "Olivia." My name sounded like chocolate on his lips. "It is a pleasure to make your acquaintance. His Majesty has spoken fondly of you."

It wasn't him I recognized, but his magic. I'd only felt the slight buzz of electricity around my mom before, of our magic speaking to one another. But then, I'd never met another sorcerer except for her. "It's a pleasure to meet you too."

"Congratulations on your engagement." His gaze moved from my ring to Sebastian. "I wish you both happiness."

I smiled, unable to resist his charms. "Thank you so much."

"Excuse me. Our king beckons." He gave us both a wink. "I'm sure we will see each other again very soon."

Once he was gone, I looked at Sebastian. "What a smooth talker."

"Yeah." He grinned. "Everyone likes Azia. He'll be a great asset to you." He didn't explain further, but I knew what he meant. When I was queen, Azia could be my sorcerer. Then, of course, I'd need one because I wouldn't be able to perform magic anymore. I'd lose the powers I just found, and that thought stole a piece of my heart. "We should dance," Sebastian said when I did a double take, looking at the door. Astor's eyes darted around the room as he searched for something or someone.

"What's Astor doing here?"

Sebastian frowned. "Maybe he realized what he lost." His hand inched down my back, pausing over the bottom of my spine in the gentlest touch. "I will find out. If he's here, then it's more than likely Gwen is, and potentially Velda."

"Wait." I tugged at his sleeve when he tried to turn, whispering gently. "If Kalon already knows, then surely Velda does. So she won't be a threat to me while we're in public."

He brought his lips close to my earlobe, sending a tingle of breath down the side of my neck as he whispered, "I'm not worried about her telling. Kalon will keep her in line. I just don't want her trying anything else."

"Like killing me."

"She would take immense pleasure in it, I'm sure." The veins in his hands bulged as he tensed. "Jealousy always was her weakest point."

"Why would she be jealous of me?" I asked.

He hesitated but hurried away before I could ask any further questions. Erianna walked to my side once he was out of sight, pulling Astor from the room. "Velda sees Seb as her... property," she answered in his place. "When she turned him, she controlled him until he broke free. Her daughter always had a silly crush on him, but for Velda, it had little to do with romance or actual feelings, if she could be capable of such things." She looked out over the room. "She likes to own things and people. If she even knows the difference between the two," she added, her lips twisting. "I believe Velda accepted, somewhat, that Seb would always be a free spirit, so it didn't hurt her, but now he's engaged to you, she might view it as you're trying to take what's hers."

"Is it possible to hate someone you've never met?" I arched a brow, thinking about the woman who'd destroyed his life. "Even if this was…." I mouthed the word "real."

"Regardless, she'll hate you for many reasons. One of them includes Kalon. So be careful around her if she is here."

Great. Another person to watch. "I'll have to find a spell to place eyes on the back of my head soon."

"Can you do that?"

I laughed. "No, but that would be terrifying."

Sebastian returned after my second glass of champagne. My mind fuzzed, and I looked around for my mom. She wasn't here. I clasped my hands together, grabbing another drink from a passing man. "Save some for the rest of us," Sebastian joked, placing the champagne on an empty tray nearby. "Astor's here because Kalon sent for Velda." Worry lined his sharp features, and his voice was hushed. "Act calm when you see them. She's going to try to make you scared. They won't try anything in front of Sargon."

The king drank from his throne, a jovial smile spreading across his face. "I'll stay calm." I was immediately drawn to the entryway when she entered. Gwen sauntered at her side, both mirror images of each other with their blonde hair and symmetrical, strong features. Velda looked straight at us, her nostrils flaring as she looked me up and down. She bared her teeth in a forced smile, showing off her long, sharpened fangs. A thinly veiled threat, but it was enough to make me want to tear her throat out. She was the one, after all, who'd come after me and my mom and utterly destroyed Sebastian's life.

I wanted her dead.

"Love." Sebastian touched my shoulder. "You're shaking."

"I'm angry. She thinks she owns you," I said simply, hoping that by some miracle she could hear me over the rising chatter and music. "Erianna told me."

"She has no power over me," he assured. "Zach is here. Good." He nodded in the direction of his friend, who wore his silvery hair in a long braid. Anna stood at his side, her eyes landing on me. Her smile was as gentle as ever, and I couldn't help but feel nervous for her in this room of bloodsuckers, even though I was just in as much danger here.

Astor saw me and took a step forward, but Gwen put an arm out, stopping him in his tracks. "Oh gods," I gasped, whispering to Sebastian. "If my mom sees Astor here, she'll kill him."

He looked around. "I don't see her."

I swallowed thickly. "Yet." I had to wonder if she was with Draven, finalizing the details of a plan I wouldn't be partaking in.

Thinking about escaping now felt wrong, leaving her to clean up everything. It would be admitting her life meant nothing.

Velda snarled when I looked at her. Sebastian stepped between our glaring exchange, stealing my attention. "Kalon is looking. So is the king. Don't think about Velda or Astor."

"She's taunting me with her face," I snapped.

"She's trying to get a reaction from you." He ran a hand over my cheek. "Hold on to me, *my love*." He twirled me into the center of the dance floor, dizzying me against my champagne high. "You are beautiful." His words should've had no effect on me. But hearing them, even if it was for show, sent butterflies swirling in my stomach. His fingers tightened against me, pulling me closer.

"Everyone's watching." The cinematic music resonated around the room.

"Good." His fingers entwined with mine as he slid his leg across the ground, pulling me with him in a move far too graceful to be my own. I looked around, pausing on Velda, whose eyes narrowed in our direction. Sitting next to her, Gwen looked as if she were trying to kill me with a single glare. Sargon smiled from his throne as our dance caught the attention of half the room, but it was forced. There was no lift in his eyes or lines forming in his cheeks.

Astor's face crumpled when I looked at him, his eyes burning with a pain I didn't want to open myself to. Others began to dance around us, but the figurative spotlight was still on us. The light notes of piano keys reached through the instrumental piece playing, and Sebastian twirled me around. Bringing his hand up to my cheek, he cupped my face. His gaze swallowed me as I fixated on him. "Don't worry about everyone else." His thumb brushed down to the corner of my lip. "They don't matter."

My shoulders relaxed as I settled my fingers on his chest. His signature scent of pine mixed with spice was suddenly intoxicating. I had to remind myself this was for show, a performance, but my body didn't get the memo, responding to every flicker of touch with a pulsating want for more. Gwen laughed loudly, snapping my attention in her direction.

Sebastian tangled his fingers in my hair and pulled my lips to his, almost touching. "Stop worrying about them. You're with me."

My hand moved to his bicep, and he laced his hand around my waist. My back arched to his touch, and the tips of our noses brushed together. I could feel his breath mixing with mine, and he inched closer. My heart raced as I lost myself in each fleck of silver in those night-blue eyes, finding the sensation of home in them.

Sebastian twirled me outward, loosening the curls from my bun, then pulled me back into his arms, leaving no distance between us. Breathless, I reached for his shoulder, and we moved together even when the music stopped playing and there was silence between songs.

Anticipation rippled between us when the music started up again. We could end this now. I was sure everyone believed our love story from that, but he didn't stop, and I didn't want to. The room melted away, and suddenly no one else mattered. I couldn't move my eyes from his. Surprise shone in his deep blues as he changed the way he looked at me.

I almost caught myself wishing this were real.

"Sebastian." I whispered his name as his grip grew more possessive. Before I could say anything else, his lips were on mine, stealing my next breath. We stopped dancing, and he cradled my head, deepening our kiss, stroking his tongue gently against mine.

I instinctively rocked against the feel of his legs pressed up against my whisper-thin dress. His gaze burned with desire, his muscles tensing as he pulled back, restraint pulling in his tortured expression.

My lips parted, barely a breath sweeping past them. He took my hand, and when we walked off the dance floor, someone spilled a goblet of blood all over the front of Sebastian's suit. He scowled, pulling me back so none of it splashed me. "Watch where you're going," he shouted after the sangaree who was mopping it up from the ground. "Did it get you?" he asked me.

"No." I looked over the dripping blood, shuddering. Then, darting between long tables of sangaree who sat watching, he pulled me out of the room. "That should be enough," he said once we were out of the throne room. "They'll think we stepped out to continue what happened in there."

I cleared my throat, shaking my head. "Right, yes, it seems we kept everyone's attention."

Hesitantly, he moved to touch my neck but stopped at the last moment. "You played that well," he said, his chest still heaving against his shirt. "I almost believed you."

"I was going to say the same to you."

He opened his mouth as if he wanted to say something but instead pushed his hands in his deep pockets, looking up at the vaulted ceiling. "You should go back inside and keep Kalon entertained while I prepare. Talk to the king. Zach will be watching you, so don't worry."

I pressed two fingers against my clavicle, tracing the way Sebastian had touched me. With one kiss, the memory of Astor felt somehow animated in comparison. Mentally kicking myself, I was reminded that this was a means to the end. I couldn't fall into some fantasy that didn't exist. He was a vampire, someone I'd never wanted to kiss, and he was only doing this because he wanted me to bestow mortality onto him. Soon enough, I would be reigning over a kingdom, and he would be free. He only cared about me as long as I put on a good show and went along with his plan. The kiss suddenly felt treacherous, and I took a step back. I wasn't doing this for him. It was for my mom.

"We shouldn't do that again," I stated firmly. "It was a mistake."

"Do you truly believe that?"

"Yes." I crossed my arms over my chest. "It crossed a line."

Something changed in his expression. "Fine. We'll keep to just touches." He caressed my hand, and I pulled it back. "Although, I didn't feel you complaining when you rocked up against me back there."

My face flooded with heat. "I was… That was nothing."

"It's okay." His lip curled up at the corner. "I won't pretend I didn't enjoy it."

With that, he left. Before I could turn back to join the ballroom, someone coughed from behind me. I whipped my head around and was greeted by Kalon's sadistic smile and hopeful eyes.

TWENTY-SIX

Kalon approached me from the other side of the foyer, taking his time, even though we both knew he could be in front of me in less than a second. Had he been watching us? Waiting from the shadows until Sebastian left?

I watched as his cloak dragged against the ground behind him. "Olivia." His gold-flecked, amber eyes narrowed. "Don't you look ravishing." He reached for a lock of my hair. I flinched back, but he grabbed a curl anyway, moving it like silk between two fingers. "I swore, in the sunlight, I saw a glimpse of red." His lip curved up. "I must have been hallucinating."

"Kalon." I addressed him by name instead of using his official title as prince.

"That was quite some show you put on back there for us. I almost caught myself believing it. Perhaps you really do love him."

My jaw clenched. "Of course I love him," I said, keeping up the pretense even though at this point I was sure there was little point.

His expression didn't falter. "It is an interesting arrangement, the two of you. Although I can see the allure with your being a sorceress," he toyed. "How long do you plan to remain at court, Olivia?"

He was testing me. Erianna said it would be driving him crazy, not knowing why I hadn't just come out and told Sargon who I was. "Not long," I assured him with a lie. "Sebastian and I will return to the city soon."

"Hmm. Oh, look, it's snowing," he stated as if I hadn't spoken at all. He curled his fingers over the stone ledge of the open arched window next to the staircase, looking out at the white-trapped horizon. "Take a walk with me," he commanded but didn't extend his arm to take like Sebastian or Sargon did. "Allow me to show you the grounds. They are spectacular in the winter months."

"Isn't it always winter here?"

"We have seasons, but they're nothing like Baldoria. Ismore is such a beautiful city. I've wanted to revisit, although I'm sure it has changed over the decades."

"I never said I was from Ismore."

"Ah." He touched the side of his head. "Old age. I must have imagined the conversation."

"I'm sure you've imagined lots of things."

His laugh was clipped. "You have your mother's mouth."

"You don't know who my mom is," I said quickly as we walked out through the double doors, forged from wood, carved into patterns of skulls and contorted bodies.

He turned to face me once we were standing on the frosted ground. "Let us not continue to lie to one another."

"Erianna is close by," I warned, my fingers trembling from the cold, or him, I wasn't sure. "They're in the hall. If you try to hurt me, they'll find out."

He lifted my chin with a bony finger, examining my face. "My dear niece, I have no plans to hurt you. Yet."

I guessed there was little point in lying. "When did you realize?"

He moved his finger and walked. I followed, anxious to be alone with him but also nervous to stay, unsure of what he would do if we didn't have this talk. "I'm not going to hurt you. The king already favors you. He foolishly thinks you will be joining his council and working for him." He rolled his eyes up to the sky. "People saw us leave together. It would be stupid of me to kill you out here, with witnesses placing us together. I'm not foolish."

That, I did believe. I hurried behind him, rubbing my arms as the cold sank through my skin, slowing my heart. He stopped, placing his cloak around my shoulders. I wanted to shrug it off, but it was the warmest thing I'd worn in weeks. Stealing the heat from the fibers, I begrudgingly matched his pace. "So, when did you know?" I repeated.

"I've seen a picture of you, dear Olivia. Velda took it for me when she was tracking you, but when you showed me your abilities at dinner, I knew for certain that the girl we'd tracked was really our lost princess. You see, we share the same gifts, Olivia. I can feel people's emotions, and it didn't go away when I was turned."

"Can you use it to change people's feelings?"

He shook his head. "No, I could only do that when I was a sorcerer."

My eyebrows shot up my forehead. "You were a sorcerer?"

"Naturally. Our father conceived me, Sargon, and our late sister with a sorceress."

Of course. It made sense when I thought about it. "Sebastian will be back soon."

"No, he won't. He's probably gone to cool down after that little dance of yours."

My mouth twisted in disgust. "You're vile," I said, not wanting to pretend anymore.

He only smiled, his expression unbothered. "Why haven't you told your father who you are?"

"I don't want any of this."

"Good," he said, his tone clipped. "The throne isn't for the faint of heart."

"I'm not scared," I said through gritted teeth. "I just don't want to become a vampire."

"Coming here wasn't the wisest idea, then."

"You see"—I chewed the inside of my lip—"I wouldn't have ever come here, but you sent your order to kill me, and then you took my mom."

"You're a threat," he explained as if what had happened was no big deal. "My brother rules this kingdom, but I pull the strings. So nothing happens here without it running by me first."

"I should tell Sargon how loyal his brother really is. I know you're making a play for his throne."

He ran a long nail around his chin, looking up in thought, his expression unmoving. "If you tell him, not that he would believe you over me, then I shall divulge your true identity, now that I know you don't want that. I can still kill a vampire version of you as much as a mortal one." He stopped walking and clasped his hands behind his back, his stare widening. "Be careful, niece. You won't always have your friends around to protect you. All it takes is you being in the wrong place at the right time, and your short, insignificant life will be over."

"Is that why you brought Velda here? Needed backup?"

"Don't bait me, child. I am not the same as most of these idiots here at court and will not be manipulated. You are in my home now, and it won't be long before you make a misstep." He turned on his heel and strode back to the castle as snowflakes caught in his red strands. "You should take the escape your mother is offering you tonight," he said as he left. "Either way, you won't last long. Keep the cloak," he added and walked back through the double doors, leaving me standing alone in the frost-bitten grounds with my heart in my throat.

He knew what my mom had planned, and she was far more competent than most. What if he knew about our plan, somehow? Even if I wanted to escape, I couldn't now, not with Kalon aware. He probably had members of Nightshade ready to follow and kill us after our escape. I had to let Sebastian know. I couldn't risk them getting killed. We'd underestimated him.

I climbed the staircases, suddenly aware of how unfit I was, as I stopped to catch my breath several times. Finally, reaching our room, I threw open the door. I could hear the shower spraying in the bathroom and Sebastian humming as steam crept through the cracks in the en-suite door.

"Sebastian," I bellowed, and the water turned off. "We need to talk, now." Urgency laced my tone.

His low voice resonated from the bathroom. "You know, I was just thinking about you."

I didn't even want to know what that meant, although it was probably him going over our plan in his head. "We can't go through with tonight," I said through the door. "When you left, Kalon found me and spoke to me. He confirmed he knows everything about me."

The door opened, and Sebastian emerged in a cloud of steam with a towel around his waist, hair dripping around the tops of his ears. "He said he knows about what we're doing?"

"Not exactly, but he knows other stuff," I said, not giving too much away. "Things he shouldn't know."

"We already guessed he was aware of who you are."

"It's not that." I cursed under my breath. "Look, my mom came to see me earlier and told me she planned for me to escape tonight with Draven. I wasn't going to do it," I said, noticing the grimace on his face, "but nonetheless, Kalon knew, and my mom isn't the type to leave loose ends. We've underestimated him."

"When were you planning on telling me about this escape plan?"

"You already don't trust me. So why would I bother?"

"Unless you were planning on leaving."

"I wasn't!" I scowled.

"Why not? Isn't it what you wanted?"

I placed my hand on my hip. "We don't have time for this right now. We need to tell Erianna and Zach to call it all off."

"Absolutely not. We don't know that he knows, and calling it off means putting your life in danger. Velda is here with half the order. Trust me when I tell you they will kill you, and it could be at any time. This is the only way to ensure your safety."

I balled my fists, my voice rising. "What if Erianna ends up paying the price for that? How many people are you willing to sacrifice for your mortality?"

"This isn't just about my mortality anymore," he shouted.

"Then what is it about?"

He opened his mouth, his tense expression melting as he stared, his eyes darting around my face. "It's about the future of Sanmorte."

My eyebrows pinched together. "Since when did you care about that?"

He didn't answer and turned away from me. "Go back to the hall and stay in sight of Zach."

I crossed my arms over my chest. "No."

"Fine, stay here and fuck our plan even more."

"We need to call it off."

"It's too late," he snapped. "It's already underway. I'm heading down there now."

"It can't be. I only just left Kalon."

"No offense, but a lot can happen in the time it takes for a mortal to climb all these stairs."

He had a point, however annoying it was. "I'm going to try to stop it."

"In about thirty minutes," he said, checking his watch, "the Princess of Asland will be a vampire, and you not being at the ball will be problematic. So I'm asking you to go down there. I will fly you down if you want."

"I am not going anywhere near your arms."

"You didn't mind it earlier."

"You are..." I searched for the right word. "Infuriating."

"And here I was thinking you were going to say something far more colorful."

I glared. "How is the plan already underway if she hasn't been changed yet?"

"Because Erianna already fed her my blood. She's been lacing her wine with it all night from their private rooms. Erianna is, let's just say, close to the castle taster and has sway over him."

"Oh, like romantically."

"Yes. Zach's job is simply to make sure the princess is killed while with Kalon."

"You didn't tell me any of this."

"We couldn't risk it."

I tapped my foot against the ground, seething. "I knew you didn't trust me. It's sad Erianna doesn't either."

"Erianna wanted to tell you. I said no."

"I'm done with you."

"Unfortunately, love, we're still in this together."

I let out a low, frustrated scream behind closed lips and stomped to the bedroom door. "I'm going to find Draven first, so he doesn't try to escape and get himself killed. He takes priority right now."

"You won't find him in time to be back." Worry replaced his mocking tone. "Let me fly you."

"No."

"Don't let your stubbornness get your friend killed and mine."

I paused, hating him for being right. "Fine, but I take zero pleasure in this."

He rolled his eyes and sped to the closet, then pulled out a new suit. I looked away as he got dressed and quickly washed his hair. At least he'd cleaned all the blood that the vampire had spilled on him in the ballroom.

"Sebastian." His name shakily left my lips. "How often do vampires spill things?"

"It can happen when they're drunk."

I thought back to the man who'd bumped into us as we were leaving. He appeared sober enough. "What if it was one of Kalon's men who spilled that goblet of blood on you, so he could get you out of the way? Kalon was waiting for me when you left to shower."

He fixed his top button and threw the blazer over his shoulder, hanging it from one finger. "If that's true, then his goal was only to get you alone. I won't leave you next time. Had I known you weren't going to go back inside, I would have stayed, blood-soaked shirt and all."

"I have a bad feeling."

"Have a little faith in us, Olivia." He swept me into his arms before I could argue my point and sped for the door. "Let's go find your friend and get back to the ball," he said as his wings extended and he flew down the wide, open staircases.

TWENTY-SEVEN

Astor saw us first as Sebastian landed in the foyer outside the ballroom, but he turned his back and disappeared before either of us could say anything. I peered inside as the music loudened, champagne flowed, and masks were lowered. Sangaree feasted on the necks of mortals on benches. Most seeming willing. Perhaps they liked the feeling that came with being bitten because while it was agony at first, that quickly turned into ecstasy.

"Nothing's happened yet," I said with a breath of relief. "How long do we have left until midnight?"

He turned over his tattooed wrist, checking his watch. "An hour and fifteen minutes until midnight. Where are you supposed to meet him?"

"Our bedroom, but I worry Kalon's people will be waiting for him there. I want to get to Draven before then." I looked around manically, my heart racing as the vastness of the castle became far more daunting. He could be anywhere.

"Careful," Sebastian said, grabbing my hand before I crashed into a tray of drinks carried by a server. I shook my head, muttering an apology as I darted through small crowds of vampires, finally bumping into Kalon.

"Young Olivia and her betrothed," he taunted, looking Sebastian up and down. "I am just stepping out. I have a young lady to entertain, but I am glad I could bump into you first. I thought I wouldn't see you again."

I gritted my teeth. "You thought wrong. I have no plans on escaping."

He lowered his voice to a whisper, smirking at Sebastian as he leaned down to my ear. "You have no reason to be afraid. I have no plans on stopping you from leaving. In fact, it would only be a good thing for me. I see you told Sebastian of your mother's plans. She would be most disappointed, especially after sending your friend looking for you. I don't imagine it will be long until he's climbing the staircases to your room." He scoffed, containing a smile. "Hmm. Well, enjoy your evening. I have somewhere I must be." Looking far calmer than he should, he strode away.

"There's no way he was ever going to just let me get away. He sent the entire order to find me," I snapped, confident no one could hear us over the rising chatter and music. Even with their hearing, it was too much noise all at once.

"Don't worry, he was just trying to get to you. We'll find Draven."

I turned, almost walking into a large ice statue of an anatomically correct mortal heart stationed above a river of red running down metal tubes from a box and into empty glasses. "Blood on ice," I said, my nose scrunching. "Are these things always so decadent?"

Sebastian nodded, making his way back into the foyer. "He's not in there."

I ran to the double doors and pushed them wide open to snow-flurried oblivion. The gusting wind caught my hair, freezing my eyelashes white. My lips trembled against the iciness until Sebastian reached my side, shielding me from the climate with one wing.

"Sebastian, if you have any idea where he could be, please, tell me."

"I'm not sure, but if we can't find him in the next five minutes, we'll need to stop. It is imperative we are in that ballroom, and in the king's line of sight, come midnight. It's bad enough we're not in there now."

"I can't leave my friend," I scolded as snowflakes landed on his wing, whooshing against them. "Unless…" I thought back to what Kalon said. "Of course, Draven will need to go up the stairs before going to our room. If we can intercept him there before, then Kalon's men won't get a chance to hurt him."

"We can't wait around on the stairs for the next hour."

"What if we go back inside and make ourselves seen? Then we can leave in half an hour. Draven should be close to going to our room by then, and we can grab him, and you can fly him down here, and we will still be here for midnight."

"It's not a good idea."

"Please." My fingers splayed over his chest, and I smiled, feeling his heartbeat race under my touch. "If I lose Draven, then I'll never be the same again. I'm already giving up everything. Please don't make me give him up too."

He hesitated, looking around, then finally closed the doors on the cold. "You're not going anywhere. At least one of us should be seen in there. I will leave, in forty minutes, and fly up. It'll only take me a minute to get to our room, and I'll search the stairs until I see him."

"Really? You'll do that?"

"Yes."

I wrapped my arms around his waist, and he stiffened against my touch, then relaxed, draping an arm around me. It was the first genuine moment between us where I wasn't thinking about scheming or hating or politics. I was just grateful. "Thank you." I pulled back. "I thought you needed to be accounted for too?"

"I won't be long, ten minutes at the most, and besides, no one should suspect me. When the princess dies, she will have been in the company of Kalon. He left to be with her now, to entertain her." He gave me a knowing look. "He's always enjoyed her since she first came to the castle. It's why I chose her, amongst other reasons."

"Why isn't she in the ball?"

"She doesn't like crowds and prefers to be entertained privately."

I arched a brow. "A royal who doesn't like the spotlight."

"It happens," he said, his hand gently pressing against my back. "Do we have a deal? I'll wait on the second staircase for Draven if you stay here?"

I swallowed thickly, gazing up into his sharp stare. He did have a better chance than me, and if it meant potentially bringing down Kalon, then I supposed it was for the best. Besides, the thought of climbing those stairs again sent a sharp dagger of pain through my lungs.

I nodded, and he linked his arm with mine. "For the next forty minutes, you need to loosen up and look like you're having fun. We need Sargon, his guards, and as many witnesses as we can gather that we were here at midnight."

Before he could escort me back inside, I pulled him to one side. "How will she die?"

"Erianna will have the taster give her a fast-acting poison. She will die in Kalon's arms, then wake up a vampire. Her guards will sound an alarm. She has around twenty of them, two of which are sorcerers."

"I bet Sargon hates that."

"Yes, he does."

"Where's Zach and Anna?"

"Anna's in her room on the side of the castle. Zach wanted her left out of this."

"Understandable."

"Zach is keeping watch over the princess and Erianna to make sure she doesn't get caught up in this. They should join us shortly after, but don't worry, no one will suspect them. They know what they're doing and know how to hide if need be."

My stomach knotted as he escorted us inside, smiling his pearly whites at Velda and Gwen as she sauntered in a skimpy, sequin dress next to her mom, who moved elegantly in a ballgown fit for royalty. "Sebby." Velda stepped in our path, reaching out to touch his chin. "I've been waiting for the chance to speak with you."

"Back off, bitch," I snapped, stepping in front of him.

Her eyes burned with a possessiveness that beat through the emotions, wrapping around us like a snake. "I wasn't talking to you, *mortal*." She somehow made the word sound like an insult. "Sebby would never speak to me like that."

"Stop calling him that."

His fingers squeezed gently on my shoulder and moved to my side. "It's okay, love."

"It's not. She's a vile snake and doesn't deserve to be anywhere near you."

Her thin, blonde eyebrows raised. "I was led to believe this engagement"—she snapped my hand in hers and wrenched me toward her to examine the ring on my finger—"was a facade, but perhaps you really do have feelings for him. It's a shame they'll never be reciprocated."

"Let her go." Sebastian took a step toward Velda, and she laughed, dropping my hand as if it were made from hot coal.

"Fear not, I don't want to touch her any more than I have to."

I rubbed my wrist, shaking my head as I glared at her up and down. "Come on, Sebastian. Let's dance."

"I was going to ask him the same question, and I'm sure he'd rather dance with me. That is, unless you want me to talk with the king right here about your treacherous little plans, or maybe I'll save myself the time and just rip your throat out."

Of course Kalon had told her everything. "You wouldn't."

"She would," Sebastian said, his tone thick with rage.

"No." I placed my hand on his chest, standing between them. "She's bluffing. Kalon has plans in place, else I'd already be dead, and Sargon would know the truth."

He tilted his head, and she observed him. I realized, out of everyone in the room, she was the only one he might fear even the slightest amount. She had, after all, killed his entire family in front of his eyes and then kept him prisoner.

"Goodbye, Velda," I said and pushed past her.

Sebastian sped to me, standing in front of me, arms crossed in case she tried to make good on her threat, but she didn't. Just as I expected, she left, with a dangerous glint in her eye that told me this wasn't over.

Gwen followed, and they met with Astor, whose smile dropped on seeing me. I turned away from him and to Sebastian. "That felt good."

He grinned, his dimple deepening. "That was pretty badass. I've never seen anyone stand up to her like that."

"I'm sure I'll pay for it later."

"Not if I have anything to do with it."

363 REBECCA L. GARCIA

"So you're not still mad at me?" I questioned. "I really had no plans on leaving."

"No." He peered over my shoulder. "Sargon is watching."

We walked out in the line of view of the throne, and Sargon lifted a glass in our direction. Sebastian shot him a charming smile, then leaned down in what looked like to kiss my cheek, but instead, he whispered, "Let's have some fun."

"Like what?"

He pulled me over to the tents, sitting us both on the benches next to them. Sargon glanced over, then back to Hamza, who only occasionally gave us a venomous glare. He hated seeing me with Sebastian, and when I turned, I saw Velda and Gwen looking in our direction too. "They all think they own us," I said, shaking my head.

His fingers brushed the inside of my arm, dancing down to my wrist. "Then we will show them they don't."

I caught myself enjoying the jealousy in Velda's eyes as Sebastian flickered touches down to my hand, and even Gwen looked annoyed. Astor's expression hardened, and I smiled toothily, leaning back against Sebastian's taut chest, placing myself on his lap.

"I think they're angry."

He brushed a kiss against my neck, trailing kisses to my clavicle. "I didn't think you had it in you."

"You wanted me to put on a show," I said, my next breath catching as he whispered against my skin.

"How do you feel?"

"Powerful," I admitted, my face flooding with heat.

"Don't be embarrassed." He moved back the fabric of my skirt, running his hand along the inside of my leg, lightly touching the inside of my thigh. Wetness gathered between my legs, and I felt his length harden under his pants. My heart palpitated, and the champagne lifted me to new highs as his fingers inched a breath higher.

Astor's jaw slacked, and Velda's glass cracked in her hand as I pressed myself against him, enjoying the feel of his hard length twitch against the curves of my buttocks.

Hamza peered over, and I turned to face Sebastian, giving in to the feeling of being watched and maybe even liking it. "You're enjoying this," I said, bringing my lips closer to his. "Don't you care that they're watching?"

He pressed his hands over my thighs, and I rocked my hips against him. "I want them to know you're mine."

"Even if I'm not?"

"Yes." He tangled one hand in my hair, bringing my lips crashing against his in a knot of lust. Desire built through me, tingling down from my stomach to my legs, until all I wanted was for him to take me on the table. I wrapped my legs around his waist, hooking him closer.

This was so unlike me, and so far, it was just kisses and touches, nothing too far, but as our kiss deepened, he twisted me from view, running a finger under my skirt and over the line of my panties.

I could feel the wet slicking through, and I rubbed myself against his fingers as he pulled back, his intrusive gaze bleeding into mine. I should have told him to stop, but every fiber of my being wanted him to continue, to take me against the wall and fuck me until I couldn't remember why I was hurting or what I was fighting for.

He slipped a finger under my panties, groaning as he touched my desire, silking it between his fingers. My nipples hardened under my dress as he pushed down, leading featherlight touches, then paused.

I moaned, and he pulled my face into his neck, noticing he'd blocked me from their view. "When I take you," he said slowly, restraint tight in his features, "it'll be somewhere I can really enjoy you."

My legs weakened, and I rocked up against his touch. He pulled back, pressing his fingers to his lips. "You don't want this here," he said, and I spotted my mom over his shoulder. Fortunately, she hadn't seen me yet.

My cheeks pinkened and the desire slowly dissolved. "Oh, gods."

"No, love, just a vampire," he said with a smirk, but his eyes undressed me where I stood. It took everything for me to fold the dress back over myself and let him move away. "I have to find Draven. As much as I want to finish this, I know you wouldn't forgive me if I let him die."

"Please, go," I pleaded, and he held me close.

"Give me a minute to cool down," he said, dancing with me in front of the throne. After a few more sways across the room, he stepped back. "I'll be back soon."

I watched him speed away, and I twirled on the dance floor, facing an open space. Hurrying toward a passing server, I took a glass of champagne, then looked at the old grandfather clock next to the ice sculpture. I hiccupped after downing half the glass, then smiled lazily in the direction of the sorcerer Azia, who glided around the room with the grace of a panther.

Velda had left with Gwen and Astor during our show, and I couldn't help but feel glad they saw it. I wanted Astor to know I wasn't his anymore and for Velda to see that Sebastian could never be hers. Even if he wasn't mine, she didn't need to know that.

I could still taste him as I looked at the groups of drunk vampires, laughing, chugging back glasses of champagne. I noticed some had mixed their blood with it and grimaced.

While I knew everything we did was for appearances, my body had betrayed me, wanting him so much I almost let him put his fingers inside of me in front of a room filled with vampires. What the fuck was I thinking? He was using me for his own means, and how many mortal women had he fucked then left? But every time I thought about him, I couldn't help but flush, unable to push his thick lips, soft strokes, and devilish smile from my thoughts.

"Sweet Olivia," Kalon said from behind me, his voice sliding over me like ice snapping me from my fantasies. "Care to dance?"

What was he doing here? Sebastian said he was entertaining the princess in her room. I made a move to walk away, to warn Sebastian, but Kalon caught my arm before I could make it a foot. "Let's not make a scene," he said, digging his nails into my skin. "The king is watching."

"I thought you were entertaining your guest?" I asked nonchalantly. "Did she grow bored with your presence?"

He let out a short, clipped laugh, his amber eyes narrowing as he swept me around. "I wanted to make sure I was here for midnight. Sebastian is truly far more gullible when he's focused on you."

Every hair on the back of my neck stood on end when he touched me. I opened my barrier to see if his was down, but he blocked me, so I did the same in return. We didn't look away from each other as we waltzed, a staring competition between cat and mouse.

I slowed as I circled him, then placed my hand on his as he spun me. "Why?"

"All the best things happen after midnight."

My intuition was right.

He knew something. I tugged my hand away, but he held me still, warning dancing in his eyes. "It's rude to leave mid-dance."

My gaze burned with fury. "I want a new partner."

He kicked my leg until I slipped back like a puppet trapped in a deadly waltz. "I'd rather you stayed."

I glanced at the door, hoping Sebastian had already found Draven and had returned, but he was nowhere to be seen. I looked up at the throne. Sargon's crown tilted around his forehead as he enjoyed what could be his hundredth glass, for all I knew.

It was hard not to notice my mom when she stepped behind the throne, standing at the king's side dressed head to toe in a blue pantsuit, standing out from everyone else in their formal wear. But then, she never did care to fit in.

I opened my mouth, desperate to get her attention, but Kalon pulled me away from their line of sight and into a crowd of thirty-something sangaree. "Let me go."

His grip tightened. "It's not long until the main event. I assure you; you don't want to miss it."

My eyes widened. "What did you do?"

His thin lips curved up into a sadistic smile. "Nothing more than what you wanted to do to me."

My nostrils flared. "I'll tell the king everything."

"No, you won't."

"Where's Draven?"

He let out a low chuckle. "He was never in danger."

"What?"

"Oh no." His shoulders slumped as he forced a regretful expression. "I hope you weren't looking for him, or worse, you sent Sebastian to the staircase."

I gritted my teeth. "You slipped that in on purpose. You wanted this."

"I have been nothing but honest with you. I truly had no plans to stop your escape. You and your friend could be on your way into the forest now, but, well." He danced his hand in the air.

"I need to find Sebastian."

He pulled me back, turning my body against his so I could watch the main doors to the room, and the clock chimed twelve. Loud chimes pierced through the music, and with them came a bloodcurdling scream. "It's time for the main event."

TWENTY-EIGHT

I wrestled against Kalon, smelling his champagne breath from over my shoulder. The eyes of the sangaree were not on us. In their hazed states, they could barely focus on each other.

A dark beat was carried in the music's undertone, ensnaring people's senses, so most danced like no one was watching. Their hands slid over each other, making mine and Sebastian's moment appear as a blip in a sea of nudity and decadence.

Alcohol sprayed over the uneven ground, splattering up the front of my dress as a mortal dancer dropped her drink, shattering glass on the stone. I noticed her neck first, defaced with a dozen bite marks leading down to one over her left breast. Then, shrugging, she walked away from the mess under the draped arm of a vampire.

The tents were little more than for show now, with the drinks lowering inhibitions, so there was little point in hiding anything. Vampires of the most eloquence embraced their shadow sides, and I wondered what else the king had laced into the alcohol.

Kalon's long nails dug into my hips, sure to leave a mark under the sheer fabric slicking around my trembling body.

"Get off me," I stormed, earning only a chuckle tickling against the top of my ear. I was sick and tired of being pulled around, fed on, and forced under the will of lesser people.

My darkness purred inside, and I called for it, thrumming my powers to the surface until they ached my fingertips, begging for release.

"I said get off."

Shockwaves rippled from my hands as I whispered a touch against his, jolting him backward. My lips curved up when his disbelieving gaze found me, realization swimming in those dark-honey pools.

I took a step forward, and he flinched under my touch. Then, sliding my arms around his neck, grappling my fingers around the back of his head, I allowed the full depth of my magic to envelop us both, frying his red curls in a blaze of smoke and flame.

His scream splashed through the room, pinching the music and quieting the musicians. Sangaree fell around us, leaving an empty circle in our space as sobriety reached through their shocked expressions, the haze lifting.

Sargon's hands were on my shoulders first, wrenching me backward. Kalon's skin melted on my fingertips, sending the stench of rotting flesh around us. "What did you do?" My father's thick voice hit me as he slammed me against the ground, knocking the air from my lungs.

"Ask your brother," I hiccupped, bathing in the dominant energy quaking in my bones, feeling power emanating from my core. I had never felt so fearless and satisfied in the knowledge that I had hurt him, and even more so that for once, I could protect myself against my enemies.

Velda rushed to Kalon's aid, whooshing past me in a gust of air. Propping myself up from the floor, I half sat up, peering around Kalon to Azia, who watched me from between both thrones, intrigue burning in his expression.

My mom was already gone from his side, and when I blinked, forcing my eyelids open to a starry vision, she was at mine. "Take my hand." She slipped her other arm around my waist, lifting me to standing.

I leaned up against her, catching my breath. A second bloodcurdling scream tore through the party, and the music stopped altogether. Only this time, the sound hadn't come from Kalon.

"Sebastian." His name followed a gasp from my lips as I found my footing.

Uneasiness crept over me as I followed the rest of the room into the foyer, pushing my way through the crowded scene until

I fell out into reason for all the commotion. A woman with tight, black curls tinged red from the blood soaking through them lay at the bottom of the staircase, her leg twisted at an unnatural angle. Crimson seeped from her skull, running rivers into cracks in the stone floor.

I raised my fingers to my lips, looking around for any sign of Erianna, Sebastian, or Zach, but none of them were near. A few feet from the dead woman, a bent tiara of white gold glittered, telling me this was the body of the princess of Asland.

A hoard of questions knotted in my mind. The plan was to poison her, not for this violent display, and I wondered if Sebastian's blood ever made it past her lips. Somehow, in all the plotting and scheming, I had forgotten about the mortal woman tied up in the middle of this. Closing my eyes, I understood how easy it was to disregard the value of life when it was talked about in the same way as a prop amongst a plot to get what we wanted. Had I become just as much of a monster as everyone else in the castle?

Bile burned my throat, stinging my tongue as I held my hand over my stomach. The princess didn't appear to be turning into anything other than the corpse she was. Her wish to become a vampire was gone, and the weight of her death hung over my head like a dark cloud. Velda and Gwen pushed me out of the way, dropping to their knees. Velda pressed her fingers into the blood, then lifted them to her lips. Astor's arm brushed mine as he watched them, his hardened glare difficult to ignore.

"She has vampire blood in her veins," Velda announced to the room.

Inhaling sharply, I tried to move back, feeling desperate to find my friends when a path was made between the sangaree for Sargon and my mom, who wore a false crown with no power. Her fingers twitched, meeting mine for a second, a gesture that ballooned my heart. I needed her help, especially knowing that Sebastian could be in trouble. I'd sent him up to the staircase, and Kalon had wanted that to happen.

This was all a part of his ploy, and I'd tangled Sebastian in the center.

Velda looked over her shoulder after examining the body and shook her head. "She has bruises on her forearms."

Sargon's expression darkened, his lip twitching as his gaze climbed up the wide staircases, looking through the space leading to the top floor. "Someone must have thrown her."

Kalon stepped to his brother's side, wearing the stench of burnt hair, his charred clothes proof of what my magic could do, even though his body had already healed. "Asland will see this as an act of war." His low voice resonated through me.

I may have gotten in a good hit first, but he was getting the last laugh. I just didn't know how yet.

"Enough," Sargon barked, showing his darker side he kept hidden behind the charm. "Who did this?"

"Nobody leaves this foyer," Kalon shouted, his voice echoing around the room. "We will get to the bottom of this," he assured Sargon.

I prayed behind the darkness of my closed eyes that Erianna had hidden and Kalon hadn't gotten to her first. In the little time I'd known her, she'd become more like family to me than most felt in a lifetime. Her kindness and strength were a rarity in this world, and against her nature and position, she had made me feel cared for.

If she died, I couldn't forgive myself for not pressing Sebastian harder to stop this plot and leave. My intuition had screamed at me that he knew, but I ignored it against my better judgment, and for once, I hated being proven right.

I didn't want to think about what Sargon would do to them, or worse, what punishment Kalon would whisper is most appropriate. My chest sank when I realized that not only was Sebastian somewhere up on these staircases when the princess was thrown off one, but so was Draven.

The princess's eyes flung open, a loud gasp escaping her lips. She reached around the ground, sitting upright with panicked breaths. When she opened her mouth, fangs protruded through her gums.

"Who did this to you?" Sargon demanded.

I stepped back through the crowd, gliding to be out of sight as quickly as possible when the immortal words left the princess's lip, stunning me to the spot.

"Sebastian Vangard," she spluttered. "H-he fed me his blood and pushed me off the staircase."

I turned slowly, watching her performance through the cracks in the crowd. She pointed a shaky finger at Kalon, tears in her brown eyes. "He was trying to frame you."

Sargon's shoulders slumped, his crown catching the light from the chandelier when his own wings expanded in a glory of purple and silver. "Then he will die for it."

"No," I shouted, turning everyone's heads in my direction.

Kalon raised his voice, pointing at me with a sneer. "She was an accomplice. Seize her."

My magic pulsated under my skin, ready at my fingertips. "You can try." I poised to attack, planting my feet apart. Sebastian stepped out from the shadows of the staircase, his hands in his pockets as if all this was no big deal.

"There's no need, love." His eyes slid over me, moving to meet Sargon's fury. "She had nothing to do with it."

"Neither did you," I snapped, but no one was paying attention. What was he playing at?

"Take them both to the dungeons." Sargon's voice lost power as his sentence slowed. "To await their execution."

"No." My eyes bulged, and when two sangaree flew at me, I willed all my power into their chest, pushing my hands against the guard's breastbone. Electricity tore through his body, disintegrating his clothes into ash.

"Don't touch her." Sebastian's roar pierced my heart, and I fought back against the second vampire who tied my wrists at my back. Magic flamed through my veins, pouring out into the guard who fell backward, screeching.

A third guard ran toward me, and my powers faltered, only for a second. "Move." The word belonged to Erianna, who appeared from the steps behind us and whizzed an ax through the air. It cut deep into the vampire's neck, nearly detaching it from his body.

"Seize them all," Sargon boomed, and twenty of his military rushed the three of us.

An arrow ripped the wing of one, and Zach ran at the speed of light, reaching us in seconds. The fight blurred against my mortal senses, and before I could grab one of them, a chain was wrapped around my neck.

Suddenly, my magic faded, numbed deep into my center. I found my mom amongst the chaos, the lines around her eyes deepening. Warning circled my eyes. If she intervened now, it would be obvious who I was. It was bad enough she helped me to my feet after I'd torched Kalon.

"Erianna," I called through a panicked breath when I saw her dragged down to the ground, chains tightening around her arms and legs.

Behind her, Sebastian was cuffed, forced to his knees.

"Sebastian," I said breathlessly when Azia appeared before us, his arm extending closer. I closed my eyes, feeling his finger touch my forehead, muddying my mind, weakening my body until blackness consumed me and all the fight in me evaporated.

TWENTY-NINE

Icy winds slithered under the heavy metal door of the dungeon, sliding between the crevices of the stone walls. Sebastian's broken body emerged from the shadows of the room as an aniccipere opened the door, flickering candlelight into the space. He was taken three hours ago for questioning by a soul vampire with a desire for violence.

I locked eyes with him across the room, swallowing thickly when I saw the long talons of the creature curl over his shoulders, his hands wrapped around Sebastian's throat.

Every moment we shared hovered between us, and I suddenly realized I couldn't leave him here, in the depths of a castle awaiting his execution date. The creature closed the door, leaving the candle melting in an alcove of the wall.

"Sebastian," I whispered, crawling as far as my chains would allow, dragging them across the uneven ground.

He raised his face to meet mine, untamed power hidden behind those deep-blue eyes. His blood-smeared lips parted, a cough escaping between them. He'd healed from whatever injuries that thing had caused him, but the reminiscence of them lingered on the ash covering his crumpled shirt with missing buttons and crimson-soaked pants.

"What did they do to you?"

"It doesn't matter." He dragged himself against the wall, resting his head back on the stone, his eyes rolling up to the gray ceiling. "You have to tell them."

"No." I prepared myself another argument, wishing I had Erianna here to back me up, but she was stuck in a distant cell with Zach. They were charged with interfering with an arrest and, fortunately, hadn't been implicated in the plot to kill the princess and frame Kalon, a crime Sebastian had taken full responsibility for to save them.

The king was going to kill him that night until I said I was involved too, and Sargon was forced to open a trial. I was a sorceress, and killing me meant him giving up a slice of potential power. It was enough to pause him, to keep us down here. It had been two days since we'd been caught, and we'd been housed in the lowest level of the dungeon meant for the worst of the worst prisoners.

"They will kill you." Sebastian rolled his shoulders back. They'd sent him cups of blood at first but laced it with some slow-acting poison that weakened his body so he couldn't break out. The latest of his food sat cold in a cup in the center of the cell.

"You should drink," I said, ignoring his statement, one I'd thought over a hundred times since being in here. Lightheaded, I attempted to stand, but my legs buckled under my weight. "Drink from my wrist."

He side-eyed me. "You're already weak. I won't take what little life is left in you."

"I can take it," I urged, although I had to wonder if he was right.

They hadn't given me a scrap of food since my arrest and very little water. Parting my parched lips, I dropped back against the wall, exhaustion pulling the strings of my consciousness.

"No, you can't."

I whispered a touch against the poppy bruise on my temple, left over from one of the soul vampires who'd knocked me out once Azia's spell to keep me subdued wore off. My magic was suppressed by the heavy chain around my neck, throbbing aches into my shoulder blades and top of my neck.

"I wish I could heal you." He winced as I touched the purple around one eye. I hadn't seen myself in a mirror since they'd beaten me to bring me here, only catching a half-glance in the reflection of Sebastian's cup, but going by Sebastian's expressions, I guessed I looked like hell.

"Your blood is laced with poison," I spluttered.

"I know." He blew out a tense breath. "You must reconsider." He continued his plight. "Only one of us has to die."

"I'm not leaving you to be killed," I whispered, my knees knocking together as I huddled my arms around them, pulling my legs to my chest.

"Do you plan on dying by my side? That's not smart, Olivia. You still have a chance here."

"I'm not leaving." I thought about my mom and the way she'd looked at me before I was made unconscious and dragged away. She would try to find a way out of this for me, and I only hoped it wouldn't cost her too much, like her life. "We underestimated Kalon."

He shook his head. "No, I underestimated you. I should have listened when you said he knew."

I fell silent, hating seeing him beat himself up like this. The life glistening behind his smirks and playful glances was gone, replaced with a constant look of regret. When I lowered my barrier, I only felt the same emptiness that came with my depression. I wanted to take it away, but he wouldn't let me.

"If you drink from me," I said slowly, "you can break out of here."

"It would take a lot more blood than you can give to give me the strength for that."

"Then change me."

He narrowed his eyes, sitting straight for the first time since being stuck in this cell. "I don't think—"

"It's my destiny anyway. You said it yourself, and the plan was always for me to become queen and turn anyway."

He averted his gaze, sliding it to a dark corner. "I know it's not what you really want."

"Since when do you care what I want?"

He rolled his shoulders back, then scoffed. "Do you think I don't care about you?" His eyebrows gathered together. "Because if that's true, then I've done a poor job of showing you."

My stomach fluttered, despite the dismal situation. "So you do?"

"Of course I do."

My heart palpitated, mostly because I wanted to ask him what that meant, but at the same time, I didn't want to sound like a child asking how he liked me because he could just mean as a friend, in the same way he felt about Erianna.

My stomach dipped when her name echoed in my mind. "What will they do to Erianna and Zach?"

He grimaced. "I don't know."

"We can help them." I inhaled sharply, readying myself for the inevitable. I'd never wanted to be a vampire, but the more I tried to hide from my fate, the more it kept catching up to me. "Once you change me."

"You don't want that."

"It was our plan all along. You knew this was going to happen. This is what you wanted."

Covering his wrist with one hand, he inhaled sharply. "Things got"—he blew out a tense breath, his eyes climbing to the ceiling—"complicated."

My eyebrows pinched together. "What does that mean?"

His shoulders hunched as he stared above, refusing to answer.

"Give me your blood then bite me," I demanded when he refused to answer me. "It doesn't matter about the poison if I'm going to die anyway. Just suck me dry and gather your strength."

"Then what?" he snapped, moving his intrusive gaze to meet mine. "We break through the door and fight our way through a small army of aniccipere and escape a heavily guarded castle?"

"My mom got away once."

"She was in a better position than us." He lifted his hands, chinking the chains. Somewhere in the distance, a pipe dripped water, and a rat scurried, squeaking into the darkness.

"It's the only choice we have."

"No, it's not." He struggled with his words, shaking his head. "You can tell them who you are. Sargon will forgive your sins and you can live."

"He'll turn me anyway, so who cares?"

He rubbed his temples, his tone sharpening. I'd never seen him so torn, as frustration burned behind his eyes. "With him, you can get away. Gain his trust, like you tried to do with us at first."

Heat pinkened my cheeks, creeping through my body. "How did you know?"

"You went from hot to cold, then hot again ten times a day trying to play nice. It was amusing to watch."

I licked my lips. "Then you know, I'm not good at it."

A ghost of a smile crossed his mouth. "It's that sharp tongue of yours, but I know you can do it. You need to survive this."

"I thought you wanted me to be queen."

"I thought so too."

The silence was deafening. Slowly, I slumped farther down the wall. "I don't want him to know who I am, and I will not leave you or Erianna and Zach to your fates. She's been nothing but amazing to me, and honestly, you have too." I let out a long exhale. "If I give up on you, then I'm just as bad as Astor."

"Don't say that."

"It's true. If I can't forgive him for saving himself and betraying his friends, then how could I forgive myself for doing the same?"

"This is nothing like that!" His fists balled as he captured my stare from across the dungeon. "Don't let some screwed-up sense of right and wrong get in the way of your survival. Do you want to die? Because they will take you outside and cut your head off along with mine, and all of this would have been for nothing."

"Not if you change me. We can get away."

"You being a sorceress is the only reason we're still alive, but it won't last long. Even Sargon will have to come to terms with the crime you foolishly admitted to. He can't pardon such treason."

I blinked back tears. "I hate her."

"Who?"

"The Princess of Asland. She lied through her teeth about you."

"She was told what to say by Kalon, I'm certain. He offered to turn her once he realized our plan."

"How did he find out?"

"Erianna's taster friend may have spilled the truth, or more likely, one of our conversations was overheard. He has spies all over the castle. I should have communicated with you on paper only." He bent forward, burying his head in his hands.

"Stop blaming yourself. This is on all of us. We shouldn't have been stupid enough to think we could have taken him on in the first place."

"If you've lost faith," he stated, "then we're all screwed."

"I was going to say the same thing to you. What happened to surrendering and having faith?"

"You got dragged into it with me, as did Erianna and Zach. I don't even want to think about what they're doing to Anna without Zach's protection."

A lump formed in my throat. I blew out a fogged breath, rubbing my arms to try to instill some measure of warmth into my icy skin. She hadn't even crossed my mind until now. "I've never been much good at anything, really," I admitted after a few minutes. "But since being here, I've finally found my powers."

"Which is why you can't lose them to vampirism. There's a reason they call it a curse."

"If only I could remove these chains."

"Only Azia can take them off," he said regretfully.

"I assumed as much." I bit down on my bottom lip, running my tongue over the dried cracks. "When I was with Astor, he let me believe I wasn't supposed to amount to much, and that was okay. At the time, I thought he accepted me when my mom wouldn't, and not having any expectations was comfortable. My mom was always pushing me, and until now, I thought it was because she was disappointed in me. I know now she wanted me to be the best version of myself."

He nodded, and I coughed, my chest heaving from the dry, cold air.

"I never thought much of myself, but now I think about how I set fire to Kalon and...."

"You did what?" he choked out.

"Oh, yeah, you weren't there. Kalon wouldn't let me go, so I electrocuted him."

"Fucking damn. I'm sorry I missed it."

"Me too," I smirked. "But that's why I can't give in yet. If I'm going out, I'm doing it on my own terms, so please, change me."

"We will die trying to escape here."

"Maybe, but at least we'll have a chance."

"Olivia—"

"Please, Sebastian, don't ask me to tell Sargon again. I'll never do it. I'm asking you to turn me. At least, think about it." I yawned, fighting against the tiredness, but the lack of sleep slowly dragged me under.

"Get some sleep. I'll think about it." Something changed when he looked at me, and I yawned again, my eyes watering.

"Promise me."

"I promise."

Closing my eyes, a dreamless sleep found me before I could utter another word.

THIRTY

I swore I could feel arms around me while I slept. For a moment, I wondered if Sebastian had lifted me in his and carried me from my cell when I heard my mom's voice. "You were close to death. My poor baby." An icy hand pressed against my forehead. I moved onto my side, noticing the absence of stone. "She still has a fever. This is all your fault."

Sargon's tone snipped hers. "How could I have known? You should have said something."

She clicked her tongue, parting my lips with a goblet, pouring a thick, cloying liquid down my throat. I choked, spluttering a cough as my eyes peeled back to reveal my mom, the king, and Azia.

"What's happening?" I sat upright, my heart racing, spindling lightness into my head.

"Careful, honey. Lie back down. You're severely malnourished. Sargon's given you some blood, but it's taking some time to work."

I gagged. Is that what that liquid was? "Sebastian."

"Don't worry about him. He won't be bothering you again."

I fisted the sheets, noticing I was lying on a four-post bed in a room I didn't recognize, decorated with the finest furnishings. "Where is he?"

Sargon spoke this time, his eyes softening when he strode to me. "He's being executed today."

"No."

I exchanged glances with my mom, her eyebrows pinched together as she stood, lost for words.

"You can't mean that? He kept you prisoner."

I moved back against a hoard of pillows. "He didn't. Who said that?"

"Sebastian did. He told us you had no part in the princess's death." My mom brushed a lock of hair back. "He called on the guards in the night, trying to bargain your identity for his life."

It suddenly dawned on me when I stared into the eyes of my father, a mirror of my own. He knows.

"Daughter."

The word chilled me.

"Sebastian saved me. He can't die." Panic seized me, and suddenly the air felt thicker than I could bring in.

"He was willing to give you up to save his own skin," Sargon snapped. "He doesn't care about you, and we know he hid you from me. Why didn't you tell me the truth?"

My heart felt ten times heavier as he approached me, a gentleness in his movements, reserved only for me. I couldn't tell him it was because we planned on killing him, but I couldn't believe Sebastian handed me over like that. He promised he'd at least think about turning me so we could escape, and now he was going to die anyway.

Anger rolled in my bones, but I didn't want to show it. I felt like an idiot for trusting him, but I couldn't let him die. "Dad," I said, softening my tone, hoping to appeal to the part of him that had craved a daughter and longed for the one he lost. "I will explain everything, but first, please, don't let Sebastian die."

"You have a fever. You don't know what you're saying."

"I do!" I flushed red. "Save him, or I will never, ever forgive either of you if he dies today. Please, I will stay here. I'll do anything you want and take my place as heir, but I beg you, let him live."

Sargon looked at my mom, who shrugged. He tugged at his collar, then opened the door with a heavy sigh. "Call off the execution of Sebastian Vangard, but keep him a prisoner."

My mom was shaking, but it couldn't have been from the cold. "Mom?"

She glanced at a black veil on a hanger over the closet door. "What's that?"

"I'm sorry. I tried to keep you from all of this."

Sargon closed the door. "You kept her from her birthright." He rushed to the veil, running a finger over the thin net. "This is what I picked out for you when you were born."

My eyes darted from him to my mom. "For what?"

She cast her eyes downward.

He cleared his throat, smiling with his eyes. "For you to become shadow kissed. I won't lose you again. You will finally take your rightful place as Princess of Sanmorte."

"But…"

"I agreed to your request for saving a traitor to the crown. Now you must stand by your word." He handed me the veil and kneeled to meet me at eye level. His emerald-green eyes glittered with excitement as he touched my cheek. "My daughter, here, at last." Brushing his thumb down from the corner of my eye to my mouth, he sighed. "I will never allow anyone to hurt you again." A smile built slowly on his lips. "My blood is healing you already. You're going to be magnificent." He took a lock of my hair between his fingers, and I noticed it was red again. "Everyone has tried to hide you from me, but now you're here. Azia confirmed it with your blood and dissolved the hair dye they made you wear." A dangerous glint crossed his expression as he stood, stepping back. "The ceremony will be prepared for Adormai."

My eyes narrowed. I knew it well, the holiday celebrated for the goddess of the heart, and the night when many got engaged or married, the one which Astor had proposed to me on. "Isn't that supposed to celebrate love?"

"Exactly, and in front of the entire court, you will declare yourself as my daughter and your love for another."

I hesitated, half wishing I was back in the dungeon. "Another?"

"Every declared heir must be married," my mom explained from behind him, her hardened glare fixed on the back of his head, her hand on one hip.

"No," I spluttered. "I'm good."

"You will choose a partner before Adormai to take. They will become prince or princess of Sanmorte with you."

"Kalon isn't married," I suddenly realized why Sebastian and Erianna had said marriage was so important in their culture.

"He was, once, but she died."

I contemplated telling him about Kalon's plans, but saving Erianna and everyone was more important. "Erianna, Zach, and Anna, I want them saved."

"I can't let prisoners go." Sargon clasped his ringed fingers together. "They are all traitors to the crown and must be punished. I have forgiven his execution as a gift to you, dear daughter, but that is all I can do."

"What will happen to them?"

"They will have their wings removed and will serve with the other mortals for the court."

My eyes widened as I imagined an aniccipere sawing off their wings, my heart swelling. Sebastian may have betrayed me, but he didn't deserve that. None of them did.

"When is Adormai?" I asked, not knowing what day it was.

"It is in five days." Sargon leaned down and kissed my cheek, then stood. "Hamza will show you to your chambers. I will have a list of suitors sent to you for your inspection."

"But I don't love anyone!"

My mom's jaw clenched. "He doesn't care about love. All that matters to your father is you choose someone so you can become a princess."

"Be careful, Ravena. I am still your king."

Her mouth twisted. "You can't threaten me. I have nothing more left to lose. You already have our daughter."

"You are blessed you still have your life," he stated before turning to me. "I will visit you tomorrow, Seraphina." He walked out, closing the door behind him, and I slumped against the bed as the name hung unfamiliar around my ears.

Now I understood why it was taking place on the night celebrating love because it would also be my wedding. Sebastian had left out the part about any heirs needing to be married, the liar, but in that cell, I could have sworn he cared. He didn't want this for me anymore, I could feel it, but then he'd given me up when I told him not to and tried to trade me for his life.

Everything hurt when I stood. My mom helped me across the floor when I fell against her. "Where's Draven?" I asked as he penetrated my thoughts.

"I kept him safe," she promised. "I've already spoken to him, and he's agreed to help you."

"Can't we still escape?" I asked half-heartedly.

"There's no way out now. Sargon has guarded the castle heavily."

"How is Draven going to help? I know he thinks he can fight himself out of any situation, but this is a little different," I said, amused at the idea of him trying to get us out of the castle with a shotgun. After all of this, I would just be happy to see him.

"He will be your husband. He's the obvious choice, unless you'd rather choose a vampire from Sargon's list."

"No!" I stood straight. "Draven will have to be turned into a vampire. I don't want that for him. I want him away from all of this."

"Honey, he's the best option for you."

"No, he's not." I batted her hand away as she tried to touch my cheek. "Everyone keeps thinking they know what's best for me, but this isn't what I want. I'm deciding not to. I won't do that to him."

"Then you'll marry a stranger. Divorce doesn't exist here, Olivia. You will have to live with whoever you choose, and you don't know anyone in this castle."

My mind slowed. "Can I pick anyone in the castle?"

"Yes, the law states it is your decision."

"Then you can tell Sargon I've already made my choice."

Her dark brows knitted together, her arms crossing over her chest. "You haven't even seen the list."

"I don't need to see it because he's not on it."

"Olivia," she warned.

"I choose Sebastian."

Her shoulders tensed, a heavy sigh whooshing through her nostrils. "You can't do that."

"The rules are I can pick anyone."

"He is in prison for treason."

That was exactly why I was picking him. Even though he'd betrayed me, it had saved my life. Being the prince of Sanmorte would be the last thing he wanted, but I would betray him his mortality and, in return, save his wings and him from a lifetime of slavery. Maybe he'd hate me for it, for taking his choice away and forcing him into marriage and a position he didn't want, but at least he wouldn't be dead or enslaved. I'd find a way to help Erianna and Zach. For now, I had to help myself.

"You can't really want him for your husband. He handed you over. He was trying to trade you."

"I don't," I admitted. "But if I have to pick someone, then I'd rather it be the devil I know."

"Olivia—" She touched my shoulder, and I shrugged her off. "Don't make this mistake."

"You know, I'm exhausted of people telling me what to do." Tears glossed my eyes as my powers ran under my skin, unleashed. I wasn't ready to give them up yet, but if I had only five days to use them, then I'd wreak havoc first, bringing Kalon, Velda, and Hamza down before I ascended the throne.

I left the room, darkness following me as I pushed past Hamza, baring my mortal teeth at him in warning. If I was going to be the princess, then I would make it my own, grabbing fate by the horns so no one would ever hurt me again.

The end... *for now*

FREE BONUS CHAPTER

Download your free bonus chapter from Sebastian's point of view, carrying over from this last chapter, when you sign up for my monthly newsletter.
Get updates on the rest of the series, enter giveaways and see cover and title reveals before anyone else.

Sign up here:

https://bit.ly/NewsletterBonusChapter

Preorder Books 2 & 3 here:

mybook.to/MidnightCrown

mybook.to/DarkestHeart

ALSO BY REBECCA L. GARCIA

THE FATE OF CROWNS SERIES

The Fate of Crowns

The Princess of Nothing

The Court of Secrets

Ruin

EMBRACING DARKNESS COLLECTION

Spellbound

Heart of a Witch

MARKED BY BLOOD SERIES

Shadow Kissed

Midnight Crown

Darkest Heart

ACKNOWLEDGMENTS

A huge thank-you, as always, to my incredible beta readers: Kelly Kortright, Jennifer Rose, Lauren Churchwell, Sherri Stovall, Sarah Rodriguez, Christine Hutton, Mallory McCartney, Carla Sosa, Val Forness, Linda Hamonou, Sophie Koufes, Heather Taylor, and Rebecca Waggner. Your comments are invaluable, and your enthusiasm and notes help me perfect the first drafts.

Thank you to my editor, Belle, and proofreader, Virgina, for helping polish, shape, and perfect this story, and thank you Belle for being a great friend to talk to and swap notes with and for just being an incredible person.

A big shout-out to She-Wolf Pack! Sarah Cradit & K. L. Kolarich, you are the dream team and I am so grateful to have you both to strategize, talk with about all the ins and outs of self-publishing, and getting writing tips and advice from. You ladies are the best and I love you.

Thank you Casey Bond, Tish Thawer, Cameo Renae, Sarah Cradit, K. L. Kolarich and Rebecca Grey for reading Shadow Kissed before publication and providing editorials. I love our community and am honored to have such talented author friends!

Thank you to my husband for entertaining our son and keeping me fed and hydrated while I worked on a deadline, and to my unborn son for giving me a tight time frame to finish this trilogy before you're born. Seriously, I would be nowhere without my beautiful family, so thank you. All these books wouldn't be possible without you all.

Last but not least, this is for you, the reader, who picked this book up and gave it a chance. Thank you for giving me a job where I can write worlds all day, and for sharing the love and enjoying these characters (I hope) as much as I do.
May we all find an escape into new worlds between the pages of books

FANTASY ROMANCE

REBECCA L. GARCIA

Rebecca lives in San Antonio, Texas, with her husband and son. Originally from England, you can find her drinking tea and writing new fantasy worlds filled with romance. She devoured every book she was given, and when she got older, her imagination grew with her.

When she's not writing or spending time with her family, you can find her traveling and hosting book signings with Spellbinding Events.

You can find more information, updates, social media, and more on her website: www.rebeccalgarciabooks.com

CPSIA information can be obtained
at www.ICGtesting.com
Printed in the USA
BVHW040039020522
635843BV00005B/7/J